編者的話

　　「中高級英語聽力檢定①」出版後，深受各界好評，許多學校都集體訂購這本書，讀者廣大的迴響，給了我很大的鼓勵。

　　有人認為，增加聽力要多聽 ICRT、多聽空中英語、多看外國影集或電影，這麼做，當然有助於聽力的訓練；但是，**多做聽力試題，才是最直接有效的方法**，因為唯有在做題目的時候，你才會全神貫注，才能使你專心去聽，不專心聽，聽一輩子也是徒勞無功。

　　證照時代來臨，英語能力愈來愈重要。「中高級英語能力檢定測驗」相當於大學轉學考試的程度，不同的是，還加考聽力與口試。因此，準備「中高級英語檢定」，就等於準備轉學考試、研究所、托福、TOEIC 等重要考試。這本「**中高級英語聽力檢定②**」，共分八回，每回考試時間約 35 分鐘，每回測驗分為三部份，完全比照教育部的「中高級英語能力檢定測驗」聽力部份的題型而編。要在聽力部份得高分，就是要不斷反覆練習，聽了再聽。聽多了，自然就會講，訓練聽力，其實也是練習會話的一種好方法，一石二鳥。

　　編輯好書，是「學習」一貫的宗旨。學英文的書，「學習」都有。我們的目標是，讀者只要讀了一本「學習」的書，就終身成為「學習」的支持者。唯有各界先進不吝批評，我們才會進步。讀者如需要什麼學英文的書，也希望能告訴我們，讓我們出得更齊全。

劉　毅

本書製作過程

　　本書之所以完成，要感謝石支齊老師編寫全部試題，由蔡文華老師改寫修訂，謝靜芳老師校訂，及美籍老師 Andy Swarzman 的再三校對。美術編輯白雪嬌小姐設計封面，黃淑貞小姐、曾怡禎小姐、紀君宜小姐負責版面設計及打字。本書難易適中，深度、廣度兼具，讀者可在短時間內，培養尖端實力。

High-Intermediate Level
Listening Comprehension Test

This listening comprehension test will test your ability to understand spoken English. In this test, each conversation, short talk and question will be spoken JUST ONE TIME. They will not be written out for you. There are three parts to this test. Special instructions will be given to you at the beginning of each part.

Part A

In part A, you will hear 15 questions. After you hear a question, read the four choices in your test book and decide which one is the best answer to the question you have heard.

Example:

<u>You will hear</u>: Mary, can you tell me what time it is?

<u>You will read</u>: A. About two hours ago.
                      B. I used to be able to, but not now.
                      C. Sure, it's half past nine.
                      D. Today is October 22.

The best answer to the question "Mary, can you tell me what time it is?" is C: "Sure, it's half past nine." Therefore, you should choose answer C.

1. A. It stops on Parker Street.
    B. The next one is in ten minutes.
    C. No, it doesn't.
    D. There are two buses going to the city hall.

2. A. Just a little relish, please.
    B. But I asked for a well-done one.
    C. I'll have a salad as well.
    D. I like to eat a big juicy burger.

3. A. No, I didn't make it.
    B. Yes. Do you like them?
    C. Without any ice, please.
    D. Yes. I designed them.

4. A. I told her to help them.
    B. No. The woman yesterday wasn't as young.
    C. I asked Tom to do it yesterday.
    D. Yes. She is the older one.

5. A. I am going by train.
    B. I am going tomorrow.
    C. I am going to the burger joint.
    D. I am going to New York City.

6. A. Sorry, my watch is broken.
    B. No, leave it off please.
    C. They're giving away free posters.
    D. You can go on in.

7. A. Sure, let's go after work.
   B. I'd love to work there.
   C. I love it. It's such a beautiful building.
   D. I like to go to museums.

8. A. It's my birthday.
   B. The club sandwich with clam chowder.
   C. Yes, we have that.
   D. Nothing is special today.

9. A. Yes, she's very nice.
   B. She said he was really quiet.
   C. That's my sister.
   D. He is her brother.

10. A. Yes. It could be scarier.
    B. Yes, there is a scarecrow on the farm.
    C. Food is scarce in this region, not to mention entertainment.
    D. I think it's overrated.

11. A. Shelly is a nice person, isn't she?
    B. Okay, I'll do that.
    C. Definitely Friday, and if we have fun, Saturday too.
    D. Don't go out on Fridays and Saturdays.

12. A. People say it would be
       a good investment.
    B. We're out of coffee
       and I'd like some
       cheese.
    C. Super Saver is a good
       name.
    D. We need grocery
       stores so we can buy
       groceries.

13. A. It's centrally located
       by the bus station.
    B. Turn left at the first
       intersection and go
       two blocks.
    C. Your office is not far
       from Central Station.
    D. My office is close to
       Central Station.

14. A. From platform four.
    B. At two o'clock.
    C. It's a six-hour trip.
    D The train goes to D.C.

15. A. I was actually looking
       for something a bit
       more economical.
    B. These CDs are very
       nice.
    C. I like the electric
       mirrors.
    D. The power in this
       model is too strong.

Part B

In part B, you will hear 15 conversations between a man and a woman. After each conversation, you will hear a question about the conversation. After you hear the question, read the four choices in your test book and choose the best answer to the question you have heard.

Example:

You will hear: (Man)   May I see your driver's license?

                     (Woman)   Yes, officer. Here it is. Was I speeding?

                     (Man)   Yes, ma'am. You were doing sixty in a forty-five mile an hour zone.

                     (Woman)   No way! I don't believe you.

                     (Man)   Well, it is true and here is your ticket.

                     Question: Why does the man ask for the woman's driver's license?

You will read: A. She was going too fast.

                    B. To check its limitations.

                    C. To check her age.

                    D. She entered a restricted zone.

The best answer to the question "Why does the man ask for the woman's driver's license?" is A: "She was going too fast." Therefore, you should choose answer A.

16. A. A bank clerk.
    B. A bookstore clerk.
    C. A student.
    D. A teacher.

17. A. A bank teller.
    B. A farmer.
    C. A supermarket cashier.
    D. A bookstore clerk.

18. A. A language expert.
    B. A foreigner.
    C. The section chief.
    D. Computer books.

19. A. Take a ship to Paris.
    B. Travel with the woman.
    C. Mail a package abroad.
    D. Send a letter.

20. A. Boston's spring weather.
    B. Boston's summer and winter.
    C. Boston's sunshine .
    D. Boston's scenery and weather.

21. A. Giving a presentation in front of her bosses.
    B. That there will be a reduction in her salary.
    C. That her boss will be fired.
    D. The possibility of layoffs.

22. A. Because she ran a red light.
    B. Because she was speeding.
    C. Because she had no registration.
    D. Because she forgot her license.

23. A. He did not say.
    B. Both of the speakers.
    C. No one.
    D. The woman.

24. A. Whatever he wishes to.
    B. Go swimming and snorkeling.
    C. Attend meetings and lectures.
    D. Gather facts about opening a hotel.

25. A. Every two weeks.
    B. She is on an irregular schedule.
    C. Three times a week.
    D. Every day.

26. A. Try on new clothes.
    B. Look out the window.
    C. Clean snow from the ground.
    D. Go for a walk.

27. A. At a hotel.
    B. At a concert.
    C. In a theater.
    D. In a video store.

28. A. He went to the wrong place.
    B. He had to go to a conference.
    C. His presentation took place in the conference room.
    D. He was late for the presentation.

29. A. To meet the man's friends.
    B. To see a movie that evening.
    C. To be invited to the man's next party.
    D. To be included in the man's future plans.

30. A. The woman has it.
    B. The man has it.
    C. They are going to buy one.
    D. It's not ready yet.

Part C

In part C, you will hear several short talks. After each talk, you will hear 2 to 3 questions about the talk. After you hear each question, read the four choices in your test book and choose the best answer to the question you have heard.

Example:

<u>You will hear:</u>

Thank you for coming to this, the first in a series of seminars on the use of computers in the classroom. As the brochure informed you, there will be a total of five seminars given in this room every Monday morning from 6:00 to 7:30. Our goal will be to show you, the teachers of our school children, how the changing technology of today can be applied to the unchanging lessons of yesterday to make your students' learning experience more interesting and relevant to the world they live in. By the end of the last seminar, you will not be computer literate, but you will be able to make sense of the hundreds of complex words and technical terms related to the field and be aware of the programs available for use in the classroom.

Question number 1: What is the subject of this seminar
                            series?

You will read: A. Self-improvement.
                       B. Using computers to teach.
                       C. Technology.
                       D. Study habits of today's students.

The best answer to the question "What is the subject of this
seminar series?" is B: "Using computers to teach." Therefore,
you should choose answer B.

Now listen to another question based on the same talk.

You will hear:
     Question number 2: What does the speaker say
                              participants will be able to do after
                              attending the seminars?

You will read: A. Understand today's students.
                       B. Understand computer terminology.
                       C. Motivate students.
                       D. Deal more confidently with people.

The best answer to the question "What does the speaker say
participants will be able to do after attending the seminars?" is
B: "Understand computer terminology." Therefore, you should
choose answer B.

31. A. The City Mayor.
    B. The polluters.
    C. The police.
    D. The company chief.

32. A. They are asking difficult questions.
    B. An incident of lead poisoning has occurred.
    C. The Mayor is late.
    D. Some lead has been stolen.

33. A. He will do everything he can to prevent further pollution.
    B. He will see to it that more lead will be produced in the area.
    C. He will do his best to see to it that all pollutants are dumped.
    D. He will work to improve the justice system.

34. A. She has to go to lunch.
    B. The hospital and the bank.
    C. The bank and the Immigration Office.
    D. To the immigration after lunch.

35. A. The bank.
    B. Immigration.
    C. To lunch.
    D. The hospital.

36. A. The banks are closed.
    B. Immigration is closed.
    C. Banks close at noon.
    D. The bank is near the house.

37. A. Citizens attending a water conservation rally.
    B. Apartment building residents.
    C. Workers at a waterpower plant.
    D. Convenience store employees.

38. A. That water is heavily polluted.
    B. That the city wants to conserve forest.
    C. That people should be free of water pollution.
    D. That water will be temporarily unavailable.

39. A. The roads are wet.
    B. Traffic is okay.
    C. It's raining a lot.
    D. Driving is slow.

40. A. By taxi.
    B. On foot.
    C. By train.
    D. By airplane.

41. A. Sales.
    B. Hiring.
    C. Advertising.
    D. Imports.

42. A. Sales.
    B. Export.
    C. Financial.
    D. Advertising.

43. A. Twice before.
    B. This is the first try.
    C. They had a TV commercial once.
    D. We can't tell.

44. A. The social conditions.
    B. The factory conditions.
    C. The weather conditions.
    D. How to get to the hills.

45. A. Fancy clothing.
    B. Winter clothing.
    C. Evening dresses.
    D. Warm clothing.

中高級聽力測驗詳解 ①

Part A

1. (**B**) Do you know when the bus comes?
   A. It stops on Parker Street.
   B. The next one is in ten minutes.
   C. No, it doesn't.
   D. There are two buses going to the city hall.

   * *city hall* 市政府

2. (**A**) Would you like some condiments for your burger?
   A. Just a little relish, please.
   B. But I asked for a well-done one.
   C. I'll have a salad as well.
   D. I like to eat a big juicy burger.

   * condiment〔ˋkɑndəmənt〕n. 調味料
     burger〔ˋbɝgɚ〕n. 牛肉漢堡　　relish〔ˋrɛlɪʃ〕n. 調味料
     well-done〔ˋwɛlˋdʌn〕adj. 全熟的　　*as well* 也
     juicy〔ˋdʒusɪ〕adj. 多汁的

3. (**B**) Are those designer glasses?
   A. No, I didn't make it.
   B. Yes. Do you like them?
   C. Without any ice, please.
   D. Yes. I designed them.

   * designer〔dɪˋzaɪnɚ〕n. 設計師
     designer glasses 名牌眼鏡

4. (**B**) Isn't that teller the same woman that helped us yesterday?

    A. I told her to help them.

    B. No. The woman yesterday wasn't as young.

    C. I asked Tom to do it yesterday.

    D. Yes. She is the older one.

    * teller〔'tɛlɚ〕*n.*（銀行）出納員

5. (**D**) Where are you going on your business trip?

    A. I am going by train.   B. I am going tomorrow.

    C. I am going to the burger joint.

    D. I am going to New York City.

    * *go on a business trip* 去出差

    joint〔dʒɔɪnt〕*n.* 地方   *burger joint* 漢堡店

6. (**C**) Excuse me, what's going on?

    A. Sorry, my watch is broken.

    B. No, leave it off please.

    C. They're giving away free posters.

    D. You can go on in.

    * *What's going on*? 發生了什麼事？   *leave off* 停止

    give away 贈送   poster〔'postɚ〕*n.* 海報

7. (**C**) How do you like working at the new museum?

    A. Sure, let's go after work.

    B. I'd love to work there.

    C. I love it. It's such a beautiful building.

    D. I like to go to museums.

    * *How do you like*～? 你覺得～如何？（= *What do you think of*～?）

8. (**B**) What's today's special?
   A. It's my birthday.
   B. The club sandwich with clam chowder.
   C. Yes, we have that.　　D. Nothing is special today.

   * special〔'spɛʃəl〕 n. 特餐
     club sandwich 總匯三明治（三片烤麵包中有夾肉、蛋、生菜
     　和蕃茄而成）
     clam〔klæm〕 n. 蛤蠣　　chowder〔'tʃaudɚ〕 n. 濃湯
     clam chowder 蛤蠣濃湯

9. (**B**) What kind of person did she say he was?
   A. Yes, she's very nice.
   B. She said he was really quiet.
   C. That's my sister.
   D. He is her brother.

10. (**D**) Was the movie as scary as people say?
    A. Yes. It could be scarier.
    B. Yes, there is a scarecrow on the farm.
    C. Food is scarce in this region, not to mention
       entertainment.
    D. I think it's overrated.

    * scary〔'skɛrɪ〕 adj. 嚇人的
      scarecrow〔'skɛr,kro〕 n. 稻草人
      scarce〔skɛrs〕 adj. 不足的
      region〔'ridʒən〕 n. 地區　　***not to mention*** 更不用說
      entertainment〔,ɛntɚ'tenmənt〕 n. 娛樂
      overrate〔'ovɚ'ret〕 v. 高估；評價過高

11. (**C**) Are you going out with Shelly on Friday or Saturday night?

    A. Shelly is a nice person, isn't she?

    B. Okay, I'll do that.

    C. Definitely Friday, and if we have fun, Saturday too.

    D. Don't go out on Fridays and Saturdays.

    * definitely〔'dɛfənɪtlɪ〕*adv.* 當然
    have fun 玩得愉快

12. (**B**) Can you think of anything we need from the grocery store?

    A. People say it would be a good investment.

    B. We're out of coffee and I'd like some cheese.

    C. Super Saver is a good name.

    D. We need grocery stores so we can buy groceries.

    * grocery〔'grosɚɪ〕*n.* 雜貨   ***grocery store*** 雜貨店
    investment〔ɪn'vɛstmənt〕*n.* 投資   ***be out of*** 用完

13. (**B**) How do I get to your office from Central Station?

    A. It's centrally located by the bus station.

    B. Turn left at the first intersection and go two blocks.

    C. Your office is not far from Central Station.

    D. My office is close to Central Station.

    * centrally〔'sɛntrəlɪ〕*adv.* 在中心地   ***be located*** 位於
    intersection〔ˌɪntɚ'sɛkʃən〕*n.* 十字路口
    block〔blɑk〕*n.* 街區

14. (**B**) What time does the train leave for D.C.?
    A. From platform four.
    B. At two o'clock.
    C. It's a six-hour trip.
    D. The train goes to D.C.

    * **D.C.** 華盛頓特區 (= *Washington, D.C.*)
      platform〔'plæt͵fɔrm〕*n.* 月台
      trip〔trɪp〕*n.* 行程

15. (**A**) This model has power windows, power seats, CD
    changer, sunroof, and multi-function AC.
    A. I was actually looking for something a bit more
       economical.
    B. These CDs are very nice.
    C. I like the electric mirrors.
    D. The power in this model is too strong.

    * model〔'mɑdḷ〕*n.* (汽車) 型號
      power〔'pauɚ〕*n.* 電動；動力   **CD changer** CD 音響
      sunroof〔'sʌn͵ruf〕*n.* (汽車) 可開閉天窗
      multi-function〔'mʌltɪ'fʌŋkʃən〕*n.* 多功能
      AC 空調 (= *air conditioning*)   **a bit** 有點
      economical〔͵ikə'nɑmɪkḷ〕*adj.* 經濟的；省錢的
      electric〔ɪ'lɛktrɪk〕*adj.* 電動的
      mirror〔'mɪrɚ〕*n.* 鏡子

Part B

16. (**B**) M : Hello. How often do you get new books in?

W : Well, let me see, usually twice a month on the 1st and the 15th.

M : Is there a catalog?

W : Yes. You can go on to our website and view the latest catalog, or we can mail it to you if you leave me your name and address.

M : That's all right. I'll just go on your website. Thanks.

Question : Who is the man talking to?

A. A bank clerk.   B. A bookstore clerk.

C. A student.   D. A teacher.

* catalog〔'kætḷˌɔg〕*n.* 目錄   website〔'wɛbˌsaɪt〕*n.* 網站
view〔vju〕*v.* 看   clerk〔klɝk〕*n.* 辦事員;店員

17. (**C**) W : I don't think you gave me the right change back.

M : Oh, I'm so sorry. I misread the price on the eggs.

W : It's all right. It's difficult to read.

M : I know but I should've known better. Here is your change, ma'am.

W : Thank you.

Question : What does the man probably do for a living?

A. A bank teller.   B. A farmer.

C. A supermarket cashier.   D. A bookstore clerk.

* change〔tʃendʒ〕*n.* 零錢   misread〔mɪs'rid〕*v.* 讀錯
living〔'lɪvɪŋ〕*n.* 生計   teller〔'tɛlɚ〕*n.* 出納員
cashier〔kæ'ʃɪr〕*n.* 出納員

18. (**D**)　W: Excuse me, where are the books on computer language?

M: At the end of this aisle, on the other side of these shelves. They are next to the foreign language section.

W: End of this aisle, behind these shelves, thanks.

Question: What does the woman want?

A. A language expert.

B. A foreigner.

C. The section chief.

D. Computer books.

* ***computer language*** 電腦語言
aisle〔aɪl〕 *n.* 走道　　shelf〔ʃɛlf〕 *n.* 書架
section〔'sɛkʃən〕 *n.* 區域；部門
expert〔'ɛkspɝt〕 *n.* 專家　***section chief*** 部門主管

19. (**C**)　W: Midway Shipping. May I help you?

M: Yes, do you offer overseas shipping services? I need to send a package to Paris.

W: I'm sorry. We only ship within the country.

M: Can you refer me to a company that does?

W: Sure. Morrison and Associates does shipping worldwide. And the rate is very reasonable.

Question：What does the man want to do?

A. Take a ship to Paris.

B. Travel with the woman.

C. Mail a package abroad.

D. Send a letter.

* shipping〔'ʃɪpɪŋ〕*n.* 運輸
  overseas〔'ovɚ'siz〕*adj.* 國外的　　ship〔ʃɪp〕*v.* 運送
  refer〔rɪ'fɝ〕*v.* 指點 < *to* >
  associate〔ə'soʃɪt〕*n.* 合夥人
  worldwide〔'wɝld'waɪd〕*adv.* 全世界地
  rate〔ret〕*n.* 費用　　reasonable〔'riznəbl̩〕*adj.* 合理的
  abroad〔ə'brɔd〕*adv.* 到國外

20.（ **D** ）M：Boston is so beautiful this time of year.

W：Yeah, the changing leaves are spectacular.

M：And I love the cooler temperatures.

W：Not to mention all those interesting historic sites
you can visit.

Question：What are they talking about?

A. Boston's spring weather.

B. Boston's summer and winter.

C. Boston's sunshine.

D. Boston's scenery and weather.

* spectacular〔spɛk'tækjələ〕*adj.* 壯觀的
  not to mention 更不用說
  historic〔hɪs'tɔrɪk〕*adj.* 歷史上有名的
  historic site 古蹟　　scenery〔'sinərɪ〕*n.* 風景

21. (**D**)　W：Where's the boss this morning?

M：I think she's in a meeting with all the other higher-ups.

W：Well, I hope they're not discussing personnel cutbacks.

M：I don't think they are. We are spread pretty thin as it is and they all know that.

W：Well, we've been barely breaking even for three quarters straight. I'm afraid that the axe is really going to come down.

Question：About what is the woman worried?

A. Giving a presentation in front of her bosses.

B. That there will be a reduction in her salary.

C. That her boss will be fired.

D. The possibility of layoffs.

* higher-up〔'haɪɚ'ʌp〕 *n.* 大人物

personnel〔͵pɝsn̩'ɛl〕 *n.* 人員

cutback〔'kʌt͵bæk〕 *n.* 減少

be spread thin 同時做太多工作

as it is 事實上　　barely〔'bɛrlɪ〕 *adv.* 幾乎不

break even 收支平衡　　quarter〔'kwɔrtɚ〕 *n.* 季

straight〔stret〕 *adv.* 連續地

axe〔æks〕 *n.* 解雇（原意爲斧頭；另一拼法爲 ax）

The axe is going to come down. 快要裁員了。

presentation〔͵prɛzn̩'teʃən〕 *n.* 上台報告

reduction〔rɪ'dʌkʃən〕 *n.* 減少

salary〔'sælərɪ〕 *n.* 薪水　　fire〔faɪr〕 *v.* 解雇

possibility〔͵pasə'bɪlətɪ〕 *n.* 可能性

layoff〔'le͵ɔf〕 *n.* 裁員

22. (**B**) M : May I see your driver's license and registration, please?

W : Here you are. What's the problem, officer?

M : You were going 45 in a 35 mile zone.

W : I can't be going that fast! It's got to be a mistake!

M : No, ma'am. I clocked you on radar. You can see it if you want.

W : No. Just give me my ticket.

Question : Why did the officer stop the woman?

A. Because she ran a red light.

B. Because she was speeding.

C. Because she had no registration.

D. Because she forgot her license.

* registration〔͵rɛdʒɪ'streʃən〕*n.* 行照　　zone〔zon〕*n.* 區
clock〔klɑk〕*v.* 測（速度）　　radar〔'redɑr〕*n.* 雷達
ticket〔'tɪkɪt〕*n.* 罰單　　***run a red light*** 闖紅燈
speed〔spid〕*v.* 超速行駛

23. (**A**) M : I just saw Mr. Brown in the elevator.

W : Did he say anything about the promotions?

M : Only that promotions won't be announced until next week.

W : I hope I'm on that promotion list.

M : You took the words right out of my mouth.

Question : Whom did Mr. Brown promote?

A. He did not say.   B. Both of the speakers.

C. No one.   D. The woman.

* promotion〔prə'moʃən〕*n.* 升遷
announce〔ə'naʊns〕*v.* 宣布　　list〔lɪst〕*n.* 名單
take the word out of one's mouth 說出某人將要說的話

24. (**C**) W: Did you say you're going away on business this weekend?

M: Yeah, I'm going on an all-expenses-paid trip to Hawaii. However, my schedule is completely booked with meetings and lectures.

W: Well, I hope you get a little time to do your own thing.

M: I won't be getting any sun; that's for sure.

W: I'm pretty sure you'll manage.

Question: What will the man do in Hawaii?

A. Whatever he wishes to.

B. Go swimming and snorkeling.

C. Attend meetings and lectures.

D. Gather facts about opening a hotel.

* ***on business*** 為了公事

  all-expenses-paid〔'ɔl,ɪk'spɛnsɪz'ped〕 *adj.* 全額給付的；公費的　　schedule〔'skɛdʒʊl〕 *n.* 行程表

  book〔bʊk〕 *v.* 預訂　　lecture〔'lɛktʃɚ〕 *n.* 演講

  for sure 確定的　　manage〔'mænɪdʒ〕 *v.* 設法；應付

  snorkel〔'snɔrkl̩〕 *v.* 浮潛　　attend〔ə'tɛnd〕 *v.* 參加

  fact〔fækt〕 *n.* 事實；細節

25. (**C**) W: Wow, I feel great! I've just started working out.

M: You look great, too. How often do you exercise?

W: Three times a week, but I'm changing to every day starting next week.

M: I wish I had your stamina and determination. I really need to start working out.

W: It's really easy. You just got to take it slow in the beginning and work your way up.

Question：How often does the woman exercise now?

A. Every two weeks.

B. She is on an irregular schedule.

C. Three times a week.

D. Every day.

* ***work out*** 運動　　stamina〔'stæmənə〕*n.* 體力

determination〔dɪ,tɜmə'neʃən〕*n.* 決心

irregular〔ɪ'rɛgjələ〕*adj.* 不定期的

26. (**C**)　W：Look at it out there.　It really came down last night.

M：I'll go out and shovel the driveway.

W：OK, but put something warmer on.

M：I think I'm going to make a snowman, too.

W：That sounds like a great idea.　Wait, I'll go
with you.

Question：What's the man going to do?

A. Try on new clothes.

B. Look out the window.

C. Clean snow from the ground.

D. Go for a walk.

* ***come down*** 下來（此指下雪）

shovel〔'ʃʌvl̩〕*v.* 用鏟子鏟

driveway〔'draɪv,we〕*n.* 車道　　***put on*** 穿上

snowman〔'sno,mæn〕*n.* 雪人　　***try on*** 試穿

go for a walk 去散步

27. (**C**)　W：I'd like two colas and one large popcorn, please.

M：Sorry, but you'll have to wait a while for the popcorn.

W：Okay, as long as I get it before the movie starts.

M：It's popping now so you should have it in a minute or so.

W：I want some salt and butter on that.

Question：Where are the speakers?

A. At a hotel.　　　　　B. At a concert.

C. In a theater.　　　　D. In a video store.

* cola〔'kolə〕*n.* 可樂

　popcorn〔'pɑp,kɔrn〕*n.* 爆米花　　*as long as* 只要

　pop〔pɑp〕*v.* 發出啪的聲響　　*or so* 大約

　salt〔sɔlt〕*n.* 鹽　　*video store* 錄影帶店

28. (**A**)　W：How was the presentation?

M：I don't know. There wasn't anybody in the conference room.

W：Well, that's because the presentation is in the dining hall.

M：And I thought everyone was late.

W：You should pay more attention to details next time.

Question：What happened to the man?

A. He went to the wrong place.

B. He had to go to a conference.

C. His presentation took place in the conference room.

D. He was late for the presentation.

* presentation〔,prɛzṇ'teʃən〕*n.* 上台報告

　conference〔'kɑnfərəns〕*n.* 會議　　*dining hall* 餐廳

29. (**D**) W：What did you guys do last night?

M：We went to a movie and then we went bowling.

W：Hey, that sounds like fun. Why don't you invite me next time you guys plan something like that?

M：We would have invited you to come along if we knew you wanted to.

W：How would you know if you never ask?

Question：What does the woman want?

A. To meet the man's friends.

B. To see a movie that evening.

C. To be invited to the man's next party.

D. To be included in the man's future plans.

* guy〔gaɪ〕*n.* 傢伙；人

bowl〔bol〕*v.* 打保齡球　***come along*** 一起來

30. (**D**) M：Have you received the sales report yet?

W：I'm afraid they are still working on it.

M：Why is it taking them so long?

W：They are bogged down with work so they are lagging behind a little.

M：They are going to drag us behind if they keep this up.

Question：Where is the sales report?

A. The woman has it.　　B. The man has it.

C. They are going to buy one.

D. It's not ready yet.

* ***be bogged down*** 不能前進；停滯不前　***lag behind*** 落後

drag〔dræg〕*v.* 拉　***keep up*** 保持

Part C

Questions 31-33 refer to the following talk.

> That's a very difficult question. I don't think anyone would be in a position to answer that question right now. I, too, have the same question. Who did it? All I can say right now is that I, as Mayor of the city, will see to it that no more dumping of pollutants continues in this area. I'm really sorry that this was brought to my attention so late. This lead poisoning incident should serve as a great warning to the rest of the nation. And I do hope that more will be done on a national level to make sure that companies committing this kind of crime are brought to justice.

** ***be in a position to V***. 有可能～　　　mayor〔ˈmeɚ〕*n*. 市長
see to it that 留意～　　　dumping〔ˈdʌmpɪŋ〕*n*. 傾倒
pollutant〔pəˈlutn̩t〕*n*. 污染物
bring sth. to one's attention 使某人注意某事
lead〔lɛd〕*n*. 鉛　　　poisoning〔ˈpɔɪznɪŋ〕*n*. 中毒
incident〔ˈɪnsədənt〕*n*. 事件　　　***serve as*** 當作
level〔ˈlɛvl̩〕*n*. 層次　　　***on a national level*** 全國性地
commit〔kəˈmɪt〕*v*. 犯（罪）　　　crime〔kraɪm〕*n*. 罪
justice〔ˈdʒʌstɪs〕*n*. 依法審判
bring sb. to justice 將某人繩之以法

31. (**A**) Who is talking?

A. The City Mayor.

B. The polluters.

C. The police.

D. The company chief.

* polluter〔pə'lutɚ〕 *n.* 製造污染的人
  chief〔tʃif〕 *n.* 老闆

32. (**B**) What seems to be the problem?

A. They are asking difficult questions.

B. An incident of lead poisoning has occurred.

C. The Mayor is late.

D. Some lead has been stolen.

33. (**A**) What has the speaker vowed to do?

A. He will do everything he can to prevent further pollution.

B. He will see to it that more lead will be produced in the area.

C. He will do his best to see to it that all pollutants are dumped.

D. He will work to improve the justice system.

* vow〔vaʊ〕 *v.* 誓言　　further〔'fɝðɚ〕 *adj.* 更進一步的
  dump〔dʌmp〕 *v.* 傾倒　　improve〔ɪm'pruv〕 *v.* 改善
  justice system 司法制度

Questions 34-36 are based on the following advice.

Silvia, I suggest you go to the bank first because if you go to the Immigration Office first, you may finish too late. The banks close at noon, you know. The bank job will be very quick, but for immigration you need a lot of time for the long queues. Besides, the banks are very strict about their time, but the immigration people will let you in even two minutes before they close the doors and once you are in you are sure to be served.

** suggest〔səˈdʒɛst〕*v.* 建議
immigration〔͵ɪməˈgreʃən〕*n.* 移民
Immigration Office 移民局
queue〔kju〕*n.* (排隊等候的) 一隊人
strict〔strɪkt〕*adj.* 嚴格的
serve〔sɝv〕*v.* 服務

34. (**C**) Where does Silvia have to go?

    A. She has to go to lunch.

    B. The hospital and the bank.

    C. The bank and the Immigration Office.

    D. To the immigration after lunch.

35. (**A**) Where should Silvia go first?

    A. The bank.

    B. Immigration.

    C. To lunch.

    D. The hospital.

36. (**C**) Which one of the following statements is true?

    A. The banks are closed.

    B. Immigration is closed.

    C. Banks close at noon.

    D. The bank is near the house.

Questions 37-38 are based on the following announcement.

> Due to the city's water conservation program, water will be shut off from 10 a.m. to 6 p.m., Monday September 5th. Tenants are advised to take appropriate measures. Water service will resume as usual following this inconvenience.

** conservation〔͵kɑnsɚˋveʃən〕*n.* 保護
program〔ˋprogræm〕*n.* 計畫　***shut off*** 關掉
tenant〔ˋtɛnənt〕*n.* 住戶　***take measures*** 採取措施
appropriate〔əˋproprɪɪt〕*adj.* 適當的
resume〔rɪˋzjum〕*v.* 恢復　***as usual*** 像往常一樣

37. (**B**)　Who is this message addressed to?
　　　A. Citizens attending a water conservation rally.
　　　B. Apartment building residents.
　　　C. Workers at a waterpower plant.
　　　D. Convenience store employees.

　　　* address〔əˋdrɛs〕*v.* 對~說話 < *to* >
　　　citizen〔ˋsɪtəzn̩〕*n.* 市民　　rally〔ˋrælɪ〕*n.* 大會
　　　resident〔ˋrɛzədənt〕*n.* 居民
　　　waterpower plant 水力發電廠

38. (**D**)　What is the main message of the announcement?
　　　A. That water is heavily polluted.
　　　B. That the city wants to conserve forest.
　　　C. That people should be free of water pollution.
　　　D. That water will be temporarily unavailable.

　　　* temporarily〔ˋtɛmpə͵rɛrəlɪ〕*adv.* 暫時地
　　　unavailable〔͵ʌnəˋveləbl̩〕*adj.* 得不到的

Questions 39-40 are based on the following talk.

Steve! You'd better tell the driver to start off for the airport now. I was just listening to the broadcast and traffic on the airport road is pretty bad today. The other things can wait. We don't want to make the same mistake as we did when Mrs. Winchester came. I was so embarrassed when she came in a taxi.

** ***start off*** 出發　　broadcast〔ˋbrɔd͵kæst〕*n.* 廣播
embarrassed〔ɪmˋbærəst〕*adj.* 尷尬的

39. (**D**) What's the traffic like?
A. The roads are wet.
B. Traffic is okay.
C. It's raining a lot.
D. Driving is slow.

40. (**A**) How did Mrs. Winchester come last time?
A. By taxi.
B. On foot.
C. By train.
D. By airplane.

* ***on foot*** 徒步

Questions 41-43 are based on the following introduction.

> We have called this meeting to plan how we are going to set up the advertising team. Mr. Roberts, of the financial department will speak first. Then Mr. Rendel from sales will give us an overview of our general requirements. This being our first venture into main media advertising, I strongly advise that we don't make decisions too quickly. I mean without giving it serious thought. Mr. Roberts has been in touch with several advertising agencies. He will give you the figures in a moment. When you see the proposed costs, I know, you will agree with me that we must move slowly. Mr. Roberts, please.

** *call a meeting* 召開會議　　*set up* 成立
advertising〔'ædvɚ͵taɪzɪŋ〕*n.* 廣告
financial〔faɪ'nænʃəl〕*adj.* 金融的
sales〔selz〕*n. pl.* 銷售；業務　　overview〔'ovɚ͵vju〕*n.* 概要
requirement〔rɪ'kwaɪrmənt〕*n.* 必要條件
venture〔'vɛntʃɚ〕*n.* 冒險
media〔'midɪə〕*n.* 媒體 (爲 medium 的複數形)
give sth. *serious thought* 仔細考慮某事
be in touch with 和～有接觸
agency〔'edʒənsɪ〕*n.* 公司　　figure〔'fɪgjɚ〕*n.* 數字
proposed〔prə'pozd〕*adj.* 被提出的

41. (**C**) What is this meeting about?
      A. Sales.   B. Hiring.
      C. Advertising.   D. Imports.

     * hiring〔'haɪrɪŋ〕*n.*（人事）雇用
      import〔'ɪmport〕*n.* 進口

42. (**C**) Which department is Mr. Roberts from?
      A. Sales.   B. Export.
      C. Financial.   D. Advertising.

     * export〔'ɛksport〕*n.* 出口

43. (**B**) How many times has the company attempted media advertising?
      A. Twice before.
      B. This is the first try.
      C. They had a TV commercial once.
      D. We can't tell.

     * attempt〔ə'tɛmpt〕*v.* 嘗試
      commercial〔kə'mɝʃəl〕*n.* 廣告

Questions 44-45 are based on the following advice.

The factory is located in the hills. Temperatures may fall very low in the evenings. It's therefore, advisable to carry some warm clothing. In fact, the weather forecast predicts some frost tomorrow morning. This is unusual for this time of year, but we've had much of that before.

** advisable〔əd'vaɪzəbḷ〕*adj.* 適當的

forecast〔'for,kæst〕*n.* 預測

predict〔prɪ'dɪkt〕*v.* 預測   frost〔frɔst〕*n.* 霜

44. (**C**) What is this advice about?

　　A. The social conditions.

　　B. The factory conditions.

　　C. The weather conditions.

　　D. How to get to the hills.

　　* condition〔kən'dɪʃən〕*n.* 狀態；情況

45. (**D**) What sort of clothing should the visitors take with them?

　　A. Fancy clothing.

　　B. Winter clothing.

　　C. Evening dresses.

　　D. Warm clothing.

　　* sort〔sɔrt〕*n.* 種類   fancy〔'fænsɪ〕*adj.* 花俏的

　　evening dress 晚禮服

High-Intermediate Level
Listening Comprehension Test

This listening comprehension test will test your ability to understand spoken English. In this test, each conversation, short talk and question will be spoken JUST ONE TIME. They will not be written out for you. There are three parts to this test. Special instructions will be given to you at the beginning of each part.

Part A

In part A, you will hear 15 questions. After you hear a question, read the four choices in your test book and decide which one is the best answer to the question you have heard.

Example:

You will hear:　Mary, can you tell me what time it is?

You will read:　A.　About two hours ago.

　　　　　　　　B.　I used to be able to, but not now.

　　　　　　　　C.　Sure, it's half past nine.

　　　　　　　　D.　Today is October 22.

The best answer to the question "Mary, can you tell me what time it is?" is C: "Sure, it's half past nine." Therefore, you should choose answer C.

1. A. That was last week, remember?
   B. Yes, it was great having a day off. I wish every week was like that.
   C. No, I've already made plans.
   D. It's great to have a holiday on Wednesday.

2. A. They both are excellent renaissance playwrights.
   B. Shakespeare was born in England.
   C. Moliere married early.
   D. I love Les Miserables.

3. A. About 20 minutes after the first show.
   B. I liked the show so much the first time, so I saw it a second time.
   C. They started to show it to me, but we ran out of time.
   D. The second show stars Tom Cruise.

4. A. Jim will be joining our new team.
   B. I'll be working out at a new health club.
   C. The facilities are all right, but the staff isn't very friendly.
   D. We'll have P.E. classes in the new gym.

5. A. I think we should buy a new copier.
   B. I think we should purchase a color printer.
   C. We are leasing a small photocopier.
   D. We should buy the Xerox.

6. A. My roommates are sloppy.
   B. I close my door and ignore them.
   C. I don't like loud noises.
   D. He can't stand my bad manners.

7. A. It runs out next year.
   B. It lasts a few weeks if you keep it refrigerated.
   C. Your hospital stay will be about a week.
   D. I don't subscribe to Newsweek.

8. A. The U.S. imports oil from a number of countries.
   B. Mexico imports the most oil from the United States.
   C. Middle Eastern countries export oil to the United States.
   D. I think it's Venezuela.

9. A. Yeah, we're both 34.
   B. Yes, this is bus number four.
   C. Yeah, it runs along that street.
   D. Yes, it goes to thirteenth and fourth.

10. A. I think Mr. Price will win the election.
    B. Elections are always held in the fall.
    C. I think prices will rise following the election.
    D. The stock prices are connected to the election.

11. A. I believe they said it was Judge Melman.
    B. It shows very bad judgment.
    C. He does much better with his hearing aid.
    D. You can't judge a man's hearing without proper equipment.

12. A. Next Monday.
    B. In room one.
    C. Cuts in the budget.
    D. No. He's going to Hawaii next week.

13. A. No. He's not with me.
    B. I have no problem hearing.
    C. Yes, he had a heart attack. His second.
    D. He was taken by ambulance to the nearest hospital.

14. A. There isn't enough room there for it.
    B. I like armchairs better than couches.
    C. The couch is a good place to sit.
    D. This is the best corner of the room.

15. A It was an hour ago.
    B. I saw that fire last night.
    C. It lasted only about thirty minutes.
    D Yes. It was over on Twelfth Street.

Part B

In part B, you will hear 15 conversations between a man and a woman. After each conversation, you will hear a question about the conversation. After you hear the question, read the four choices in your test book and choose the best answer to the question you have heard.

Example:

You will hear:　(Man)　　May I see your driver's license?

　　　　　　　(Woman)　Yes, officer. Here it is. Was I speeding?

　　　　　　　(Man)　　Yes, ma'am. You were doing sixty in a forty-five mile an hour zone.

　　　　　　　(Woman)　No way! I don't believe you.

　　　　　　　(Man)　　Well, it is true and here is your ticket.

　　　　　　　Question:　Why does the man ask for the woman's driver's license?

You will read:　A. She was going too fast.
　　　　　　　B. To check its limitations.
　　　　　　　C. To check her age.
　　　　　　　D. She entered a restricted zone.

The best answer to the question "Why does the man ask for the woman's driver's license?" is A: "She was going too fast." Therefore, you should choose answer A.

16. A. The man's mother.
    B. The man's stepmother.
    C. The man's mother-in-law.
    D. A woman from the company.

17. A. The man and the woman.
    B. The woman.
    C. The company secretary.
    D. The man.

18. A. Buying airline tickets.
    B. Reserving a table for dinner.
    C. Purchasing theater tickets.
    D. Showing a house.

19. A. Return with the woman's lunch.
    B. Help the woman complete her work.
    C. Wait for the woman to complete her work.
    D. Skip lunch.

20. A. Check selected parts of his report.
    B. Write his report.
    C. Present his report.
    D. Do some research.

21. A. All departments must reduce their expenses.
    B. Accounting must increase expenditures.
    C. The accounting department must reduce expenses.
    D. The woman's department is over budget.

22. A. He finds hot weather intolerable.
    B. He believes the woman is insensitive.
    C. The woman should buy a new fan.
    D. Fans and air conditioners work equally well.

23. A. They are coming to
       take Mr. Biggs.
    B. They are coming to
       take the old
       computer.
    C. There is something
       wrong with the old
       monitor.
    D. It's lunch time.

24. A. Washing his car.
    B. Rushing to work.
    C. Waiting for his
       girlfriend.
    D. Getting a haircut.

25. A. Once a month.
    B. Twice a month.
    C. Three times a month.
    D. Every other Wednesday.

26. A. 1:30.
    B. 2:00.
    C. 2:30.
    D. 2:45.

27. A. After supper.
    B. On Saturday
       morning.
    C. The following
       afternoon.
    D. Sometime Sunday
       evening.

28. A. To rent a furnished
       apartment.
    B. To become a realtor.
    C. To sell her furniture.
    D. To find a roommate.

29. A. Pass her driving test.
    B. Have her moped
       repaired.
    C. Sell her moped.
    D. Buy a car.

30. A. Tennis.
    B. Basketball.
    C. Racquetball.
    D. Golf.

Part C

In part C, you will hear several short talks. After each talk, you will hear 2 to 3 questions about the talk. After you hear each question, read the four choices in your test book and choose the best answer to the question you have heard.

Example:

You will hear:

Thank you for coming to this, the first in a series of seminars on the use of computers in the classroom. As the brochure informed you, there will be a total of five seminars given in this room every Monday morning from 6:00 to 7:30. Our goal will be to show you, the teachers of our school children, how the changing technology of today can be applied to the unchanging lessons of yesterday to make your students' learning experience more interesting and relevant to the world they live in. By the end of the last seminar, you will not be computer literate, but you will be able to make sense of the hundreds of complex words and technical terms related to the field and be aware of the programs available for use in the classroom.

Question number 1: What is the subject of this seminar series?

You will read: A. Self-improvement.
                  B. Using computers to teach.
                  C. Technology.
                  D. Study habits of today's students.

The best answer to the question "What is the subject of this seminar series?" is B: "Using computers to teach." Therefore, you should choose answer B.

Now listen to another question based on the same talk.

You will hear:
        Question number 2: What does the speaker say participants will be able to do after attending the seminars?

You will read: A. Understand today's students.
                  B. Understand computer terminology.
                  C. Motivate students.
                  D. Deal more confidently with people.

The best answer to the question "What does the speaker say participants will be able to do after attending the seminars?" is B: "Understand computer terminology." Therefore, you should choose answer B.

31. A. A plastic surgery clinic.
    B. A private business.
    C. A non-profit agency.
    D. An employment agency.

32. A. Frames.
    B. Glass.
    C. Paper.
    D. Paint.

33. A. Sales.
    B. Banking and loan.
    C. Accounting and
       investment.
    D. Word processing and
       graphic design.

34. A. The newly built factory.
    B. The newly hired
       workers.
    C. The company's
       performance.
    D. The new products.

35. A. The company
       expanded its
       operational scale.
    B. The company fired
       thirty workers.
    C. The company hired
       a new manager.
    D. Profits remained the
       same while costs fell.

36. A. Profits dropped.
    B. A loss was registered.
    C. We can't tell.
    D. There was no change.

37. A. They are overstocked.
    B. It is their anniversary.
    C. It is going out of
       business.
    D. Every Christmas
       they have a sale.

38. A. Menswear.
    B. Sportswear.
    C. The shoe department.
    D. The electronics department.

39. A. To himself.
    B. To Mrs. Smith.
    C. To Dr. Schuler.
    D. To someone on the phone.

40. A. Nobody knows.
    B. In the bathroom.
    C. Probably on his way.
    D. In the operation room.

41. A. Four to five minutes ago.
    B. Forty minutes ago.
    C. Three quarters of an hour ago.
    D. Not so long ago.

42. A. Calling back one of their products.
    B. Introducing a new brand of pet food.
    C. Interviewing their customers.
    D. Recruiting new workers.

43. A. It contains steroids.
    B. It's lacking in calcium.
    C. It has a high level of salinity.
    D. Customers don't want it.

44. A. Help with finding a new home.
    B. Catering for home parties.
    C. Interior design.
    D. Housecleaning.

45. A. It is free.
    B. It is very speculative.
    C. It is not available at night.
    D. It is convenient.

中高級聽力測驗詳解 ②

Part A

1. (**A**) I'm not sure, but isn't next Wednesday a holiday?

    A. That was last week, remember?

    B. Yes, it was great having a day off. I wish every week was like that.

    C. No, I've already made plans.

    D. It's great to have a holiday on Wednesday.

    * off〔ɔf〕adj. 休假的

2. (**A**) Do you like the plays of Shakespeare and Moliere?

    A. They both are excellent renaissance playwrights.

    B. Shakespeare was born in England.

    C. Moliere married early.

    D. I love Les Miserables.

    * play〔ple〕n. 戲劇

      Shakespeare〔'ʃek͵spɪr〕n. 莎士比亞（英國詩人劇作家）

      Moliere〔͵molɪ'ɛr〕n. 莫里哀（法國劇作家）

      renaissance〔͵rɛnə'zɑns〕adj. 文藝復興時期的

      playwright〔'ple͵raɪt〕n. 劇作家

      Les Miserables 悲慘世界（著名的音樂劇，改編自雨果的小説）

3. (**A**) What time does the second show start?

    A. About 20 minutes after the first show.

    B. I liked the show so much the first time, so I saw it a second time.

    C. They started to show it to me, but we ran out of time.

    D. The second show stars Tom Cruise.

    * ***run out of*** 用完   star〔stɑr〕*v.* 由～主演

4. (**C**) What do you think of that new gym that you joined?

    A. Jim will be joining our new team.

    B. I'll be working out at a new health club.

    C. The facilities are all right, but the staff isn't very friendly.

    D. We'll have P.E. classes in the new gym.

    * gym〔dʒɪm〕*n.* 體育館；健身房
    work out 運動   ***health club*** 健身俱樂部
    facilities〔fə'sɪlətɪz〕*n. pl.* 設施
    staff〔stæf〕*n.* （全體）工作人員
    P.E. class 體育課（= *physical education class*）

5. (**D**) Which photocopier do you think we should purchase?

    A. I think we should buy a new copier.

    B. I think we should purchase a color printer.

    C. We are leasing a small photocopier.

    D. We should buy the Xerox.

    * photocopier〔ˌfotə'kɑpɪɚ〕*n.* 影印機（= *copier*）
    purchase〔'pɝtʃəs〕*v.* 購買   printer〔'prɪntɚ〕*n.* 印表機
    lease〔lis〕*v.* 租賃   Xerox〔'zɪrɑks〕*n.* 全錄影印機

6. (**B**) How do you tolerate your noisy roommates?
   A. My roommates are sloppy.
   B. I close my door and ignore them.
   C. I don't like loud noises.
   D. He can't stand my bad manners.

   * tolerate〔'tɑlə͵ret〕v. 忍受　　sloppy〔'slɑpɪ〕adj. 懶散的
   ignore〔ɪg'nor〕v. 不理會　　stand〔stænd〕v. 忍受
   manners〔'mænəz〕n. pl. 規矩

7. (**A**) When does your subscription to *Medical Week* expire?
   A. It runs out next year.
   B. It lasts a few weeks if you keep it refrigerated.
   C. Your hospital stay will be about a week.
   D. I don't subscribe to *Newsweek*.

   * subscription〔səb'skrɪpʃən〕n. 訂閱 < *to* >
   Medical Week 醫學週刊　　expire〔ɪk'spaɪr〕v. 到期
   run out 到期　　last〔læst〕v. 保持良好狀態
   refrigerate〔rɪ'frɪdʒə͵ret〕v. 冷凍
   stay〔ste〕v. 停留時間
   subscribe〔səb'skraɪb〕v. 訂閱 < *to* >

8. (**D**) Which country exports the most oil to the United States?
   A. The U.S. imports oil from a number of countries.
   B. Mexico imports the most oil from the United States.
   C. Middle Eastern countries export oil to the United States.
   D. I think it's Venezuela.

   * export〔ɪks'port〕v. 出口
   import〔ɪm'port〕v. 進口　　***a number of*** 許多
   Middle Eastern countries 中東國家
   Venezuela〔͵vɛnə'zwilə〕n. 委內瑞拉

9. (**C**) Do you know if this bus goes to 34th Street?

    A. Yeah, we're both 34.

    B. Yes, this is bus number four.

    C. Yeah, it runs along that street.

    D. Yes, it goes to thirteenth and fourth.

    * run〔rʌn〕*v.* 行駛

10. (**C**) In your opinion, will stock prices rise or fall after the election?

    A. I think Mr. Price will win the election.

    B. Elections are always held in the fall.

    C. I think prices will rise following the election.

    D. The stock prices are connected to the election.

    * stock〔stɑk〕*n.* 股票　　election〔ɪ'lɛkʃən〕*n.* 選舉
    hold〔hold〕*v.* 舉行　　***be connected to*** 和~有關

11. (**A**) Who's the presiding judge on the Milton hearing?

    A. I believe they said it was Judge Melman.

    B. It shows very bad judgment.

    C. He does much better with his hearing aid.

    D. You can't judge a man's hearing without proper equipment.

    * presiding〔prɪ'zaɪdɪŋ〕*adj.* 主席的
    judge〔dʒʌdʒ〕*n.* 法官　*v.* 判斷
    presiding judge 審判長
    hearing〔'hɪrɪŋ〕*n.* 聽證會;聽力
    judgment〔'dʒʌdʒmənt〕*n.* 判決;判斷力
    hearing aid 助聽器　　proper〔'prɑpɚ〕*adj.* 適當的
    equipment〔ɪ'kwɪpmənt〕*n.* 設備

12. (**A**) Did Mark say when he'd like to take vacation?

    A. Next Monday.

    B. In room one.

    C. Cuts in the budget.

    D. No. He's going to Hawaii next week.

    * cut〔kʌt〕n. 削減　　budget〔'bʌdʒɪt〕n. 預算

13. (**C**) What happened to Sam? I heard he's in the hospital.

    A. No. He's not with me.

    B. I have no problem hearing.

    C. Yes, he had a heart attack. His second.

    D. He was taken by ambulance to the nearest hospital.

    * ***have no problem + V-ing*** 做～沒問題

    heart attack 心臟病

    ambulance〔'æmbjələns〕n. 救護車

14. (**A**) If you move the couch to the corner, the room will look better.

    A. There isn't enough room there for it.

    B. I like armchairs better than couches.

    C. The couch is a good place to sit.

    D. This is the best corner of the room.

    * couch〔kautʃ〕n. 長沙發

    armchair〔'arm͵tʃɛr〕n. 扶手椅

15. (**D**) Do you know where that fire was last night?

    A. It was an hour ago.

    B. I saw that fire last night.

    C. It lasted only about thirty minutes.

    D. Yes. It was over on Twelfth Street.

    * last〔læst〕v. 持續

Part B

16. (**C**) M：Are we having company this weekend, honey?

    W：Yes, dear. My mother is coming on Saturday.

    M：Oh, that's right. We'll have to prepare the guest room.

    W：She volunteered to look after the kids for us for the weekend.

    M：Great! We can finally get some time to ourselves.

    Question：Who's coming on Saturday?

    A. The man's mother.

    B. The man's stepmother.

    C. The man's mother-in-law.

    D. A woman from the company.

    * company〔'kʌmpənɪ〕n. 客人；公司

    guest room 客房

    volunteer〔،vɑlən'tɪr〕v. 自願　　*look after* 照顧

    stepmother〔'stɛp،mʌðɚ〕n. 繼母

    mother-in-law〔'mʌðərɪn،lɔ〕n. 岳母

17. (**A**)　W: I'm going home. Can you recheck the data before
　　　　　　　you go?

　　　　　　M: No, I'm going, too. Let's do it tomorrow.

　　　　　　W: Well, all right. I guess we both need some rest.

　　　　　　M: I really wish we could get it done tonight, but I am
　　　　　　　just burnt out.

　　　　　　W: Yeah, me too. See you tomorrow.

　　　　　　Question: Who will recheck the data?

　　　　　　A. The man and the woman.　　B. The woman.

　　　　　　C. The company secretary.　　D. The man.

　　　　　　* data〔'detə〕*n. pl.* 資料　　***burn out*** 使體力耗盡

18. (**C**)　M: Two front-row tickets, please.

　　　　　　W: For which show, sir?

　　　　　　M: The last one.

　　　　　　W: I'm sorry, sir. That show is sold out.

　　　　　　M: Then how about the one before it?

　　　　　　W: Let me see… Here are your tickets, sir. Enjoy
　　　　　　　the show.

　　　　　　Question: What is the man doing?

　　　　　　A. Buying airline tickets.

　　　　　　B. Reserving a table for dinner.

　　　　　　C. Purchasing theater tickets.

　　　　　　D. Showing a house.

　　　　　　* row〔ro〕*n.* 排　　***sell out*** 賣光
　　　　　　reserve〔rɪ'zɝv〕*v.* 預訂
　　　　　　purchase〔'pɝtʃəs〕*v.* 購買

19. (**A**) M: How about meeting me for lunch?

W: I wish I could, but I have to finish this report before tomorrow.

M: Okay. I'll bring something back for you.

W: Nothing too greasy, okay?

M: How about a turkey sandwich?

W: That sounds great. Thanks.

Question: What will the man do?

A. Return with the woman's lunch.

B. Help the woman complete her work.

C. Wait for the woman to complete her work.

D. Skip lunch.

* greasy〔'grizɪ〕 *adj.* 油膩的　　turkey〔'tɜkɪ〕 *n.* 火雞肉
complete〔kəm'plit〕 *v.* 完成　　skip〔skɪp〕 *v.* 略過

20. (**A**) M: I'm so far behind on this report. Can you help me?

W: Sure, what can I do?

M: Just edit the first and the last parts for me.

W: Can I make corrections as I see fit?

M: Please do.

Question: What does the man want the woman to do?

A. Check selected parts of his report.

B. Write his report.　　　C. Present his report.

D. Do some research.

* behind〔bɪ'haɪnd〕 *adv.* 落後　　edit〔'ɛdɪt〕 *v.* 校訂
correction〔kə'rɛkʃən〕 *n.* 修正　　fit〔fɪt〕 *adj.* 恰當的
selected〔sə'lɛktɪd〕 *adj.* 指定的
present〔prɪ'zɛnt〕 *v.* 提出　　research〔'risɜtʃ〕 *n.* 研究

21. (**C**)　W：The new survey says we have to cut our expenses by half this year.

M：That only pertains to the accounting department.

W：Oh, that's good.　Our department is running over budget already.

M：But we still need to watch our expenditures because if we don't shape up, we may be next.

W：You're right.　We need to have a departmental meeting.

Question：What is the result of the new survey?

A. All departments must reduce their expenses.

B. Accounting must increase expenditures.

C. The accounting department must reduce expenses.

D. The woman's department is over budget.

* survey〔'sɝve〕*n.* 調查　　expense〔ɪk'spɛns〕*n.* 支出
pertain〔pɚ'ten〕*v.* 有關 < *to* >
accounting〔ə'kaʊntɪŋ〕*n.* 會計　　***run over*** 超過
expenditure〔ɪk'spɛndɪtʃɚ〕*n.* 支出　　***shape up*** 採取行動
departmental〔dɪ,part'mɛntḷ〕*adj.* 部門的
reduce〔rɪ'djus〕*v.* 減少　　budget〔'bʌdʒɪt〕*n.* 預算

22. (**A**)　M：How did you survive the summer without an air conditioner?

W：I left my fan on all the time.

M：You must not be as sensitive to warm weather as I am.

W：If I had my choice, I would love to have an air conditioner.　But since I don't, a fan will have to do.

M：I hear you.

Question : What does the man mean?

A. He finds hot weather intolerable.

B. He believes the woman is insensitive.

C. The woman should buy a new fan.

D. Fans and air conditioners work equally well.

* survive〔sə'vaɪv〕v. 從~中存活
  air conditioner 冷氣機   fan〔fæn〕n. 電風扇
  on〔ɑn〕adj. 使用中的
  sensitive〔'sɛnsətɪv〕adj. 對~敏感的 < to >
  do〔du〕v. 夠;可以   **I hear you.** 我了解。
  intolerable〔ɪn'tɑlərəbl〕adj. 無法忍受的
  equally〔'ikwəlɪ〕adv. 同樣地

23. (**C**) W: Mr. Biggs, the technicians are here.

M: Have they brought a new monitor with them?

W: I suppose so. They are carrying a big box.

M: Wonderful! Hurry up and show them in.

W: Yes, sir.

Question : Why have the technicians come?

A. They are coming to take Mr. Biggs.

B. They are coming to take the old computer.

C. There is something wrong with the old monitor.

D. It's lunch time.

* technician〔tɛk'nɪʃən〕n. 技術人員
  monitor〔'mɑnətə·〕n. 顯示器;螢幕
  hurry up 趕緊
  show sb. **in** 帶領某人進入

24. (**D**) M: Could you take a little off the top and trim the sides?

W: Sure. Would you like me to wash it first?

M: No, I'm in a bit of a hurry.

W: Okay. You'll be done in a jiffy.

Question: What's the man doing?

A. Washing his car.

B. Rushing to work.

C. Waiting for his girlfriend.

D. Getting a haircut.

* top〔tɑp〕n. 頭頂　　trim〔trɪm〕v. 修剪
  side〔saɪd〕n. 旁邊　　jiffy〔'dʒɪfɪ〕n. 瞬間
  in a jiffy 一下子　　rush〔rʌʃ〕v. 趕
  haircut〔'hɛr,kʌt〕n. 剪髮

25. (**A**) W: This memo states the date of our monthly meeting is changing.

M: What's it changing to?

W: From the second Wednesday of the month to the fourth.

M: Might as well. That way we can have clearer monthly reports at the meeting.

Question: How often do they have a meeting?

A. Once a month.

B. Twice a month.

C. Three times a month.

D. Every other Wednesday.

* memo〔'mɛmo〕n. 備忘錄　　state〔stet〕v. 敘述；說
  might as well 無妨；這樣也好　　***every other ~*** 每隔一～

26. (**B**) W: Is Flight 205 still scheduled to leave at 1:30?

M: No, I'm sorry, madame. It's been delayed for 30 minutes.

W: What happened? What's the delay?

M: There seemed to be some minor mechanical problems. We are really sorry for the inconvenience.

W: I see. Thank you very much.

Question: When will the flight probably leave?

A. 1:30.   B. 2:00.

C. 2:30.   D. 2:45.

* flight〔flaɪt〕n. 班機　　schedule〔'skɛdʒʊl〕v. 預定
　madame〔'mædəm〕n. 女士
　delay〔dɪ'le〕v. 延誤　　n. 延遲
　minor〔'maɪnɚ〕adj. 不嚴重的
　mechanical〔mə'kænɪkl̩〕adj. 機械的
　inconvenience〔͵ɪnkən'vinjəns〕n. 不便

27. (**C**) W: My sister wants to come and visit us this weekend. You don't mind, do you?

M: Of course not. When will she arrive?

W: She was planning on driving up tomorrow in the afternoon to be here in time for dinner.

M: Maybe we can have a barbecue tomorrow.

W: Yeah. And we can invite Mike over. They seemed to have hit it off pretty well the last time she was here.

Question: When will the woman's sister arrive?

A. After supper.   B. On Saturday morning.

C. The following afternoon.

D. Sometime Sunday evening.

* *plan on* 打算　　barbecue〔'bɑrbɪ͵kju〕n. 烤肉
　hit it off 相處融洽　　supper〔'sʌpɚ〕n. 晚餐

28. (**A**) W: Do you lease only unfurnished apartments?

M: Yes, none of our apartments are furnished.

W: Oh, I see.　Thanks anyway.

M: Wait!　I can find some other properties that are furnished for you.

W: That'll be great.　Thanks.

Question: What does the woman want?

A. To rent a furnished apartment.

B. To become a realtor.

C. To sell her furniture.

D. To find a roommate.

* lease〔lis〕v. 出租

　unfurnished〔ʌnˈfɝnɪʃt〕adj. 沒有傢俱的

　property〔ˈprɑpətɪ〕n. 房屋

　realtor〔ˈriəltə〕n. 房地產經紀人

　furniture〔ˈfɝnɪtʃə〕n. 傢俱

29. (**D**) M: Why did you get rid of your moped?

W: It was in pretty bad shape, and besides, I think it's time I got a car.

M: Well, a car is a much bigger investment.

W: Yes, it is.　But I'm just tired of riding around rain or shine.

M: You're right.　A car does keep the weather out.

Question：What is the woman going to do?

A. Pass her driving test.

B. Have her moped repaired.

C. Sell her moped.

D. Buy a car.

* **get rid of** 擺脫　　moped〔ˋmopɛd〕n. 機車

　in bad shape 狀況不佳

　investment〔ɪnˋvɛstmənt〕n. 投資

　be tired of 厭倦

　rain or shine 不論晴雨　　**keep out** 關在外面

30. (**A**) M：Do you prefer clay or grass courts?

W：Clay. I serve better on clay.

M：Me, too. We'll have to get together for a game.

W：How about tomorrow afternoon?

M：You're on.

Question：What are they discussing?

A. Tennis.

B. Basketball.

C. Racquetball.

D. Golf.

* clay〔kle〕n. 黏土；泥土　　grass〔græs〕n. 草地

　court〔kort〕n. 網球場　　serve〔sɝv〕v. 發（球）

　You're on. 好的。

　racquetball〔ˋrækɪtˌbɔl〕n. 迴力球

Part C

Questions 31-33 refer to the following recording.

Laser Shop is a privately owned business dedicated to producing top quality, professional resumes. Just bring a copy of your old resume or a list of relevant personal information and in one day, with help from the latest computer technology on the market, we'll hand you back a masterpiece. We offer endless colors and types of paper, and any size, style or color of font you could possibly imagine.

Your suggestions are welcome, or you can let our staff of professionals in word processing and graphic design create a resume that will suit your needs perfectly. When you really want the job, come to Laser Shop.

** laser〔'lezɚ〕*n.* 雷射　　dedicate〔'dɛdəˌket〕*v.* 致力於 < *to* >
professional〔prə'fɛʃənḷ〕*adj.* 專業的　*n.* 技術專家
resume〔ˌrɛzʊ'me〕*n.* 履歷表　　copy〔'kɑpɪ〕*n.* 份
list〔lɪst〕*n.* 表；清單　　relevant〔'rɛləvənt〕*adj.* 相關的
personal〔'pɝsṇḷ〕*adj.* 個人的　　hand〔hænd〕*v.* 交給
masterpiece〔'mæstɚˌpis〕*n.* 傑作
endless〔'ɛndlɪs〕*adj.* 不計其數的　　font〔fɑnt〕*n.* 字體
word processing 文書處理　　graphic〔'græfɪk〕*adj.* 繪圖的
graphic design 製圖　　suit〔sut〕*v.* 適合
perfectly〔'pɝfɪktɪ〕*adv.* 完全地

31. (**B**)　What is Laser Shop?

　　　A.　A plastic surgery clinic.

　　　B.　A private business.

　　　C.　A non-profit agency.

　　　D.　An employment agency.

　　　* plastic〔'plæstɪk〕*adj.* 整形的
　　　　surgery〔'sɝdʒərɪ〕*n.* 外科
　　　　plastic surgery 整形外科　　clinic〔'klɪnɪk〕*n.* 診所
　　　　non-profit〔nɑn'prɑfɪt〕*adj.* 非營利的
　　　　agency〔'edʒənsɪ〕*n.* 機構
　　　　employment agency 職業介紹所

32. (**C**)　What does Laser Shop offer in endless colors and types?

　　　A.　Frames.　　　　　　B.　Glass.

　　　C.　Paper.　　　　　　D.　Paint.

　　　* frame〔frem〕*n.* 外框　　paint〔pent〕*n.* 顏料

33. (**D**)　What kind of professionals work for Laser Shop?

　　　A.　Sales.

　　　B.　Banking and loan.

　　　C.　Accounting and investment.

　　　D.　Word processing and graphic design.

　　　* banking〔'bæŋkɪŋ〕*n.* 銀行業務　　loan〔lon〕*n.* 貸款
　　　　accounting〔ə'kaʊntɪŋ〕*n.* 會計
　　　　investment〔ɪn'vɛstmənt〕*n.* 投資

Questions 34-36 are based on the following report.

> Our operational costs increased by about 3.7 percent. But this is only because we actually grew bigger compared to last year. The most notable change is that we expanded our production plant by nearly forty percent and hired thirty more workers. In spite of the increase in costs, our profit margin remained the same. The new product seems to have kept us up.

** operational 〔͵ɑpə'reʃəṇ〕 *adj.* 操作上的
   operational cost 營運成本
   compare 〔kəm'pɛr〕 *v.* 比較 < *to* >
   notable 〔'notəḅl〕 *adj.* 值得注意的
   expand 〔ɪk'spænd〕 *v.* 擴大
   production 〔prə'dʌkʃən〕 *n.* 生產
   plant 〔plænt〕 *n.* 工廠
   in spite of 儘管　　margin 〔'mɑrdʒɪn〕 *n.* 利潤
   profit margin 利潤　　***keep～up*** 使～不下降

34. (**C**) What is this report about?

    A. The newly built factory.

    B. The newly hired workers.

    C. The company's performance.

    D. The new products.

    * performance〔pɚˈfɔrməns〕*n.* 業績

35. (**A**) Which one of the following statements is true?

    A. The company expanded its operational scale.

    B. The company fired thirty workers.

    C. The company hired a new manager.

    D. Profits remained the same while costs fell.

    * scale〔skel〕*n.* 規模

36. (**D**) What happened to the profit margin?

    A. Profits dropped.

    B. A loss was registered.

    C. We can't tell.

    D. There was no change.

    * drop〔drɑp〕*v.* 下降
    register〔ˈrɛdʒɪstɚ〕*v.* 記帳；記錄

Questions 37-38 _refer to the following information._

Regent's Department Store is closing its doors forever. Starting Monday, all merchandise will be reduced by 40 to 75 percent. All furniture, all sporting goods, all housewares must go! Our electronics department has gone completely mad, offering home stereos for up to an amazing 80 percent off the retail price. So remember, if you want deals starting this Monday, Regent's is the place to go.

** merchandise〔'mɜtʃənˌdaɪz〕_n._ 商品

reduce〔rɪ'djus〕_v._ 降低

furniture〔'fɜnɪtʃɚ〕_n._ 傢俱

sporting goods 體育用品

housewares〔'hausˌwɛrz〕_n. pl._ 家庭用品

electronics〔ɪˌlɛk'tranɪks〕_n._ 電器用品

go mad 發瘋　　stereo〔'stɛrɪo〕_n._ 立體音響

_up to_ 高達　　amazing〔ə'mezɪŋ〕_adj._ 驚人的

retail〔'ritel〕_n._ 零售　　deal〔dil〕_n._ 交易

37. (**C**) Why is Regent's Department Store having such a
big sale?
A. They are overstocked.
B. It is their anniversary.
C. It is going out of business.
D. Every Christmas they have a sale.

* overstock〔,ovəˈstɑk〕v. 使存貨過多
anniversary〔,ænəˈvɝsərɪ〕n. 週年紀念
go out of business 歇業

38. (**D**) Which of the following is offering 80 percent off its
merchandise?
A. Menswear.
B. Sportswear.
C. The shoe department.
D. The electronics department.

* menswear〔ˈmɛnz,wɛr〕n. 男裝
sportswear〔ˈsports,wɛr〕n. 運動服

Questions 39-41 are based on the following talk.

> Oh! Mrs. Smith. Please take a seat. Dr. Schuler should be in any minute. He knows you are coming. In fact, he was here all morning, but he had to go to the ER about 45 minutes ago. He won't be long. He's just going to pick up his pen. You know how forgetful he is… but he certainly won't forget your appointment.

** ***ER*** 急診室（= *emergency room*）　　***pick up*** 拿取
forgetful〔fə'gɛtfəl〕*adj.* 健忘的

39. (**B**) Who's the man talking to?
    A. To himself.　　　　B. To Mrs. Smith.
    C. To Dr. Schuler.　　　D. To someone on the phone.

40. (**C**) Where is Dr. Schuler?
    A. Nobody knows.　　　B. In the bathroom.
    C. Probably on his way. D. In the operation room.

    * ***on*** *one's* ***way*** 在途中
    operation〔ˌɑpə'reʃən〕*n.* 手術　　***operation room*** 手術房

41. (**C**) When did Dr. Schuler leave his office?
    A. Four to five minutes ago.
    B. Forty minutes ago.
    C. Three quarters of an hour ago.
    D. Not so long ago.

    * quarter〔'kwɔrtɚ〕*n.* 十五分鐘

Questions 42-43 are based on the following talk.

> Apollo Foods is recalling all its Staron brand of canned dog food from its stores around the country. Customers who may have bought canned dog food dated July 16, 1994, should return it to the store from which they bought it. The food is said to contain too much salt, which can cause unexpected health problems in young puppies.

** recall〔rɪˈkɔl〕*v.* 撤回；收回　　brand〔brænd〕*n.* 牌子
canned〔kænd〕*adj.* 罐頭的　***around the country*** 全國
date〔det〕*v.* 註明日期於　　contain〔kənˈten〕*v.* 含有
unexpected〔͵ʌnɪkˈspɛktɪd〕*adj.* 意外的
puppy〔ˈpʌpɪ〕*n.* 小狗

42. (**A**) What is Apollo Foods doing?
　　A. Calling back one of their products.
　　B. Introducing a new brand of pet food.
　　C. Interviewing their customers.
　　D. Recruiting new workers.
　　* ***call back*** 收回　　recruit〔rɪˈkrut〕*v.* 招募

43. (**C**) Which one of the following statements is true about the dog food from Apollo Foods?
　　A. It contains steroids.　　B. It's lacking in calcium.
　　C. It has a high level of salinity.
　　D. Customers don't want it.
　　* steroid〔ˈstɛrɔɪd〕*n.* 類固醇　lacking〔ˈlækɪŋ〕*adj.* 不足的
　　calcium〔ˈkælsɪəm〕*n.* 鈣　　level〔ˈlɛvḷ〕*n.* 含量
　　salinity〔səˈlɪnətɪ〕*n.* 鹽分

Questions 44-45 are based on the following advertisement.

> Do you have to clean up the house for a special occasion, but you don't have the time or energy to do it? Try Rent-a-Maid. For just $49, we'll send a professional maid to your home within an hour of your call. Any time of the day or night, 24-hours a day. Bathrooms, kitchens, dining rooms, garages, even windows. No job is too big for our staff. For more information, call us today at 555-1255.

** occasion〔ə'keʒən〕*n.* 場合　　maid〔med〕*n.* 女傭
　　professional〔prə'fɛʃən!〕*adj.* 專業的
　　staff〔stæf〕*n.*（全體）工作人員

44. (**D**)　What service is being offered?
　　　A. Help with finding a new home.
　　　B. Catering for home parties.
　　　C. Interior design.　　　D. Housecleaning.

　　* catering〔'ketərɪŋ〕*n.* 外燴
　　　interior〔ɪn'tɪrɪɚ〕*adj.* 內部的
　　　housecleaning〔'haʊs,klinɪŋ〕*n.* 打掃房屋；大掃除

45. (**D**)　What can be said about the service?
　　　A. It is free.　　　　　　B. It is very speculative.
　　　C. It is not available at night.
　　　D. It is convenient.

　　* speculative〔'spɛkjə,letɪv〕*adj.* 投機的；冒險的
　　　available〔ə'veləb!〕*adj.* 可得到的

High-Intermediate Level
Listening Comprehension Test

This listening comprehension test will test your ability to understand spoken English. In this test, each conversation, short talk and question will be spoken JUST ONE TIME. They will not be written out for you. There are three parts to this test. Special instructions will be given to you at the beginning of each part.

Part A

In part A, you will hear 15 questions. After you hear a question, read the four choices in your test book and decide which one is the best answer to the question you have heard.

Example:

<u>You will hear</u>: Mary, can you tell me what time it is?

<u>You will read</u>: A. About two hours ago.
B. I used to be able to, but not now.
C. Sure, it's half past nine.
D. Today is October 22.

The best answer to the question "Mary, can you tell me what time it is?" is C: "Sure, it's half past nine." Therefore, you should choose answer C.

1. A. All but one. I'll have
   it in a few minutes.
   B. Just put it on my desk.
   C. You'll be reporting to
   Jerry Mcquire.
   D. Yes, we must report
   on the change to our
   boss.

2. A. No, I don't think so.
   B. Really? I like the
   other one.
   C. You have to submit to
   the court's judgment.
   D. I think this one is by
   far the best.

3. A. Don't let your troubles
   keep you awake at
   night.
   B. Yeah, your face is as
   red as a tomato, too.
   C. Yes, we need to get
   some sun block lotion.
   D. Yes, I usually get
   nervous before a test.

4. A. Two weeks, and it was
   wonderful.
   B. I went to Florida to see
   my parents.
   C. I haven't decided yet.
   D. I'll take a week off to
   Hawaii.

5. A. Yes, the meeting room
   is under renovation.
   B. The meeting won't be
   over for another hour.
   C. I think just one would
   be enough.
   D. Right away. How
   long will you need it?

6. A. I'm sorry, but the job's
   been filled.
   B. Yes, computer skills
   are important.
   C. Frank Jones, Director
   of Human Resources.
   D. Please address him as
   Dr.

7. A. Yes, dinner was simply delightful!
   B. Yes, I was all set for hiking.
   C. Everybody must've left.
   D. I have a liking for sweets.

8. A. Yes, it's solar powered.
   B. Yes, it's a minivan, you know.
   C. No problem. My scooter is very secure.
   D. Of course, it has a capacity of 2 liters.

9. A. My eyesight isn't so good.
   B. Your watch keeps very good time.
   C. Sure, what's it about?
   D. I have something emergency.

10. A. You're one to talk!
    B. No, the soup is too bland for me.
    C. Certainly, my dear.
    D. Please show me your pass.

11. A. I have a meeting at six.
    B. I'll come at six on the dot.
    C. It's on the house.
    D. Sure, I'll buy you a heater.

12. A. Christmas is around the corner.
    B. That's a great idea. Where's the phone?
    C. I'm planning to spend time with my family.
    D. Maybe she's out visiting her neighbors.

13. A. I'll spend two days doing it.
    B. I'm going to read.
    C. You can bet I'll give it my all.
    D. Sure, here you are.

14. A. Sure, hop in.
    B. I have to lose some weight first.
    C. I'm sorry. My arms aren't what they used to be.
    D This box is too heavy to lift.

15. A. No. My family likes it here too much.
    B. Yes. Starting tomorrow.
    C. Not unless the company covers my moving expenses.
    D. I'm going to transfer to a new branch in Atlanta.

Part B

In part B, you will hear 15 conversations between a man and a woman. After each conversation, you will hear a question about the conversation. After you hear the question, read the four choices in your test book and choose the best answer to the question you have heard.

Example:

<u>You will hear</u>: (Man)   May I see your driver's license?
            (Woman)   Yes, officer. Here it is. Was I speeding?
            (Man)   Yes, ma'am. You were doing sixty in a forty-five mile an hour zone.
            (Woman)   No way! I don't believe you.
            (Man)   Well, it is true and here is your ticket.

            Question: Why does the man ask for the woman's driver's license?

<u>You will read</u>: A. She was going too fast.
            B. To check its limitations.
            C. To check her age.
            D. She entered a restricted zone.

The best answer to the question "Why does the man ask for the woman's driver's license?" is A: "She was going too fast." Therefore, you should choose answer A.

16. A. The woman is very sorry.
    B. The man doesn't have time.
    C. The woman is required to sign.
    D. The account has been frozen.

17. A. Go on vacation.
    B. See Tom.
    C. Quit his job.
    D. Cancel his plans.

18. A. Cindy is working overtime.
    B. There is a meeting.
    C. The office equipment will be serviced.
    D. Technicians will be working.

19. A. The striped one.
    B. The green one.
    C. The black one.
    D. The plain one.

20. A. She's a headhunter.
    B. She's a student.
    C. She's a headmistress.
    D. She has a low position.

21. A. Insurance.
    B. Advertising.
    C. Inflation.
    D. Pricing.

22. A. The works of Michelangelo.
    B. Computer programming.
    C. Computer viruses.
    D. The death of Michelangelo.

23. A. He's meeting a guest.
    B. He's looking for a room.
    C. He's looking for a job.
    D. He's looking for his glasses.

24. A. She's washing her hands.
　　 B. She's handling something dangerous.
　　 C. She's looking for some soap.
　　 D. She's eating.

25. A. He's looking for something to eat.
　　 B. He wants the address of the food company.
　　 C. Samples from another company.
　　 D. A place for sampling food.

26. A. She wants to get some money.
　　 B. She forgot her account number.
　　 C. She wants to check her account.
　　 D. She wants to open an account.

27. A. Headhunter.
　　 B. A go-between.
　　 C. A prosecutor.
　　 D. A consultant.

28. A. John is arranging the room.
　　 B. The man is writing an order.
　　 C. John is not doing his job.
　　 D. The order slip is missing.

29. A. The man is afraid of the crash in stock market.
　　 B. Gold price affects the man's business.
　　 C. The woman is not interested in buying gold.
　　 D. Gold price is rising.

30. A. They are needed on Sunday.
　　 B. They will be given to the printers.
　　 C. They are remainders from the exhibition.
　　 D. They are needed for the exhibition.

Part C

In part C, you will hear several short talks. After each talk, you will hear 2 to 3 questions about the talk. After you hear each question, read the four choices in your test book and choose the best answer to the question you have heard.

Example:

<u>You will hear</u>:

Thank you for coming to this, the first in a series of seminars on the use of computers in the classroom. As the brochure informed you, there will be a total of five seminars given in this room every Monday morning from 6:00 to 7:30. Our goal will be to show you, the teachers of our school children, how the changing technology of today can be applied to the unchanging lessons of yesterday to make your students' learning experience more interesting and relevant to the world they live in. By the end of the last seminar, you will not be computer literate, but you will be able to make sense of the hundreds of complex words and technical terms related to the field and be aware of the programs available for use in the classroom.

Question number 1: What is the subject of this seminar
series?

You will read: A. Self-improvement.
B. Using computers to teach.
C. Technology.
D. Study habits of today's students.

The best answer to the question "What is the subject of this
seminar series?" is B: "Using computers to teach." Therefore,
you should choose answer B.

Now listen to another question based on the same talk.

You will hear:
Question number 2: What does the speaker say
participants will be able to do after
attending the seminars?

You will read: A. Understand today's students.
B. Understand computer terminology.
C. Motivate students.
D. Deal more confidently with people.

The best answer to the question "What does the speaker say
participants will be able to do after attending the seminars?" is
B: "Understand computer terminology." Therefore, you should
choose answer B.

31. A. Outdoors away from buildings.
    B. In the basement of a building.
    C. Inside a car.
    D. Inside a cupboard.

32. A. So they can hear the approaching storm.
    B. It will help reduce damage to the home.
    C. So rescuers can get inside to help them.
    D. It will make it easier for them to escape.

33. A. It is an explanation of how to earn a medical degree.
    B. It is a college graduation ceremony.
    C. It is the introduction of an important research doctor.
    D. It is an advertisement for Bio2000.

34. A. At Adams Medical School.
    B. At Bio2000.
    C. At Madison College.
    D. During this presentation.

35. A. 1939.
    B. 1938.
    C. 1949.
    D. 1948.

36. A. Four thousand dollars.
    B. $1.2 million.
    C. $40 million.
    D. $2 million.

37. A. Doctors.
    B. Lawyers.
    C. College students.
    D. Those who want to borrow money.

38. A. Affordability.
    B. Flexibility.
    C. Convenience.
    D. Reliability.

39. A. Us Today.
    B. Dream Alone.
    C. Dream Loans.
    D. Dream's Today.

40. A. Make a person eat less.
    B. Help digestion.
    C. Cause traffic accidents.
    D. Make a person gain weight.

41. A. The body compensates by reducing other intake.
    B. Calories from alcohol are not healthy.
    C. The body notices calories from alcohol.
    D. Calories from alcohol are not noticed by the body.

42. A. A child.
    B. A young woman.
    C. An old man.
    D. An elderly woman.

43. A. A child's toy.
    B. Some keys.
    C. A wallet.
    D. A butterfly.

44. A. A grand opening sale.
    B. A clearance sale.
    C. A liquidation sale.
    D. A Christmas sale.

45. A. 25%-75%.
    B. 20%-40%.
    C. 15%-20%.
    D. 20%-50%.

中高級聽力測驗詳解 ③

Part A

1. (**A**) Have all the productivity reports been handed in?

   A. All but one. I'll have it in a few minutes.

   B. Just put it on my desk.

   C. You'll be reporting to Jerry Mcquire.

   D. Yes, we must report on the change to our boss.

   * productivity〔,prodʌk'tɪvətɪ〕 n. 生產力　***hand in*** 繳交

2. (**D**) Which of these designs should we submit?

   A. No, I don't think so.

   B. Really? I like the other one.

   C. You have to submit to the court's judgment.

   D. I think this one is by far the best.

   * submit〔səb'mɪt〕 v. 呈遞；服從 < *to* >
     court〔kort〕 n. 法院
     judgment〔'dʒʌdʒmənt〕 n. 判決
     by far 最～；顯然（修飾比較級和最高級）

3. (**D**) Are you suffering from insomnia?

   A. Don't let your troubles keep you awake at night.

   B. Yeah, your face is as red as a tomato, too.

   C. Yes, we need to get some sun block lotion.

   D. Yes, I usually get nervous before a test.

   * ***suffer from*** 受～之苦　　insomnia〔ɪn'samnɪə〕 n. 失眠
     sun block〔'sʌn'blak〕 n. 防曬乳
     lotion〔'loʃən〕 n. 乳液

4. (**B**)　Where did you go on your vacation?

    A.　Two weeks, and it was wonderful.

    B.　I went to Florida to see my parents.

    C.　I haven't decided yet.

    D.　I'll take a week off to Hawaii.

    * *take off* 休假

5. (**D**)　Can you see if the meeting room is available at two tomorrow?

    A.　Yes, the meeting room is under renovation.

    B.　The meeting won't be over for another hour.

    C.　I think just one would be enough.

    D.　Right away.　How long will you need it?

    * available〔ə'veləbḷ〕*adj.* 可用的；可獲得的
    renovation〔͵rɛnə'veʃən〕*n.* 整修
    right away 立刻

6. (**C**)　To whom should I address my cover letter?

    A.　I'm sorry, but the job's been filled.

    B.　Yes, computer skills are important.

    C.　Frank Jones, Director of Human Resources.

    D.　Please address him as Dr.

    * address〔ə'drɛs〕*v.* 寫（信）給～ < *to* >；稱呼 < *as* >
    cover letter 附函　　fill〔fɪl〕*v.* 填補（空缺）
    director〔də'rɛktɚ〕*n.* 主任
    human resources 人力資源

7. (**A**) Was everything to your liking?

    A. Yes, dinner was simply delightful!

    B. Yes, I was all set for hiking.

    C. Everybody must've left.

    D. I have a liking for sweets.

    * ***to one's liking*** 合某人口味　　simply 〔ˈsɪmplɪ 〕 *adv.* 實在

      delightful 〔 dɪˈlaɪtfəl 〕 *adj.* 令人愉快的

      be (all) set for 準備好~

      have a liking for 喜歡~　　sweets 〔 swits 〕 *n. pl.* 甜食

8. (**B**) Is your car big enough for the six of us?

    A. Yes, it's solar powered.

    B. Yes, it's a minivan, you know.

    C. No problem. My scooter is very secure.

    D. Of course, it has a capacity of 2 liters.

    * solar 〔ˈsolɚ 〕 *adj.* 太陽的　　power 〔ˈpaʊɚ 〕 *v.* 供給（電力）

      minivan 〔ˈmɪnɪˌvæn 〕 *n.* 小貨車

      scooter 〔ˈskutɚ 〕 *n.* 摩托車

      secure 〔 sɪˈkjʊr 〕 *adj.* 牢固的；安全的

      capacity 〔 kəˈpæsətɪ 〕 *n.* 容量　　liter 〔ˈlitɚ 〕 *n.* 公升

9. (**C**) Could I possibly see you for a minute?

    A. My eyesight isn't so good.

    B. Your watch keeps very good time.

    C. Sure, what's it about?

    D. I have something emergency.

    * eyesight 〔ˈaɪˌsaɪt 〕 *n.* 視力

      keep good time （鐘、錶）走得準

      emergency 〔 ɪˈmɝdʒənsɪ 〕 *n.* 緊急

10. (**C**) Can you pass the salt?

    A. You're one to talk!

    B. No, the soup is too bland for me.

    C. Certainly, my dear.

    D. Please show me your pass.

    * pass〔pæs〕*v.* 傳遞　*n.* 通行證
      bland〔blænd〕*adj.*（味道）淡的

11. (**A**) Why can't you come to my housewarming party?

    A. I have a meeting at six.

    B. I'll come at six on the dot.

    C. It's on the house.

    D. Sure, I'll buy you a heater.

    * housewarming〔'haʊs,wɔrmɪŋ〕*n.* 喬遷喜宴
      on the dot 準時地　　*on the house* 免費的
      heater〔'hitɚ〕*n.* 暖氣機

12. (**D**) Why do you think your mother hasn't called? She always calls us on Christmas morning.

    A. Christmas is around the corner.

    B. That's a great idea. Where's the phone?

    C. I'm planning to spend time with my family.

    D. Maybe she's out visiting her neighbors.

    * *around the corner* 即將來臨

13. (**B**) How are you going to pass the time?

    A. I'll spend two days doing it.

    B. I'm going to read.

    C. You can bet I'll give it my all.

    D. Sure, here you are.

    * ***pass the time*** 打發時間　　bet〔bɛt〕*v.* 確信

    give it *one's* ***all*** 全力以赴

14. (**A**) Can you give me a lift?

    A. Sure, hop in.

    B. I have to lose some weight first.

    C. I'm sorry. My arms aren't what they used to be.

    D. This box is too heavy to lift.

    * lift〔lɪft〕*n.* 順便搭載　 *v.* 舉起

    give *sb.* ***a lift*** 載某人一程（ = *give sb. a ride*）

    hop〔hɑp〕*v.* 跳上（汽車、火車）　 ***Hop in.*** 上車吧。

    weight〔wet〕*n.* 體重

15. (**B**) Rumor has it that you're moving to Sales. Is that true?

    A. No. My family likes it here too much.

    B. Yes. Starting tomorrow.

    C. Not unless the company covers my moving expenses.

    D. I'm going to transfer to a new branch in Atlanta.

    * rumor〔'rumɚ〕*n.* 謠言　 ***Rumor has it that*** ～ 謠傳說～

    move〔muv〕*v.* 遷移；搬家

    cover〔'kʌvɚ〕*v.* 給付　 ***moving expenses*** 搬遷費用

    transfer〔træns'fɝ〕*v.* 調職　 branch〔bræntʃ〕*n.* 分行

Part B

16. (**C**) W : I don't have enough time to drop by and pick up my check. Just send it to my account like you did last time.

M : I'm sorry we can't do that. We need the recipient's signature.

W : But I have done this before. There was no problem… Excuse me, but are you new?

M : Yes, ma'am. I am new. But the new policy requires everyone to sign for their paychecks. Unless you've set up a direct deposit account at the designated bank.

W : This is the first time I've heard of it.

Question : Which one of the following statements is true?

A. The woman is very sorry.

B. The man doesn't have time.

C. The woman is required to sign.

D. The account has been frozen.

* ***drop by*** 順便到（某處）　　***pick up*** 領取

account〔ə'kaʊnt〕*n.* 帳戶

recipient〔rɪ'sɪpənt〕*n.* 受領者

signature〔'sɪgnətʃɚ〕*n.* 簽名　　policy〔'pɑləsɪ〕*n.* 政策

sign for 簽收　　paycheck〔'peˌtʃɛk〕*n.* 薪水支票

set up 設立　　deposit〔dɪ'pɑzɪt〕*n.* 存款

direct deposit account 存款專戶

designated〔'dɛzɪgˌnetɪd〕*adj.* 指定的

freeze〔friz〕*v.* 凍結（銀行存款）

17. (**D**) W: Frank, I think you'll have to reschedule your vacation.

M: But my wife is already getting ready to go.

W: Sorry, but Tom has just fallen sick and no one else can do his job.

M: Oh, come on. You can't do this to me. I'm sure there are people who can do it.

W: I'm sorry. You are it.

Question: What does Frank have to do?

A. Go on vacation.

B. See Tom.

C. Quit his job.

D. Cancel his plans.

* reschedule〔͵ri'skɛdʒʊl〕v. 重新安排

  fall sick 生病　　***You are it.*** 就是你了。

  quit〔kwɪt〕v. 辭（職）

18. (**D**) M: Cindy, you can't work past 5 PM today.

W: Why? I've got work to finish before the meeting tomorrow.

M: The technicians are coming to change all the fuses in the building at five.

W: I don't know if I'll be done before that.

M: Well, I'm sorry to say, but you'll just have to try.

Question：What's happening tonight?

A. Cindy is working overtime.

B. There is a meeting.

C. The office equipment will be serviced.

D. Technicians will be working.

* technician〔tɛkˋnɪʃən〕*n.* 技術人員

fuse〔fjuz〕*n.* 保險絲

overtime〔ˋovɚˏtaɪm〕*adv.* 加班地

equipment〔ɪˋkwɪpmənt〕*n.* 設備

service〔ˋsɝvɪs〕*v.* 維修

19. (**B**) W：I kind of like the other shirt.

M：The green one?

W：Oooo… You have good taste. That's one of our finest.

M：Can I try this on?

W：Sure. The fitting room is right over there.

Question：Which shirt does the woman like?

A. The striped one.

B. The green one.

C. The black one.

D. The plain one.

* *kind of* 有點兒　　taste〔test〕*n.* 品味

try on 試穿　　*fitting room* 試衣間

striped〔straɪpt〕*adj.* 有條紋的

plain〔plen〕*adj.* 無花紋的

20. (**A**) M：Hello Jane. We are looking for a very highly
            motivated college graduate for this position. Can
            you do some headhunting for us?

       W：Certainly, there are already a few names coming
            to my mind. I'll fax you a list of candidates this
            afternoon.

       M：That'll be wonderful. I hope one of them will work
            out.

       W：Hey. When have I ever let you down?

       Question：What's the woman's job?

       A. She's a headhunter.

       B. She's a student.

       C. She's a headmistress.

       D. She has a low position.

       * motivated〔'motə,vetɪd〕*adj.* 積極的

          graduate〔'grædʒʊɪt〕*n.* 畢業生

          position〔pə'zɪʃən〕*n.* 職務；職位

          headhunting〔'hɛd,hʌntɪŋ〕*n.* 徵才

          candidate〔'kændə,det〕*n.* 應徵者

          work out 有預期的結果   ***let down*** 使失望

          headhunter〔'hɛd,hʌntɚ〕*n.* 負責徵才之主管

          headmistress〔'hɛd'mɪstrɪs〕*n.* 女校長

21. (**D**) M: How should we calculate our prices?

W: Well, let's see. Freight, packing, insurance, tariffs, taxes, storage and decide what profit margin you want.

M: Seventeen per cent.

W: Let's plug all the variables into this formula and we should get a rough estimation.

M: Wow! It all looks so easy.

Question: What are they talking about?

A. Insurance.

B. Advertising.

C. Inflation.

D. Pricing.

* calculate〔'kælkjə,let〕*v.* 計算

 freight〔fret〕*n.* 運費　　packing〔'pækɪŋ〕*n.* 包裝

 insurance〔ɪn'ʃurəns〕*n.* 保險

 tariff〔'tærɪf〕*n.* 關稅　　storage〔'storɪdʒ〕*n.* 倉儲費

 margin〔'mardʒɪn〕*n.* 利潤　　*profit margin* 利潤

 per cent 百分之～的 (= *percent*)

 plug〔plʌg〕*v.* 填塞　　variable〔'vɛrɪəbḷ〕*n.* 變數

 formula〔'fɔrmjələ〕*n.* 公式

 rough〔rʌf〕*adj.* 粗略的

 estimation〔,ɛstə'meʃən〕*n.* 估算

 advertising〔'ædvə,taɪzɪŋ〕*n.* 廣告

 inflation〔ɪn'fleʃən〕*n.* 通貨膨脹

 pricing〔'praɪsɪŋ〕*n.* 定價

22. (**C**) W: Can you elaborate on your knowledge of computer viruses?

M: I have created over 2000 anti-virus programs myself.

W: Does that include the cure for the Michelangelo?

M: Yes, of course.

W: Great! We are always looking for talents with working knowledge of computer viruses.

Question: What are the man and woman talking about?

A. The works of Michelangelo.

B. Computer programming.

C. Computer viruses.   D. The death of Michelangelo.

* elaborate〔ɪˈlæbəˌret〕v. 詳細說明 < on >
 virus〔ˈvaɪrəs〕n. 病毒
 program〔ˈprogræm〕n. 程式   v. 設計程式
 anti-virus program 掃毒程式
 cure〔kjʊr〕n. 治療（此指電腦病毒的「解毒方法」）
 Michelangelo〔ˌmaɪklˈændʒəˌlo〕n. 米開朗基羅
   （此指「米開朗基羅電腦病毒」）
 talent〔ˈtælənt〕n. 人才
 working knowledge 足以應付工作的知識
 work〔wɜk〕n. 作品

23. (**D**) M: I checked out this morning, but I think I might have forgotten my glasses in the room. Could I go back and take a look?

W: Sorry sir. Your room has already been cleaned and the maids did not notice anything. In fact, we already have another guest in the room.

M: I know this is a little strange, but could you ring the room? I think I dropped them under the bed.

W: I'll try, sir, but I can't promise anything.

Question：What's the man looking for?

A. He's meeting a guest.

B. He's looking for a room.

C. He's looking for a job.

D. He's looking for his glasses.

* ***check out*** 結帳退房　　guest〔gɛst〕*n.* 客人

　　ring〔rɪŋ〕*v.* 打電話

24.(**B**)　M：That bottle contains some deadly chemicals. Be

　　　　　　very, very careful.

　　　　W：Don't worry.

　　　　M：Be careful. And please wash your hands in hot

　　　　　　soapy water.

　　　　W：I know what I'm doing. I've done this many times

　　　　　　before.

　　　　M：You can never be too careful.

　　　　Question：What is the woman doing?

A. She's washing her hands.

B. She's handling something dangerous.

C. She's looking for some soap.

D. She's eating.

* contain〔kən'ten〕*v.* 含有　　deadly〔'dɛdlɪ〕*adj.* 致命的

　chemical〔'kɛmɪkḷ〕*n.* 化學藥品

　soapy〔'sopɪ〕*adj.* 肥皂的

　You can never be too careful. 再怎麼小心也不為過。

　handle〔'hændḷ〕*v.* 拿；搬動

　soap〔sop〕*n.* 肥皂

25. (**C**)　M: Does anyone know where the samples are?

　　　　　W: What samples?

　　　　　M: The ones from the food company.

　　　　　W: You mean those cookies?

　　　　　M: Yeah. What happened to them?

　　　　　W: Umm… We thought they were snacks and we ate them about an hour ago.

　　　　Question: What is the man looking for?

　　　　A. He's looking for something to eat.

　　　　B. He wants the address of the food company.

　　　　C. Samples from another company.

　　　　D. A place for sampling food.

　　　　* sample〔'sæmpl〕*n.* 樣品　*v.* 品嚐
　　　　　snack〔snæk〕*n.* 零食；點心

26. (**C**)　W: Hello. I'm calling to check if my money has been sent to my account.

　　　　　M: O.K. What's your account number, ma'am?

　　　　　W: Sorry, I don't have it with me.

　　　　　M: That's all right. What is your name and social security number?

　　　　　W: Mary Allen and my SSN is 012-225-1650.

　　　　Question: Why did the woman call the bank?

　　　　A. She wants to get some money.

　　　　B. She forgot her account number.

　　　　C. She wants to check her account.

　　　　D. She wants to open an account.

　　　　* *social security number* 社會安全碼（= SSN）
　　　　　open an account 開戶

27. (**D**) M: Our company intends to go into manufacturing. Do you have any special advice?

W: That's a new area for us, too. We haven't done much in that area yet. All I can say is that we expect a lot of changes to take place in the financial sector and some of the changes do not favor companies of your size.

M: Actually, we are currently working out a merger with two other companies. Size is not going to be a problem for us.

W: Well then, that certainly changes the perspective, wouldn't you say?

Question: What is the woman's profession?

A. Headhunter.
B. A go-between.
C. A prosecutor.
D. A consultant.

* **go into** 從事

manufacturing〔͵mænjəˈfæktʃərɪŋ〕 *n.* 製造業

area〔ˈɛrɪə〕 *n.* 領域

financial〔faɪˈnænʃəl〕 *adj.* 財務的

sector〔ˈsɛktə〕 *n.* 部門　　favor〔ˈfevə〕 *v.* 有利於

currently〔ˈkɝəntlɪ〕 *adv.* 現在

work out 周密地擬定　　merger〔ˈmɝdʒə〕 *n.* 合併

perspective〔pəˈspɛktɪv〕 *n.* 前景；（將來的）前途

Wouldn't you say? 不是嗎？

profession〔prəˈfɛʃən〕 *n.* 職業

go-between〔ˈgobəˏtwin〕 *n.* 媒人

prosecutor〔ˈprɑsɪˏkjutə〕 *n.* 檢察官

consultant〔kənˈsʌltənt〕 *n.* 顧問

28. (**C**) W: How come the order slip is still lying around here?

M: Well, something came up and John probably forgot about it.

W: What if it's an urgent order?

M: I'm sorry. It won't happen again.

Question: What's happening?

A. John is arranging the room.

B. The man is writing an order.

C. John is not doing his job.

D. The order slip is missing.

* slip〔slɪp〕n. 紙條　　**order slip** 訂單
come up 發生　　**What if ~?** 如果~該怎麼辦？
urgent〔'ɝdʒənt〕adj. 緊急的　　arrange〔ə'rendʒ〕v. 布置
missing〔'mɪsɪŋ〕adj. 失蹤的

29. (**B**) M: I think the price of gold is going to go down.

W: That's good news. I want some good jewelry.

M: Not for me. The company is going to go in the red if that happens.

W: That's right. You are in commodity trading.

Question: Which one of the following statements is true?

A. The man is afraid of the crash in stock market.

B. Gold price affects the man's business.

C. The woman is not interested in buying gold.

D. Gold price is rising.

* jewelry〔'dʒuəlrɪ〕n. 珠寶　　**in the red** 虧損
commodity〔kə'madətɪ〕n. 期貨
trading〔'tredɪŋ〕n. 交易　　crash〔kræʃ〕n. 崩盤
stock〔stɑk〕n. 股票　　rise〔raɪz〕v. 上升

30. (**D**)　M：Can you call the printers and find out if they have done our brochures yet?

W：I already called, but it seems they are closed today.

M：We have to get the brochures ready before the opening of the exhibition on Friday.

W：I'll do that first thing tomorrow morning.

Question：What are the brochures needed for?

A. They are needed on Sunday.

B. They will be given to the printers.

C. They are remainders from the exhibition.

D. They are needed for the exhibition.

* printer〔'prɪntɚ〕*n.* 印刷業者

brochure〔bro'ʃʊr〕*n.* 小冊子

opening〔'opənɪŋ〕*n.* 開幕

exhibition〔͵ɛksə'bɪʃən〕*n.* 展覽會

remainder〔rɪ'mendɚ〕*n.* 剩下的東西

Part C

Questions 31-32 are based on the following report.

> This is a hurricane warning. The National Weather Service has issued a hurricane warning. High winds and severe thunderstorms are expected to hit the metropolitan area within hours. All residents should remain in their homes and take refuge in the basement of the house or building. If you do not have a basement, a closet will offer you some protection. Open one window on the west and one window on the east side of your home. Should the hurricane winds strike your home, this will act as a pressure release and your home will suffer less damage.

** hurricane 〔'hɝɪ͵ken 〕 *n.* 颶風（每小時風速 73 英哩以上的風暴，在東半球稱 typhoon「颱風」，西半球稱 hurricane「颶風」）

warning 〔'wɔrnɪŋ 〕 *n.* 警報

National Weather Service 國家氣象局

issue 〔'ɪʃjʊ 〕 *v.* 發佈　　severe 〔 sə'vɪr 〕 *adj.* 強烈的

thunderstorm 〔'θʌndɚ͵stɔrm 〕 *n.* 雷雨

hit 〔 hɪt 〕 *v.* 襲擊　　metropolitan 〔͵mɛtrə'pɑlətn̩ 〕 *adj.* 首都的

resident 〔'rɛzədənt 〕 *n.* 居民　　refuge 〔'rɛfjudʒ 〕 *n.* 避難所

take refuge in 避難於～　　basement 〔'besmənt 〕 *n.* 地下室

closet 〔'klɑzɪt 〕 *n.* 衣櫥　　protection 〔 prə'tɛkʃən 〕 *n.* 保護

should 〔 ʃʊd 〕 *aux.* 萬一　　strike 〔 straɪk 〕 *v.* 襲擊

act as 做為　　release 〔 rɪ'lis 〕 *n.* 釋放

suffer 〔'sʌfɚ 〕 *v.* 遭受　　damage 〔'dæmɪdʒ 〕 *n.* 損失

31. (**B**) Where is the best place to stay during the hurricane?

    A. Outdoors away from buildings.

    B. In the basement of a building.

    C. Inside a car.

    D. Inside a cupboard.

    * cupboard〔'kʌbəd〕 *n.* 碗櫃

32. (**B**) Why are home owners advised to leave windows open?

    A. So they can hear the approaching storm.

    B. It will help reduce damage to the home.

    C. So rescuers can get inside to help them.

    D. It will make it easier for them to escape.

    * advise〔əd'vaɪz〕 *v.* 建議

      approaching〔ə'protʃɪŋ〕 *adj.* 接近的

      reduce〔rɪ'djus〕 *v.* 減少

      rescuer〔'rɛskjuə〕 *n.* 救援人員

Questions 33-34 *refer to the following speech.*

It is a great honor for me to present a woman who I'm sure many of you have admired over the years. She began her impressive career at Madison College, where she majored in biology and graduated at the top of her class. From there she went on to Adams Medical School, one of the finest medical research institutions in the nation, where she first began to show an interest in genetic technology. After graduating from Adams, again with honors, she continued to work in the field of genetics, at the advanced think tank Bio2000. It was at Bio2000 that she developed a method to repair genetic material that has led to a great number of advances in curing birth defects and detecting genetic illnesses. She continues to be a pioneer in the field of genetics at Bio2000. You will not find a finer research doctor anywhere in the world. So, without any further delay, it is my pleasure to present Dr. Brenda Walsh.

** honor〔'ɑnɚ〕*n.* 榮譽；優異成績　　present〔prɪ'zɛnt〕*v.* 介紹
impressive〔ɪm'prɛsɪv〕*adj.* 令人印象深刻的　　*major in* 主修
go on 繼續　　*medical school* 醫學院
research〔'risɝtʃ〕*n.* 研究　　institution〔,ɪnstə'tjuʃən〕*n.* 機構
genetic〔dʒə'nɛtɪk〕*adj.* 基因的　　*with honors* 以優異成績
field〔fild〕*n.* 領域　　genetics〔dʒə'nɛtɪks〕*n.* 遺傳學
advanced〔əd'vænst〕*adj.* 先進的　　*think tank* 智囊團
material〔mə'tɪrɪəl〕*n.* 物質　　*lead to* 導致
a great number of 很多　　advance〔əd'væns〕*n.* 進步
defect〔'difɛkt〕*n.* 缺陷　　*birth defect* 先天缺陷
detect〔dɪ'tɛkt〕*v.* 查出　　pioneer〔,paɪə'nɪr〕*n.* 先驅
research doctor 研究醫生
further〔'fɝðɚ〕*adj.* 更多的；更進一步的

33. (**C**) What is the purpose of this speech?

A. It is an explanation of how to earn a medical degree.

B. It is a college graduation ceremony.

C. It is the introduction of an important research doctor.

D. It is an advertisement for Bio2000.

* explanation〔,ɛksplə'neʃən〕*n.* 解釋；說明
earn〔ɝn〕*v.* 得到　　degree〔dɪ'gri〕*n.* 學位
graduation〔,grædʒu'eʃən〕*n.* 畢業
ceremony〔'sɛrə,monɪ〕*n.* 典禮
advertisement〔,ædvɚ'taɪzmənt〕*n.* 廣告

34. (**A**) When did Dr. Walsh first become interested in genetics?

A. At Adams Medical School.

B. At Bio2000.　　　　C. At Madison College.

D. During this presentation.

* presentation〔,prɛzn̩'teʃən〕*n.* 介紹

Questions 35-36 are based on the following announcement.

Construction of the Manstown Dam was started in May of 1938 during the Great Depression as part of the federal government's efforts to gainfully employ America's unemployed workers. Over four thousand men and women worked on the project. It was completed in December of the following year at a cost of $1.2 million, which would be about $14 million in today's money. The dam generates enough electricity to power the city of Manstown and neighboring Hinesville. It is also crucial to the control of spring floods. Feel free to take photos, folks.

** construction〔kən'strʌkʃən〕*n.* 修築　　dam〔dæm〕*n.* 水壩
depression〔dɪ'prɛʃən〕*n.* 蕭條；不景氣
Great Depression 經濟大恐慌（美國 1930 年代的經濟蕭條）
federal〔'fɛdərəl〕*adj.* 聯邦的
gainfully〔'genfəlɪ〕*adv.* 有收入地
employ〔ɪm'plɔɪ〕*v.* 雇用
unemployed〔ˌʌnɪm'plɔɪd〕*adj.* 失業的
project〔'prɑdʒɛkt〕*n.* 工程　　complete〔kəm'plit〕*v.* 完成
at a cost of 以～的代價　　generate〔'dʒɛnəˌret〕*v.* 產生
power〔'pauɚ〕*v.* 供給（電力）
neighboring〔'nebərɪŋ〕*adj.* 鄰近的
crucial〔'kruʃəl〕*adj.* 重要的　　flood〔flʌd〕*n.* 洪水
feel free to 隨意　　folks〔foks〕*n. pl.* 各位

35. (**A**) In what year was construction of Manstown Dam completed?

    A. 1939.

    B. 1938.

    C. 1949.

    D. 1948.

36. (**B**) How much did it cost to build the dam at that time?

    A. Four thousand dollars.

    B. $1.2 million.

    C. $40 million.

    D. $2 million.

Questions 37-39 refer to the following advertisement.

Haven't you always dreamed that your daughter would go to the college of her choice? That she would become a doctor or a lawyer, or whatever she wanted to be in life? But then reality steps in. How are you going to pay for this dream? That's where we step in. We're Dream Loans, and we've built a business helping people just like you achieve their dreams. Dream Loans offers low interest loans that are affordable, flexible, and convenient.

** *of one's choice* 自選的;心目中的
reality〔rɪˈælətɪ〕 *n.* 現實　 *step in* 介入
loan〔lon〕 *n.* 貸款　 achieve〔əˈtʃiv〕 *v.* 達到;實現
interest〔ˈɪntərɪst〕 *n.* 利率
affordable〔əˈfɔrdəbḷ〕 *adj.* 負擔得起的
flexible〔ˈflɛksəbḷ〕 *adj.* 有彈性的

37. (**D**) Who is this announcement for?

    A. Doctors.

    B. Lawyers.

    C. College students.

    D. Those who want to borrow money.

    * announcement〔əˋnaʊnsmənt〕*n.* 通告

38. (**D**) Which of the following is NOT mentioned as an attribute?

    A. Affordability.

    B. Flexibility.

    C. Convenience.

    D. Reliability.

    * attribute〔ˋætrəˏbjut〕*n.* 特性

    affordability〔əˏfɔrdəˋbɪlətɪ〕*n.* 價格實在

    flexibility〔ˏflɛksəˋbɪlətɪ〕*n.* 彈性

    reliability〔rɪˏlaɪəˋbɪlətɪ〕*n.* 可靠

39. (**C**) What is the name of the company?

    A. Us Today.

    B. Dream Alone.

    C. Dream Loans.

    D. Dream's Today.

Questions 40-41 refer to the following news item.

A team of researchers confirmed through two studies what beer drinkers have figured out for themselves — that beer does not reduce appetite. They published their findings in September's issue of The Australian Journal of Clinical Nutrition. "We found that the body does not seem to notice the calories from alcohol or compensate by reducing other intake," said Talbot University professor Robert Gomsum. "The result is a higher caloric intake whether you are eating a high- or low-fat-diet, you stand to gain more weight."

** confirm〔kən'fɜm〕*v.* 證實　　***figure out*** 理解
***for* oneself** 獨自　　reduce〔rɪ'djus〕*v.* 降低
appetite〔'æpə͵taɪt〕*n.* 胃口　　publish〔'pʌblɪʃ〕*v.* 出版
finding〔'faɪndɪŋ〕*n.* 發現　　issue〔'ɪʃjʊ〕*n.*（報刊）一期
journal〔'dʒɝnḷ〕*n.* 期刊　　clinical〔'klɪnɪkḷ〕*adj.* 臨床的
nutrition〔nju'trɪʃən〕*n.* 營養
calorie〔'kælərɪ〕*n.* 卡路里　　alcohol〔'ælkə͵hɔl〕*n.* 酒
compensate〔'kɑmpən͵set〕*v.* 調節
intake〔'ɪn͵tek〕*n.* 吸收　　caloric〔kə'lɔrɪk〕*adj.* 熱量的
stand〔stænd〕*v.* 處於～狀態

40. (**A**) What does beer NOT do?

    A. Make a person eat less.

    B. Help digestion.

    C. Cause traffic accidents.

    D. Make a person gain weight.

    * digestion〔daɪ'dʒɛstʃən〕*n.* 消化

      gain〔gen〕*v.* 增加

41. (**D**) What does professor Gomsum say about the body and calories from alcohol?

    A. The body compensates by reducing other intake.

    B. Calories from alcohol are not healthy.

    C. The body notices calories from alcohol.

    D. Calories from alcohol are not noticed by the body.

    * notice〔'notɪs〕*v.* 注意到

Questions 42-43 are based on the following announcement.

Attention shoppers.　An elderly customer has lost her keychain somewhere in the store.　It's made of leather and has a silver metal butterfly on it.　It is holding seven keys, including two for a car.　The customer says she was shopping in the furniture department and the children's toys department and may have set it down there.　If anyone has found a keychain, please bring it to the customer service desk at the front of the store on the first floor.　The customer is very anxious and is offering a reward of $25 for the person who finds it for her.　Again, it's made of leather and has a metal butterfly design on it.　Thank you.

** elderly〔'ɛldəlɪ〕_adj._ 年長的

keychain〔'ki,tʃen〕_n._ 鑰匙圈

leather〔'lɛðə〕_n._ 皮革　　silver〔'sɪlvə〕_adj._ 銀的

metal〔'mɛtl〕_n._ 金屬

butterfly〔'bʌtə,flaɪ〕_n._ 蝴蝶　　hold〔hold〕_v._ 包含

furniture〔'fɜnɪtʃə〕_n._ 傢俱　　**set down** 放下

service desk 服務台　　anxious〔'æŋkʃəs〕_adj._ 焦急的

reward〔rɪ'wɔrd〕_n._ 獎賞

design〔dɪ'zaɪn〕_n._ 圖案

42. (**D**) Who has lost something in the store?
      A. A child.
      B. A young woman.
      C. An old man.
      D. An elderly woman.

43. (**B**) What has been lost?
      A. A child's toy.
      B. Some keys.
      C. A wallet.
      D. A butterfly.

      * wallet〔'wɑlɪt〕*n.* 皮夾

Questions 44-45 refer to the following advertisement.

Stewart's Hardware is relocating to Matin Street in Belmar. But before they move they need help carrying some of the stuff out of their store on Front Street, so they've slashed all their prices by 20 to 50 percent. This weekend will be your last chance to get in on this great clearance sale. So get on down to Stewart's Hardware on Front Street and help them say good-bye to their old location!

** hardware〔'hɑrd͵wɛr〕*n.* 五金（此指 hardware store「五金行」）
relocate〔ri'loket〕*v.* 遷徙   slash〔slæʃ〕*v.* 大幅度削減
clearance〔'klɪrəns〕*n.* 清倉   **get on** 前進

44. (**B**) What is the announcement about?
    A. A grand opening sale.   B. A clearance sale.
    C. A liquidation sale.   D. A Christmas sale.

   * grand〔grænd〕*adj.* 盛大的
    liquidation〔͵lɪkwɪ'deʃən〕*n.* 清算
    liquidation sale 法拍

45. (**D**) By how much are they cutting their prices?
    A. 25%-75%.   B. 20%-40%.
    C. 15%-20%.   D. 20%-50%.

   * cut〔kʌt〕*v.* 減少

High-Intermediate Level
Listening Comprehension Test

This listening comprehension test will test your ability to understand spoken English. In this test, each conversation, short talk and question will be spoken JUST ONE TIME. They will not be written out for you. There are three parts to this test. Special instructions will be given to you at the beginning of each part.

Part A

In part A, you will hear 15 questions. After you hear a question, read the four choices in your test book and decide which one is the best answer to the question you have heard.

Example:

You will hear: Mary, can you tell me what time it is?

You will read: A. About two hours ago.
B. I used to be able to, but not now.
C. Sure, it's half past nine.
D. Today is October 22.

The best answer to the question "Mary, can you tell me what time it is?" is C: "Sure, it's half past nine." Therefore, you should choose answer C.

1. A. I'm going to buy the ring next Tuesday.
   B. Sometime in the spring.
   C. I'll settle it out of court.
   D. I'll set the wedding presents tomorrow.

2. A. That's a great idea. Let's reserve a tee-time.
   B. I took private lessons for a couple of years.
   C. Pretty good. I got three A's and two B's.
   D. We made too much money and spent too little.

3. A. No, thanks. I'm too busy as it is.
   B. No, but thanks for asking.
   C. Thanks, Mr. Crawford.
   D. Thanks. Could you put him through, please?

4. A. No, I'm not busy at all.
   B. It's six-thirty.
   C. What do you have in mind?
   D. I have no time to talk now.

5. A. Yes, it's unseasonably mild.
   B. I didn't catch the weather forecast.
   C. Yes, it certainly was.
   D. Yes, I love rainy days.

6. A. I'm sorry; I'm not wearing my watch today.
   B. I thought the test was fairly difficult.
   C. I'll have a look at them after lunch.
   D. I can't eat that because I have to watch my figure.

7. A. No. Take the number 51, over there.
   B. Yes, I'd like to go.
   C. Yes, I agree.
   D. No. You have to transfer at the train station.

8. A. I'll be with you in a moment.
   B. Someone's already helping me, thanks.
   C. I'm helping another customer right now.
   D. I'm beyond help.

9. A. We can buy you some fruit.
   B. We can hold a public press conference.
   C. We might buy you a new lamp.
   D. We can go to that limestone cave.

10. A. Yes, that was a key decision.
    B. I think there's one down the hall.
    C. Sure — it is a little drafty in here.
    D. Here. I have the key.

11. A. I don't like dancing.
    B. Just fill out this form and pay the fee.
    C. Yes, we have two places left.
    D. The dance school is not registered.

12. A. Honolulu is a good place to take a honeymoon.
    B. It was pleasant to say the least.
    C. AF 021.
    D. Flying to Hawaii is great.

13. A. They didn't say where they were going.

B. Installing a new security system.

C. The elevator's out of order.

D. They went downstairs already.

14. A. Where do you think you left it?

B. Approximately seven business days.

C. It arrived an hour ago.

D. It will be sent to your house.

15. A. I think it means "to buy".

B. No, but Lisa is French and can probably help you.

C. Yes, I think you'd better look it up in the dictionary.

D. Yes, I speak both French and English.

Part B

In part B, you will hear 15 conversations between a man and a woman. After each conversation, you will hear a question about the conversation. After you hear the question, read the four choices in your test book and choose the best answer to the question you have heard.

Example:

You will hear:	(Man)	May I see your driver's license?
	(Woman)	Yes, officer. Here it is. Was I speeding?
	(Man)	Yes, ma'am. You were doing sixty in a forty-five mile an hour zone.
	(Woman)	No way! I don't believe you.
	(Man)	Well, it is true and here is your ticket.
	Question:	Why does the man ask for the woman's driver's license?

You will read: A. She was going too fast.

B. To check its limitations.

C. To check her age.

D. She entered a restricted zone.

The best answer to the question "Why does the man ask for the woman's driver's license?" is A: "She was going too fast." Therefore, you should choose answer A.

16. A. They are going to a
       football game.
    B. They are going to go
       to a restaurant.
    C. They are going to go
       to the airport.
    D. They are going to the
       movies.

17. A. going to fight on
       Tuesday.
    B. not going to Vietnam.
    C. flying on Tuesday
       evening.
    D. arriving on Tuesday
       evening.

18. A. He needs to have a
       fax sent to the ministry.
    B. He needs to import
       some feed stock.
    C. He needs to meet with
       the minister.
    D. He needs some
       information on the
       new policy.

19. A. The job was not what
       she wanted.
    B. The job was too
       difficult for her.
    C. She did not make
       enough money.
    D. The company fired her.

20. A. The man can't read
       French.
    B. The explanation about
       the product is bad.
    C. Customers have
       mishandled the
       products.
    D. The French
       instructor is not there.

21. A. The fax machine is
       missing.
    B. Mr. Tracy wants to
       borrow the fax machine.
    C. The fax machine is
       not working.
    D. Mr. Tracy thinks the
       fax is too expensive.

22. A. They want to create a file.
    B. They want to draft a contract.
    C. They want to copy a file.
    D. They want to review a contract.

23. A. After he opens a letter of credit.
    B. After she pays back the debt.
    C. After she presents her credit card.
    D. After she opens a letter of credit.

24. A. It's beginning to rain.
    B. It's snowing.
    C. The man is cold.
    D. The man is hot.

25. A. Banking.
    B. Making money.
    C. The stock market.
    D. Drawing lots.

26. A. James.
    B. Tyler.
    C. The manager.
    D. Al.

27. A. expanding.
    B. downsizing.
    C. going to handle general merchandise.
    D. owned by Stella and four others.

28. A. In time to arrive before the 1st.
    B. Anytime after the 1st.
    C. He doesn't have to go.
    D. On the 1st.

29. A. It depends on Jack.
    B. He can't see them.
    C. He has already seen them.
    D. After he runs.

30. A. Why the woman is depressed.
    B. The reason why people eat more during a recession.
    C. Why businesses fail.
    D. How the woman's business succeeded.

Part C

In part C, you will hear several short talks. After each talk, you will hear 2 to 3 questions about the talk. After you hear each question, read the four choices in your test book and choose the best answer to the question you have heard.

Example:

<u>You will hear:</u>

Thank you for coming to this, the first in a series of seminars on the use of computers in the classroom. As the brochure informed you, there will be a total of five seminars given in this room every Monday morning from 6:00 to 7:30. Our goal will be to show you, the teachers of our school children, how the changing technology of today can be applied to the unchanging lessons of yesterday to make your students' learning experience more interesting and relevant to the world they live in. By the end of the last seminar, you will not be computer literate, but you will be able to make sense of the hundreds of complex words and technical terms related to the field and be aware of the programs available for use in the classroom.

Question number 1: What is the subject of this seminar
series?

You will read: A. Self-improvement.
B. Using computers to teach.
C. Technology.
D. Study habits of today's students.

The best answer to the question "What is the subject of this
seminar series?" is B: "Using computers to teach." Therefore,
you should choose answer B.

Now listen to another question based on the same talk.

You will hear:
Question number 2: What does the speaker say
participants will be able to do after
attending the seminars?

You will read: A. Understand today's students.
B. Understand computer terminology.
C. Motivate students.
D. Deal more confidently with people.

The best answer to the question "What does the speaker say
participants will be able to do after attending the seminars?" is
B: "Understand computer terminology." Therefore, you should
choose answer B.

31. A. Second place winners
    were announced.
    B. The project "Life on
    Tundras" won first
    prize in biology.
    C. Only the first place
    winners will be shown
    on the bulletin board.
    D. John Lasota won
    first prize in
    chemistry.

32. A. On a middle school
    intercom.
    B. On the principal's
    telephone.
    C. Outside, in front of
    the school.
    D. On the bulletin
    board.

33. A. Ed Williams.
    B. Dave Trout.
    C. John Lasota.
    D. Not known.

34. A. To announce a new air
    route.
    B. To cancel a planned air
    route.
    C. To ask for permission
    to land planes.
    D. To extend the waiting
    period.

35. A. Illegal maneuvers on
    the part of the airline.
    B. Long waiting periods.
    C. Stubborn government
    resistance.
    D. A different air route.

36. A. A plane has been
    hijacked in Miami,
    Florida.
    B. An airplane had to
    land in the ocean.
    C. An airplane has
    crashed in Bermuda.
    D. A plane was fired on
    by terrorists.

37. A. 737.
    B. More than 400.
    C. 150.
    D. Authorities are not
       sure.

38. A. The exact location of
       the plane.
    B. That he was trying to
       land on an island.
    C. That passengers were
       injured in the attack.
    D. That smoke was
       coming from the
       plane's engine.

39. A. Business reports.
    B. Tickets to a sports
       event.
    C. A special dictionary.
    D. Scissors and a ruler.

40. A. It costs less than
       other newspapers.
    B. It is selling at a
       discount now.
    C. By keeping you
       informed of the
       market.
    D. By giving you
       shopping coupons.

41. A. Commercial vehicles
       only.
    B. Only not-commercial
       vehicles.
    C. All properly registered
       vehicles.
    D. Vehicles owned by
       residents of Alberd.

42. A. Propose that an alternate route be built.
    B. Approve a plan to ban commercial traffic.
    C. Fund a study of the region's vehicle usage.
    D. Approve funding for construction of the new road.

43. A. Increased revenue from users' fees.
    B. An increase in jobs for local residents.
    C. Better access for tourists and vacationers.
    D. Reduced congestion on the existing highway.

44. A. A department store.
    B. An airport paging system.
    C. A subway system operator.
    D. A radio station disc jockey.

45. A. Purchase music cassettes and CD's.
    B. Make reservations.
    C. Request a song.
    D. Voice your opinion.

中高級聽力測驗詳解 ④

Part A

1. (**B**) When's the wedding set for?
   A. I'm going to buy the ring next Tuesday.
   B. Sometime in the spring.
   C. I'll settle it out of court.
   D. I'll set the wedding presents tomorrow.

   * wedding〔'wɛdɪŋ〕 n. 婚禮
   set〔sɛt〕 v. 確定；指定
   settle〔'sɛtḷ〕 v. 解決　　 **settle sth. out of court** 庭外和解

2. (**B**) Five under par?! Where did you learn to golf so well?
   A. That's a great idea. Let's reserve a tee-time.
   B. I took private lessons for a couple of years.
   C. Pretty good. I got three A's and two B's.
   D. We made too much money and spent too little.

   * par〔par〕 n. 標準桿數　　 golf〔gɔlf〕 v. 打高爾夫球
   reserve〔rɪ'zɝv〕 v. 預訂　　 tee〔ti〕 n. (高爾夫球) 球座
   tee-time〔'ti,taɪm〕 n. 高爾夫球開球時間
   a couple of 幾個

3. (**D**) Mr. Crawford is calling about the Johnson case.
   A. No, thanks. I'm too busy as it is.
   B. No, but thanks for asking.
   C. Thanks, Mr. Crawford.
   D. Thanks. Could you put him through, please?

   * case〔kes〕 n. 事件；案件　　 **as it is** 事實上
   put sb. through 替某人轉接

4. (**B**) Do you have the time?

    A. No, I'm not busy at all.

    B. It's six-thirty.

    C. What do you have in mind?

    D. I have no time to talk now.

    * ***Do you have the time?*** 請問現在幾點？

      （注意不要和 *Do you have time?*「你有空嗎？」混淆）

    have sth. ***in mind*** 想某事

5. (**A**) Nice weather we're having, eh?

    A. Yes, it's unseasonably mild.

    B. I didn't catch the weather forecast.

    C. Yes, it certainly was.

    D. Yes, I love rainy days.

    * unseasonably〔ʌn'siznəblɪ〕*adv.* 不合季節地

    mild〔maɪld〕*adj.* 溫暖的   catch〔kætʃ〕*v.* 趕上

    forecast〔'for͵kæst〕*n.* 預測

6. (**C**) Do you have time to review these figures?

    A. I'm sorry; I'm not wearing my watch today.

    B. I thought the test was fairly difficult.

    C. I'll have a look at them after lunch.

    D. I can't eat that because I have to watch my figure.

    * review〔rɪ'vju〕*v.* 檢閱

    figure〔'fɪgjɚ〕*n.* 數字；身材

    fairly〔'fɛrlɪ〕*adv.* 相當地

7. (**A**) Does this bus go to the train station?

    A. No. Take the number 51, over there.

    B. Yes, I'd like to go.

    C. Yes, I agree.

    D. No. You have to transfer at the train station.

    * transfer〔træns'fɝ〕v. 換車

8. (**B**) May I help you?

    A. I'll be with you in a moment.

    B. Someone's already helping me, thanks.

    C. I'm helping another customer right now.

    D. I'm beyond help.

    * *in a moment* 立刻
    I'm beyond help. 我已經無藥可救了。

9. (**B**) What can you do to get me in the limelight?

    A. We can buy you some fruit.

    B. We can hold a public press conference.

    C. We might buy you a new lamp.

    D. We can go to that limestone cave.

    * limelight〔'laɪm,laɪt〕n. 聚光燈（= *spotlight*）
    in the limelight 引人注目的   press〔prɛs〕n. 新聞界
    conference〔'kɑnfərəns〕n. 會議
    press conference 記者會   lamp〔læmp〕n. 檯燈
    limestone〔'laɪm,ston〕n. 石灰岩
    cave〔kev〕n. 洞穴

10. (**C**) Could you please close the door?

A. Yes, that was a key decision.

B. I think there's one down the hall.

C. Sure — it is a little drafty in here.

D. Here. I have the key.

* key〔ki〕 *adj.* 關鍵的　*n.* 鑰匙　　hall〔hɔl〕 *n.* 大廳

drafty〔'dræftɪ〕 *adj.* 有風的

11. (**B**) How do I register for a dance class?

A. I don't like dancing.

B. Just fill out this form and pay the fee.

C. Yes, we have two places left.

D. The dance school is not registered.

* register〔'rɛdʒɪstɚ〕 *v.* 登記；註冊　　***fill out*** 填寫

fee〔fi〕 *n.* 費用

12. (**B**) How was your flight from Hawaii?

A. Honolulu is a good place to take a honeymoon.

B. It was pleasant to say the least.

C. AF 021.

D. Flying to Hawaii is great.

* flight〔flaɪt〕 *n.* 飛行

Honolulu〔͵hɑnə'lulu〕 *n.* 檀香山 (夏威夷州的首府)

honeymoon〔'hʌnɪ͵mun〕 *n.* 蜜月

pleasant〔'plɛznt〕 *adj.* 令人愉快的

to say the least 還算是；至少可以這麼說

fly〔flaɪ〕 *v.* 搭飛機

13. (**B**) What are those men doing downstairs?

    A. They didn't say where they were going.

    B. Installing a new security system.

    C. The elevator's out of order.

    D. They went downstairs already.

    * downstairs〔'daʊn'stɛrz〕*adv.* 在樓下
    install〔ɪn'stɔl〕*v.* 安裝   security〔sɪ'kjʊrətɪ〕*n.* 安全
    security system 保全系統   elevator〔'ɛlə,vetɚ〕*n.* 電梯
    out of order 故障的

14. (**B**) How long does it take for an order to be sent out, after it's been placed?

    A. Where do you think you left it?

    B. Approximately seven business days.

    C. It arrived an hour ago.

    D. It will be sent to your house.

    * place〔ples〕*v.* 開出（訂單）
    approximately〔ə'prɑksəmɪtlɪ〕*adv.* 大約
    business day 工作天

15. (**B**) Do you have a French-English dictionary?

    A. I think it means "to buy".

    B. No, but Lisa is French and can probably help you.

    C. Yes, I think you'd better look it up in the dictionary.

    D. Yes, I speak both French and English.

    * *had better + V.* 最好   *look up* 查閱
    look sth. *up in the dictionary* 查字典

Part B

16. (**B**) M: What kind of food would you like to have?

W: I want something light. What do you want?

M: I was thinking of some burritos.

W: That's not exactly what I have in mind, but I can deal with it.

M: We can eat something else if you like.

W: No, burritos are fine.

Question: What are the man and woman going to do?

A. They are going to a football game.

B. They are going to go to a restaurant.

C. They are going to go to the airport.

D. They are going to the movies.

* light〔laɪt〕adj. 清淡的

burrito〔bɚˋrito〕n. 類似潤餅的一種墨西哥食物

deal with 應付；接受

17. (**C**) W: Are you ready for the Vietnam trip?

M: Yes, I'm looking forward to it.

W: Your flight is on Tuesday, at 7 pm.

M: What would you like me to bring back for you?

W: Nothing. Besides, I don't know what they have in Vietnam.

Question：The man is

A. going to fight on Tuesday.

B. not going to Vietnam.

C. flying on Tuesday evening.

D. arriving on Tuesday evening.

* Vietnam〔͵viɛt'næm〕n. 越南

look forward to + V-ing 期待　　fight〔faɪt〕v. 打架

18.(**D**)　W：I understand the government has changed import
regulations. Can you request a copy of the
statement issued by the ministry spokesman?

M：We already got a fax and Steve is analyzing it.

W：I need some feedback quickly.

M：It's already being worked on. You'll have it as
soon as it's done.

W：Okay, I'm just anxious.

Question：What does the man need?

A. He needs to have a fax sent to the ministry.

B. He needs to import some feed stock.

C. He needs to meet with the minister.

D. He needs some information on the new policy.

* regulation〔͵rɛgjə'leʃən〕n. 規則
request〔rɪ'kwɛst〕v. 要求　　copy〔'kapɪ〕n.（一）份
statement〔'stetmənt〕n. 正式聲明　　issue〔'ɪʃju〕v. 發佈
ministry〔'mɪnɪstrɪ〕n.（政府的）部
spokesman〔'spoksmən〕n. 發言人
analyze〔'ænl͵aɪz〕v. 分析　　feedback〔'fid͵bæk〕n. 意見
anxious〔'æŋkʃəs〕adj. 焦急的
feed stock〔'fid'stɑk〕n. 原料
minister〔'mɪnɪstɚ〕n. 部長　　policy〔'paləsɪ〕n. 政策

19. (**A**) M : Why did you stop working for Texon?

W : The primary reason is that I couldn't use my skills to the fullest extent. The work was… what shall I say, not challenging?

M : Well, you can look forward to a lot of challenges here.

W : Great. That's exactly what I'm looking for.

Question : Why did the woman stop working for Texon?

A. The job was not what she wanted.

B. The job was too difficult for her.

C. She did not make enough money.

D. The company fired her.

* primary〔'praɪˌmɛrɪ〕*adj.* 主要的
  extent〔ɪk'stɛnt〕*n.* 程度　　***to the fullest extent*** 完全地
  challenging〔'tʃælɪndʒɪŋ〕*adj.* 有挑戰性的
  challenge〔'tʃælɪndʒ〕*n.* 挑戰

20. (**B**) W : I think these instructions are not very clear. We have to improve them.

M : Well, most of us have very limited knowledge of French. So…

W : Find a good translator if you have to. We don't want to have a situation where customers mishandle our product due to vague instructions.

M : Good translators don't come by cheap and they are really hard to find.

W : I'm sure you can figure something out.

Question：What is the problem?

A. The man can't read French.

B. The explanation about the product is bad.

C. Customers have mishandled the products.

D. The French instructor is not there.

* instructions〔ɪn'strʌkʃənz〕n. pl. 說明
improve〔ɪm'pruv〕v. 改善
limited〔'lɪmɪtɪd〕adj. 有限的
translator〔træns'letɚ〕n. 翻譯者
situation〔,sɪtʃʊ'eʃən〕n. 情況
mishandle〔mɪs'hændl〕v. 處理錯誤　　*due to* 由於
vague〔veg〕adj. 模糊不清的　　*come by* 得到
figure out 想出　　explanation〔,ɛksplə'neʃən〕n. 說明
instructor〔ɪn'strʌktɚ〕n. 教師；指導者

21.(**C**)　M：The fax machine is out of order.　Can you get it fixed?

W：Sure, Mr. Tracy.

M：Maybe we should just ask for another one.

W：That would be best, but it could take weeks for
the requisition to work its way up the chain.

M：You're right.　Let's just get it fixed.

Question：What's the problem?

A. The fax machine is missing.

B. Mr. Tracy wants to borrow the fax machine.

C. The fax machine is not working.

D. Mr. Tracy thinks the fax is too expensive.

* requisition〔,rɛkwə'zɪʃən〕n. 請求
work one's *way* 慢慢地前進
chain〔tʃen〕n. 一連串 (在此指一層層的關卡)

22. (**D**)　W: Do you still have a copy of the contract we drafted
　　　　　　 last week?

　　　　　M: I think I can access it. Do you remember the
　　　　　　 filename?

　　　　　W: I think it's CONT1.DOC.

　　　　　M: You're right. Here it is. Hold on a second while
　　　　　　 I print this out.

　　　　　W: Okay. Thanks.

　　　　　Question: What do they want to do?

　　　A. They want to create a file.

　　　B. They want to draft a contract.

　　　C. They want to copy a file.

　　　D. They want to review a contract.

　　　* contract〔'kɑntrækt〕 *n.* 契約　　draft〔dræft〕 *v.* 草擬
　　　　access〔'æksɛs〕 *v.* 由電腦取出（資料）
　　　　filename〔'faɪl,nem〕 *n.* 檔名　　 ***hold on*** 等候
　　　　print〔prɪnt〕 *v.* 列印　　file〔faɪl〕 *n.* 檔案
　　　　review〔rɪ'vju〕 *v.* 審查

23. (**D**)　M: If your company can open a letter of credit, we'll
　　　　　　 be in a position to do business with you.

　　　　　W: I can assure you that there won't be any problem
　　　　　　 at all regarding opening a letter of credit.

　　　　　M: Well, we look forward to doing business with you
　　　　　　 as soon as possible.

　　　　　W: Likewise.

Question：When will the man make a business
 commitment with the woman?

A. After he opens a letter of credit.

B. After she pays back the debt.

C. After she presents her credit card.

D. After she opens a letter of credit.

* ***letter of credit*** 信用狀　　position〔pəˈzɪʃən〕 *n.* 立場
 be in a position to + V. 能夠
 assure〔əˈʃur〕 *v.* 向～保證
 regarding〔rɪˈgardɪŋ〕 *prep.* 關於（= *about*）
 likewise〔ˈlaɪkˌwaɪz〕 *adv.* 同樣地；我也是
 commitment〔kəˈmɪtmənt〕 *n.* 承諾
 debt〔dɛt〕 *n.* 債務　　present〔prɪˈzɛnt〕 *v.* 出示

24.（ **A** ）W：It looks like it's going to rain soon.

M：I don't know. But the weatherman didn't predict
 any rain.

W：Sometimes the forecasts are incorrect. Look!
 It's raining.

M：You're right. It's really pouring out there. You
 can never believe what the weatherman says.

Question：What is happening?

A. It's beginning to rain.　B. It's snowing.

C. The man is cold.　　　D. The man is hot.

* weatherman〔ˈwɛðɚˌmæn〕 *n.* 氣象播報員
 predict〔prɪˈdɪkt〕 *v.* 預報
 forecast〔ˈforˌkæst〕 *n.* 預測
 pour〔por〕 *v.* 下傾盆大雨

25. (**B**)　W: Why are you drawing so much money today?

　　　　M: Well, with the interest rates so low, I figured I could try my luck in the stock market.

　　　　W: That sounds interesting. Are you saying it's good to try the stock market when interest rates are low?

　　　　M: Exactly. But you need to figure out which stock will make you money beforehand.

　　　　W: Maybe you can give some tips on investments.

　　Question：What is this conversation about?

　　A. Banking.　　　　　B. Making money.

　　C. The stock market.　　D. Drawing lots.

　　* draw〔drɔ〕v. 領取；抽（籤）　　*interest rate* 利率
　　figure〔'fɪgjɚ〕v. 估計　　*stock market* 股票市場
　　figure out 了解　　beforehand〔bɪ'for͵hænd〕adv. 事先
　　tip〔tɪp〕n. 秘訣　　investment〔ɪn'vɛstmənt〕n. 投資
　　banking〔'bæŋkɪŋ〕n. 銀行業務　　lot〔lɑt〕n. 籤

26. (**A**)　W: James, do you have a minute? Tom is here to see you.

　　　　M: Can you send him over to Tyler, please?

　　　　W: Tyler is not in this afternoon.

　　　　M: I can't interview him just yet. He'll have to finish all his paperwork before we can do that.

　　　　W: Where should I send him then?

　　　　M: Have Al finish his paperwork and bring him back here.

Question : Whom does Tom want to speak to?

A. James.　　　　　　　B. Tyler.

C. The manager.　　　　D. Al.

* interview〔'ɪntəˌvju〕v. 會見

paperwork〔'pepəˌwɝk〕n. 文書工作；書面工作

27. (**A**) M : Tomorrow we'll be doing the interviewing for our new branch office personnel.

W : Have we decided who is going to handle that yet?

M : Stella of General Affairs and four other people.

W : I know Stella is pretty sharp. But I don't know about the other four.

M : I'm sure they'll manage.

Question : The company is

A. expanding.

B. downsizing.

C. going to handle general merchandise.

D. owned by Stella and four others.

* interview〔'ɪntəˌvju〕v. 面談　　branch〔bræntʃ〕n. 分行

personnel〔ˌpɝsn̩'ɛl〕n. 人員　　handle〔'hændl̩〕v. 處理

general affairs 總務　　sharp〔ʃɑrp〕adj. 精明的

expand〔ɪk'spænd〕v. 擴大

downsize〔'daʊn'saɪze〕v. 裁員

merchandise〔'mɝtʃənˌdaɪz〕n. 商品

28. (**A**)　W：Greg, your flight has been canceled. What shall…

M：Find out if they can put me on a different airline, even one leaving early. I have to be in Mexico before the 1st.

W：I'll try and get back to you as soon as possible.

Question：When is Greg going to Mexico?

A. In time to arrive before the 1st.

B. Anytime after the 1st.

C. He doesn't have to go.

D. On the 1st.

* airline〔'ɛr,laɪn〕*n.* 航空公司

29. (**A**)　M：Do you think it's possible to look at the microfilms today?

W：I don't know yet. I have to check with Jack.

M：Can you please find out? I'm running out of time.

W：Let me call him now and find out.

M：That'll be great. Thanks.

Question：When can the man look at microfilms?

A. It depends on Jack.

B. He can't see them.

C. He has already seen them.

D. After he runs.

* microfilm〔'maɪkrə,fɪlm〕*n.* 微縮膠卷
run out of 用完　　***depend on*** 視～而定

30. (**D**) M: How was your company able to expand so much during a recession?

W: Well, we are in the food business and people always need food. In fact, people eat more when they are depressed and the recession was very depressing, indeed.

M: But, other businesses in your line failed. How do you explain that?

W: Those were just the wrong investments in the wrong times. We look at them as good learning experiences. That way we won't make the same mistakes again.

M: Thank you for having this talk with me. I hope to do this with you again soon.

Question: What is the man asking?

A. Why the woman is depressed.

B. The reason why people eat more during a recession.

C. Why businesses fail.

D. How the woman's business succeeded.

* recession〔rɪ'sɛʃən〕*n.* 不景氣

depressed〔dɪ'prɛst〕*adj.* 沮喪的

indeed〔ɪn'did〕*adv.* 的確

line〔laɪn〕*n.* 行業

investment〔ɪn'vɛstmənt〕*n.* 投資

Part C

Questions 31-33 refer to the following announcement.

Attention, please! We would like to announce the first place winners of this year's science fair. In biology, it was Ed Williams and Dave Trout with their project "Life on Tundras." In physics, "Windmill Electricity" by John Lasota was the winning exhibit. All winners, including runners up, will be acknowledged on the bulletin board in front of the school. Thanks to all the participants in this year's contest and congratulations to all the winners.

** announce〔ə'naʊns〕*v.* 宣布　　***first place*** 第一名
science fair 科展　　biology〔baɪ'ɑlədʒɪ〕*n.* 生物學
project〔'prɑdʒɛkt〕*n.*（科學研究）項目
tundra〔'tʌndrə〕*n.* 凍原　　physics〔'fɪzɪks〕*n.* 物理學
windmill〔'wɪnd,mɪl〕*n.* 風車
exhibit〔ɪg'zɪbɪt〕*n.* 展覽作品
runner up〔'rʌnɚ'ʌp〕*n.* 亞軍
acknowledge〔ək'nɑlɪdʒ〕*v.* 公告　　***bulletin board*** 佈告欄
participant〔pɚ'tɪsəpənt〕*n.* 參加者
contest〔'kɑntɛst〕*n.* 競賽

31. (**B**) Which statement is true about this announcement?

    A. Second place winners were announced.

    B. The project "Life on Tundras" won first prize in biology.

    C. Only the first place winners will be shown on the bulletin board.

    D. John Lasota won first prize in chemistry.

    * *second place* 第二名   *first prize* 第一名
    chemistry〔'kɛmɪstrɪ〕*n.* 化學

32. (**A**) Where does this announcement most likely take place?

    A. On a middle school intercom.

    B. On the principal's telephone.

    C. Outside, in front of the school.

    D. On the bulletin board.

    * *take place* 發生   *middle school* 中學
    intercom〔'ɪntɚ͵kɑm〕*n.* 內部通訊系統；內部廣播
    (= *intercommunication system*)
    principal〔'prɪnsəpl̩〕*n.* 校長

33. (**C**) Who won first prize in physics with the project "Windmill Electricity?"

    A. Ed Williams.

    B. Dave Trout.

    C. John Lasota.

    D. Not known.

Questions 34-35 refer to the following speech.

> We are ready to begin service to the Paris airports. However, we have not been given permission by the French airport authority to land our planes there. We went through the proper channels in asking for this permission, and have waited longer than the standard waiting period. Therefore, it is with regret that we must announce today that our New York/Paris schedule will not be opening as planned this week.

** service〔'sɜ˞vɪs〕*n.*（交通工具的）來往

permission〔pɚ'mɪʃən〕*n.* 許可

authority〔ə'θɔrətɪ〕*n.* 當局　　land〔lænd〕*v.* 降落

go through 通過　　channel〔'tʃænḷ〕*n.* 管道

standard〔'stændɚd〕*adj.* 一般的　　***with regret*** 遺憾地

announce〔ə'naʊns〕*v.* 宣布　　schedule〔'skɛdʒʊl〕*n.* 計畫

open〔'opən〕*v.* 使營業

34. (**B**) What is the purpose of this speech?

    A. To announce a new air route.

    B. To cancel a planned air route.

    C. To ask for permission to land planes.

    D. To extend the waiting period.

    * route〔rut〕*n.* 航線　　planned〔plænd〕*adj.* 計畫好的
    extend〔ɪk'stɛnd〕*v.* 延長

35. (**C**) What is hinted at in this speech?

    A. Illegal maneuvers on the part of the airline.

    B. Long waiting periods.

    C. Stubborn government resistance.

    D. A different air route.

    * hint〔hɪnt〕*v.* 作暗示　　illegal〔ɪ'ligl〕*adj.* 非法的
    maneuver〔mə'nuvɚ〕*n.* 策略
    on the part of 在～方面
    stubborn〔'stʌbɚn〕*adj.* 頑固的
    resistance〔rɪ'zɪstəns〕*n.* 反對

Questions 36-38 refer to the following announcement.

We interrupt this program for a special news bulletin: a Gerro Airlines 737 airliner flying from Miami, Florida to Bermuda with 150 passengers on board was forced to make a water landing in the Atlantic Ocean after an apparent engine fire.

Aircraft control stations monitoring the plane's broadcasts say that the pilot reported black smoke pouring from one of the engines. As the nearest islands are more than 400 miles away, the pilot was forced to land the plane in the water. The Coast Guard has already reached the downed aircraft and is rescuing passengers. There are no reports of casualties.

** interrupt 〔͵ɪntə'rʌpt〕 v. 中斷　bulletin 〔'bʊlətɪn〕 n. 新聞快報
airliner 〔'ɛr͵laɪnɚ〕 n. 大型班機
Bermuda 〔bɚ'mjudə〕 n. 百慕達（群島）　　*on board* 在機上
be forced to 被迫　　landing 〔'lændɪŋ〕 n. 降落
apparent 〔ə'pærənt〕 adj. 明顯的
aircraft 〔'ɛr͵kræft〕 n. 飛機　　monitor 〔'mɑnətɚ〕 v. 監聽
broadcast 〔'brɔd͵kæst〕 n. 廣播　　pilot 〔'paɪlət〕 n. 駕駛員
pour 〔por〕 v. 冒出　　*Coast Guard* 海岸防衛隊
downed 〔daʊnd〕 adj. 迫降的　　rescue 〔'rɛskju〕 v. 拯救
casualties 〔'kæʒʊəltɪz〕 n. pl. 死傷者

36. (**B**) What has happened?

    A. A plane has been hijacked in Miami, Florida.

    B. An airplane had to land in the ocean.

    C. An airplane has crashed in Bermuda.

    D. A plane was fired on by terrorists.

    * hijack〔'haɪ,dʒæk〕v. 劫機　　crash〔kræʃ〕v. 墜毀
    fire〔faɪr〕v. 射擊　　terrorist〔'tɛrərɪst〕n. 恐怖份子

37. (**C**) How many passengers was the plane carrying?

    A. 737.

    B. More than 400.

    C. 150.

    D. Authorities are not sure.

    * authorities〔ə'θɔrətɪɪz〕n. pl. 當局

38. (**D**) What was reported by the pilot of the aircraft?

    A. The exact location of the plane.

    B. That he was trying to land on an island.

    C. That passengers were injured in the attack.

    D. That smoke was coming from the plane's engine.

    * exact〔ɪg'zækt〕adj. 確切的
    injure〔'ɪndʒə〕v. 傷害
    attack〔ə'tæk〕n. 攻擊

Questions 39-40 are based on the following advertisement.

　　With a subscription to The Daily Tribune, you get the news of the world delivered to your doorstep each and every morning of the year. For just 32 cents a day, you'll always know what's going on in international and national affairs, state and local concerns, business, sports and culture. And every Sunday in our Shopper's Guide you'll find special coupons that will save you money when you go shopping. You can subscribe for three months, six months or a year. Subscribe anytime in April and we'll send you a copy of our popular News Reader's Dictionary, a $29 value, absolutely free.

** subscription〔səb'skrɪpʃən〕n. 訂閱 < to >
　　tribune〔'trɪbjun〕n. 論壇（此應譯爲「論壇報」）
　　doorstep〔'dor,stɛp〕n. 門口的階梯　　affair〔ə'fɛr〕n. 事情
　　state〔stet〕adj. 州的　　local〔'lokḷ〕adj. 地方的
　　concern〔kən'sɝn〕n. 重要的事
　　coupon〔'kupɑn〕n. 折價券
　　subscribe〔səb'skraɪb〕v. 訂閱　　copy〔'kɑpɪ〕n.（一）本
　　absolutely〔,æbsə'lutlɪ〕adv. 完全地

39. (**C**) Which of the following does the advertisement say subscribers will receive for free?

A. Business reports.

B. Tickets to a sports event.

C. A special dictionary.

D. Scissors and a ruler.

* subscriber〔səb'skraɪbɚ〕 *n.* 訂閱者

   for free 免費地　　sports〔sports〕 *adj.* 運動的

   event〔ɪ'vɛnt〕 *n.*（比賽）項目

   scissors〔'sɪzɚz〕 *n. pl.* 剪刀　　ruler〔'rulɚ〕 *n.* 尺

40. (**D**) How does The Daily Tribune say it can help you save money?

A. It costs less than other newspapers.

B. It is selling at a discount now.

C. By keeping you informed of the market.

D. By giving you shopping coupons.

* discount〔'dɪskaʊnt〕 *n.* 折扣

   informed〔ɪn'fɔrmd〕 *adj.* 消息靈通的；了解情況的

Questions 41-43 are based on the following speech.

Two years ago the Regional Roads Commission approved the funding for construction of a commuter road linking the town of Alberd with the city of Dalond. It gives me great pleasure to be here today to mark the opening of Route Three-Sixteen. It is quite an accomplishment to finish a project of this size in only two years.

The new road will be open only to non-commercial traffic, which will ease congestion for commuters, as well as improve the flow for commercial traffic on the old highway. Ladies and gentlemen, without further ado, I will now cut the ribbon, and officially open Route Three-Sixteen.

** **regional** 〔'ridʒənḷ〕 *adj.* 地方的
　commission 〔kə'mɪʃən〕 *n.* 委員會
　approve 〔ə'pruv〕 *v.* 同意　　**funding** 〔'fʌndɪŋ〕 *n.* 資助
　construction 〔kən'strʌkʃən〕 *n.* 建築
　commuter 〔kə'mjutɚ〕 *n.* 通勤者
　commuter road 市郊往返的道路
　link 〔lɪŋk〕 *v.* 連接　　**mark** 〔mɑrk〕 *v.* 使顯著
　route 〔rut〕 *n.* 路線；道路
　accomplishment 〔ə'kɑmplɪʃmənt〕 *n.* 成就
　project 〔'prɑdʒɛkt〕 *n.* 工程
　non-commercial 〔'nɑn͵kə'mɝʃəl〕 *adj.* 非營利的
　ease 〔iz〕 *v.* 減輕　　**congestion** 〔kən'dʒɛstʃən〕 *n.* 阻塞
　flow 〔flo〕 *n.* (交通) 流量　　**ado** 〔ə'du〕 *n.* 麻煩
　without further ado 不再囉嗦　　**ribbon** 〔'rɪbən〕 *n.* 緞帶
　officially 〔ə'fɪʃəlɪ〕 *adv.* 正式地

41. (**B**) What kind of vehicles can use Route Three-Sixteen?

    A. Commercial vehicles only.

    B. Only non-commercial vehicles.

    C. All properly registered vehicles.

    D. Vehicles owned by residents of Alberd.

    * vehicle ﹝'viɪkḷ﹞ *n.* 車輛
      commercial ﹝kə'mɝʃəl﹞ *adj.* 營利的
      properly ﹝'prɑpəlɪ﹞ *adv.* 適當地
      registered ﹝'rɛdʒɪstəd﹞ *adj.* 登記的
      resident ﹝'rɛzədənt﹞ *n.* 居民

42. (**D**) What did the Regional Roads Commission do?

    A. Propose that an alternate route be built.

    B. Approve a plan to ban commercial traffic.

    C. Fund a study of the region's vehicle usage.

    D. Approve funding for construction of the new road.

    * propose ﹝prə'poz﹞ *v.* 提議
      alternate ﹝'ɔltənɪt﹞ *adj.* 替代的   ban ﹝bæn﹞ *v.* 禁止
      fund ﹝fʌnd﹞ *v.* 出資   region ﹝'ridʒən﹞ *n.* 地區
      usage ﹝'jusɪdʒ﹞ *n.* 使用

43. (**D**) What benefit does route Three-Sixteen bring to the region?

    A. Increased revenue from users' fees.

    B. An increase in jobs for local residents.

    C. Better access for tourists and vacationers.

    D. Reduced congestion on the existing highway.

    * benefit ﹝'bɛnəfɪt﹞ *n.* 好處   revenue ﹝'rɛvə,nju﹞ *n.* 收入
      access ﹝'æksɛs﹞ *n.* 通道
      vacationer ﹝ve'keʃənə﹞ *n.* 渡假的人
      reduced ﹝rɪ'djust﹞ *adj.* 減少的
      existing ﹝ɪg'zɪstɪŋ﹞ *adj.* 現有的

Questions 44-45 are based on the following announcement.

> This is D.J. Dan, rocking you through the night. If you have something you'd like to hear, give me a call. My number here is 789-7899. Again, it's 789-7899. And don't worry, any request is okay, no matter how old it is. That's the advantage of a late night show — anything is possible.

** D.J. 電台主持人（= *disc jockey*） 　　rock〔rɑk〕*v.* 使搖擺
request〔rɪ'kwɛst〕*n.* 點播歌曲　*v.* 點播
advantage〔əd'væntɪdʒ〕*n.* 好處

44. (**D**) Who is making this announcement?
　　　A. A department store.
　　　B. An airport paging system.
　　　C. A subway system operator.
　　　D. A radio station disc jockey.

　　　* page〔pedʒ〕*v.* 廣播叫（人） 　　*paging system* 廣播系統
subway〔'sʌb,we〕*n.* 地下鐵
operator〔'ɑpə,retə〕*n.* 操作員

45. (**C**) What can you do by calling the number announced?
　　　A. Purchase music cassettes and CD's.
　　　B. Make reservations.
　　　C. Request a song. 　　　D. Voice your opinion.

　　　* purchase〔'pɝtʃəs〕*v.* 購買　cassette〔kæ'sɛt〕*n.* 錄音帶
reservation〔,rɛzə'veʃən〕*n.* 預訂
voice〔vɔɪs〕*v.* 說出；表達

High-Intermediate Level
Listening Comprehension Test

This listening comprehension test will test your ability to understand spoken English. In this test, each conversation, short talk and question will be spoken JUST ONE TIME. They will not be written out for you. There are three parts to this test. Special instructions will be given to you at the beginning of each part.

Part A

In part A, you will hear 15 questions. After you hear a question, read the four choices in your test book and decide which one is the best answer to the question you have heard.

Example:

<u>You will hear</u>:　Mary, can you tell me what time it is?

<u>You will read</u>:　A.　About two hours ago.
　　　　　　　　　　　B.　I used to be able to, but not now.
　　　　　　　　　　　C.　Sure, it's half past nine.
　　　　　　　　　　　D.　Today is October 22.

The best answer to the question "Mary, can you tell me what time it is?" is C: "Sure, it's half past nine." Therefore, you should choose answer C.

1. A. It's over there on the corner.
   B. From 9-5.
   C. I saw her there a moment ago.
   D. I need to buy some stamps.

2. A. Yes, go ahead.
   B. Not at all.
   C. You're welcome.
   D. I don't mind your smoking here.

3. A. I've done my share of the work.
   B. That's my duty.
   C. We should share all.
   D. I think advertisements can boost sales.

4. A. We're getting married next month.
   B. A few weeks ago.
   C. I'm very busy now.
   D. I'm engaged to Peter.

5. A. I worked part-time.
   B. That you need to be patient.
   C. I studied for three years.
   D. I met a lot of patients.

6. A. Yes, with cream and sugar.
   B. Yes, only at 10:00 and 3:00.
   C. Yes, they're flexible.
   D. I want it black, please.

7. A. Yes, it cost $12.00.
   B. Yes, this book looks
      interesting.
   C. Yes, he's due soon.
   D. Yes, I'm going to
      return it now.

8. A. As often as I can.
   B. Jim wants to stay
      healthy.
   C. In a few days.
   D. It's just a few blocks
      away.

9. A. Yes, I like that.
   B. No problem, sir.
   C. Just around the corner.
   D. You may take a taxi.

10. A. I think he's a good
       manager.
    B. He's going to apply
       for computer
       engineer.
    C. He was promoted
       last year.
    D. General Manager.

11. A. It's 10 o'clock.
    B. I'm not exactly sure.
    C. The cities are very
       different.
    D. I'm still suffering
       from the jet lag.

12. A. I haven't got the
       slightest idea.
    B. I believe so. Let me
       check.
    C. The line is engaged now.
    D. There's a phone booth
       over there.

14. A. She's an actress.
    B. She likes horror
       movies.
    C. The movie is the hit
       of the year.
    D. She said they were
       sold out.

13. A. I wasn't planning to call
       the airline.
    B. No, I don't think it's
       necessary.
    C. Yes, I'll have spaghetti,
       please.
    D. Yes, these seats are
       reserved for special
       guests.

15. A. I plan to go to the
       beach.
    B. It rained all day
       yesterday.
    C. It will clear up soon.
    D. It should be hot and
       humid.

Part B

In part B, you will hear 15 conversations between a man and a woman. After each conversation, you will hear a question about the conversation. After you hear the question, read the four choices in your test book and choose the best answer to the question you have heard.

Example:

You will hear: (Man)   May I see your driver's license?
               (Woman)   Yes, officer. Here it is. Was I speeding?
               (Man)   Yes, ma'am. You were doing sixty in a forty-five mile an hour zone.
               (Woman)   No way! I don't believe you.
               (Man)   Well, it is true and here is your ticket.

               Question: Why does the man ask for the woman's driver's license?

You will read: A. She was going too fast.
                B. To check its limitations.
                C. To check her age.
                D. She entered a restricted zone.

The best answer to the question "Why does the man ask for the woman's driver's license?" is A: "She was going too fast." Therefore, you should choose answer A.

16. A. Call Paul.
    B. Meet Paul at the club.
    C. Page Paul.
    D. Answer the phone.

17. A. Seven hours.
    B. Two hours.
    C. Nine hours.
    D. At seven.

18. A. She took the sample copy.
    B. She left a sample copy on the desk.
    C. She read all the copies.
    D. She gave away some copies.

19. A. No, not at all.
    B. Definitely so in the US.
    C. Only in Third World markets.
    D. Products should be cheap.

20. A. She's not going to meet Melvin.
    B. She's going back home.
    C. She's meeting someone else for lunch.
    D. She's going back to the office.

21. A. To operate on a large scale.
    B. To transfer the man.
    C. To become more competitive.
    D. To lay off the man.

22. A. The woman is well qualified for the job.
    B. The man will surely be hired for the job.
    C. They don't seem to understand each other.
    D. The man's documents are insufficient.

23. A. She's returning to the office.
    B. She's going to have a shower.
    C. She may climb Mt. Hood.
    D. She will go rock-climbing.

24. A. At the visa office.
    B. The woman's house.
    C. In the drawer.
    D. It's lost.

25. A. The directors.
    B. The day's plan.
    C. The clock.
    D. A meeting.

26. A. He wants to deliver the order now.
    B. He's going to get another job.
    C. He's going on holiday.
    D. He needs the order quickly.

27. A. The manager is leaving for Japan.
    B. A guest is arriving.
    C. Mr. Kiley is leaving at 1:30.
    D. There should always be someone going.

28. A. It has run out of gas.
    B. It won't start.
    C. It has a flat tire.
    D. Its brakes don't work well.

29. A. The printer is jammed.
    B. The woman doesn't know how to use it.
    C. The printer is broken.
    D. They don't have enough printers.

30. A. To work on Saturday.
    B. To find a new job.
    C. To take Saturday off.
    D. To finish work early.

Part C

In part C, you will hear several short talks. After each talk, you will hear 2 to 3 questions about the talk. After you hear each question, read the four choices in your test book and choose the best answer to the question you have heard.

Example:

<u>You will hear</u>:

Thank you for coming to this, the first in a series of seminars on the use of computers in the classroom. As the brochure informed you, there will be a total of five seminars given in this room every Monday morning from 6:00 to 7:30. Our goal will be to show you, the teachers of our school children, how the changing technology of today can be applied to the unchanging lessons of yesterday to make your students' learning experience more interesting and relevant to the world they live in. By the end of the last seminar, you will not be computer literate, but you will be able to make sense of the hundreds of complex words and technical terms related to the field and be aware of the programs available for use in the classroom.

Question number 1:　What is the subject of this seminar
series?

You will read:　A.　Self-improvement.
　　　　　　　　　B.　Using computers to teach.
　　　　　　　　　C.　Technology.
　　　　　　　　　D.　Study habits of today's students.

The best answer to the question "What is the subject of this
seminar series?" is B: "Using computers to teach." Therefore,
you should choose answer B.

Now listen to another question based on the same talk.

You will hear:
　　Question number 2:　What does the speaker say
　　　　　　　　　　　　　participants will be able to do after
　　　　　　　　　　　　　attending the seminars?

You will read:　A.　Understand today's students.
　　　　　　　　　B.　Understand computer terminology.
　　　　　　　　　C.　Motivate students.
　　　　　　　　　D.　Deal more confidently with people.

The best answer to the question "What does the speaker say
participants will be able to do after attending the seminars?" is
B: "Understand computer terminology." Therefore, you should
choose answer B.

31. A. By radio.
    B. By television.
    C. By telephone.
    D. By satellite.

32. A. Three.
    B. Two.
    C. One.
    D. Four.

33. A. Once.
    B. Twice.
    C. Four times.
    D. Nine times.

34. A. Mayor.
    B. Congressman.
    C. President.
    D. Governor.

35. A. Cut income and property taxes.
    B. Reduce the size of government.
    C. Increase job opportunities.
    D. Fight crime in the city.

36. A. A consultant.
    B. An immigration officer.
    C. A travel agent.
    D. A bank clerk.

37. A. The data is incomplete.
    B. They don't have data on incomes.
    C. The information is dependable.
    D. The information covers the domestic market.

38. A. At six o'clock.
    B. On the 6th.
    C. On the 16th.
    D. Anytime.

39. A. 16.
    B. 4.
    C. 24.
    D. 6.

40. A. A book about
       mathematical proofs.
    B. An instruction manual.
    C. A historical periodical.
    D. A novel.

41. A. There is a strike.
    B. There is a problem with
       production.
    C. Some workers have
       been declared redundant.
    D. The factory is unsafe
       to work.

42. A. They want a pay raise.
    B. They want the CEO
       fired.
    C. They want shorter
       working hours.
    D. They want to take over
       the company.

43. A. Tomorrow afternoon.
    B. It's already finished.
    C. It's difficult to tell.
    D. After the next
       communiqué.

44. A. Baseball.
    B. Basketball.
    C. Hockey.
    D. Football.

45. A. Houston and
       Cleveland.
    B. Cleveland and
       Chicago.
    C. Chicago and Green
       Bay.
    D. Houston and Green
       Bay.

中高級聽力測驗詳解 ⑤

Part A

1. (**A**) Can you tell me where the post office is?

   A. It's over there on the corner.

   B. From 9-5.

   C. I saw her there a moment ago.

   D. I need to buy some stamps.

   * stamp〔 stæmp 〕*n.* 郵票

2. (**B**) Do you mind if I make a suggestion?

   A. Yes, go ahead.

   B. Not at all.

   C. You're welcome.

   D. I don't mind your smoking here.

   * suggestion〔 sə'dʒɛstʃən 〕*n.* 建議
   Go ahead. 請說。　　***Not at all.*** 一點也不。

3. (**D**) How can we increase our market share?

   A. I've done my share of the work.

   B. That's my duty.

   C. We should share all.

   D. I think advertisements can boost sales.

   * share〔 ʃɛr 〕*n.* 市場佔有率；一份　*v.* 分享
   duty〔'djutɪ 〕*n.* 責任
   advertisement〔ˌædvɚ'taɪzmənt 〕*n.* 廣告
   boost〔 bust 〕*v.* 提昇　　sales〔 selz 〕*n. pl.* 銷售量

4. (**B**) When did you get engaged?

    A. We're getting married next month.

    B. A few weeks ago.

    C. I'm very busy now.

    D. I'm engaged to Peter.

    * engaged〔ɪn'gedʒd〕*adj.* 訂婚的

       be engaged to 和～訂婚

5. (**B**) What did you learn in medical school?

    A. I worked part-time.

    B. That you need to be patient.

    C. I studied for three years.

    D. I met a lot of patients.

    * medical〔'mɛdɪkl̩〕*adj.* 醫學的

       medical school 醫學院

       part-time〔'pɑrt'taɪm〕*adv.* 打工地

       patient〔'peʃənt〕*adj.* 有耐心的　*n.* 病人

6. (**C**) Can you take coffee breaks whenever you want?

    A. Yes, with cream and sugar.

    B. Yes, only at 10:00 and 3:00.

    C. Yes, they're flexible.

    D. I want it black, please.

    * **coffee break** 休息時間　　cream〔krim〕*n.* 奶精

       flexible〔'flɛksəbl̩〕*adj.* 有彈性的

       black〔blæk〕*adj.*（咖啡）不加牛奶和奶精的

7. (**D**) Did you get this book from the library?

    A. Yes, it cost $12.00.

    B. Yes, this book looks interesting.

    C. Yes, he's due soon.

    D. Yes, I'm going to return it now.

    * due〔dju〕*adj.* 預定到達的

8. (**A**) How often do you go to the gym?

    A. As often as I can.

    B. Jim wants to stay healthy.

    C. In a few days.

    D. It's just a few blocks away.

    * gym〔dʒɪm〕*n.* 健身房；體育館

    as ~ as one can 儘可能

    block〔blɑk〕*n.* 街區

9. (**C**) Excuse me, where can I get a cab?

    A. Yes, I like that.

    B. No problem, sir.

    C. Just around the corner.

    D. You may take a taxi.

    * cab〔kæb〕*n.* 計程車（= *taxi*）

    around the corner 在街角；附近

10. (**D**) What is Mr. Stern's position?

　　A. I think he's a good manager.

　　B. He's going to apply for computer engineer.

　　C. He was promoted last year.

　　D. General Manager.

　　* position〔pəˈzɪʃən〕 n. 職務　　***apply for*** 應徵

　　　engineer〔͵ɛndʒəˈnɪr〕 n. 工程師

　　　promote〔prəˈmot〕 v. 升遷　　***general manager*** 總經理

11. (**B**) What's the time difference between New York and Tokyo?

　　A. It's 10 o'clock.

　　B. I'm not exactly sure.

　　C. The cities are very different.

　　D. I'm still suffering from the jet lag.

　　* ***time difference*** 時差　　suffer〔ˈsʌfɚ〕 v. 受苦 < *from* >

　　　jet lag 時差所引起的不舒服症狀

12. (**B**) Do you have change for the phone?

　　A. I haven't got the slightest idea.

　　B. I believe so. Let me check.

　　C. The line is engaged now.

　　D. There's a phone booth over there.

　　* change〔tʃendʒ〕 n. 零錢　　slight〔slaɪt〕 adj. 微小的

　　　I haven't got the slightest idea. 我完全不知道。

　　　engaged〔ɪnˈgedʒd〕 adj. (電話)使用中

　　　The line is engaged. 電話佔線中。

　　　booth〔buθ〕 n. 公用電話亭

13. (**B**) Are you planning to make dinner reservations?

    A. I wasn't planning to call the airline.

    B. No, I don't think it's necessary.

    C. Yes, I'll have spaghetti, please.

    D. Yes, these seats are reserved for special guests.

    * reservation ﹝ˌrɛzəˋveʃən ﹞ *n.* 預訂
      airline ﹝ˋɛrˌlaɪn ﹞ *n.* 航空公司
      spaghetti ﹝ spəˋgɛtɪ ﹞ *n.* 義大利麵
      reserve ﹝ rɪˋzɝv ﹞ *v.* 保留   guest ﹝ gɛst ﹞ *n.* 客人

14. (**D**) Did she get tickets for the movie?

    A. She's an actress.

    B. She likes horror movies.

    C. The movie is the hit of the year.

    D. She said they were sold out.

    * actress ﹝ˋæktrɪs ﹞ *n.* 女演員
      horror ﹝ˋharə ﹞ *n.* 恐怖   ***horror movie*** 恐怖片
      hit ﹝ hɪt ﹞ *n.* 風行一時的事物   ***be sold out*** 賣完

15. (**D**) What's the forecast for the weekend?

    A. I plan to go to the beach.

    B. It rained all day yesterday.

    C. It will clear up soon.

    D. It should be hot and humid.

    * forecast ﹝ˋforˌkæst ﹞ *n.* 預測
      clear up 放晴   humid ﹝ˋhjumɪd ﹞ *adj.* 潮濕的

Part B

16. (**D**) M：I'm going out to lunch now. If Paul calls, tell him to meet me at the club at seven.

W：So, you won't be back for the day?

M：I don't intend to, but if there's anything important, you can page me.

W：Okay. Have fun then.

Question：What is the woman supposed to do?

A. Call Paul.　　　　　B. Meet Paul at the club.

C. Page Paul.　　　　　D. Answer the phone.

* club〔klʌb〕*n.* 俱樂部　　intend〔ɪn'tɛnd〕*v.* 打算

page〔pedʒ〕*v.* 用呼叫器呼叫（某人）

be supposed to 應該　　***answer the phone*** 接電話

17. (**B**) W：What time is breakfast here?

M：You can have your breakfast anytime between 7 and 9.

W：That's very convenient indeed.

M：We try our best to make our guests feel at home, ma'am.

W：How very thoughtful of you.

Question：How long is breakfast served for?

A. Seven hours.　　　　B. Two hours.

C. Nine hours.　　　　　D. At seven.

* indeed〔ɪn'did〕*adv.* 真地；實在

try one's best 盡力　　***feel at home*** 感到舒適

thoughtful〔'θɔtfəl〕*adj.* 體貼的　　serve〔sɜv〕*v.* 供應

18. (**B**)　M：Christy, is the sample copy ready yet?

W：It's all ready. In fact, I left a copy on your desk this morning.

M：I didn't see anything on my desk.

W：It's there. You'll just have to look through that disaster area you call your desk.

M：Ha. Ha. I'm not amused at all.

Question：What did the woman do?

A. She took the sample copy.

B. She left a sample copy on the desk.

C. She read all the copies.

D. She gave away some copies.

* sample〔'sæmpl〕n. 樣本　　copy〔'kɑpɪ〕n. 一份
sample copy 樣書；樣本　　*look through* 仔細檢查
disaster〔dɪz'æstə〕n. 災害　　*disaster area* 災區
amuse〔ə'mjuz〕v. 使覺得有趣　　*give away* 贈送

19. (**B**)　M：How important is packaging in the sale of products?

W：It's very important in the United States. I don't know about Third World consumers, but I'm sure every consumer wants something attractive.

M：That'll be interesting to find out.

W：We have a survey in the works. That should at least give us some ideas.

Question : Does packaging affect product sales?

A. No, not at all.

B. Definitely so in the US.

C. Only in Third World markets.

D. Products should be cheap.

* packaging〔'pækɪdʒɪŋ〕*n.* 包裝

 product〔'prɑdəkt〕*n.* 產品

 Third World 第三世界（泛指全球未開發或開發中國家）

 consumer〔kən'sjumɚ〕*n.* 消費者

 survey〔'sɝve〕*n.* 調查

 in the works 順利進行中　　***at least*** 至少

 not at all 一點也不　　definitely〔'dɛfənɪtlɪ〕*adv.* 一定

20. (**C**) M : Are you coming to lunch with us?

 W : Sorry, I can't. I have to meet Melvin for lunch.

 M : Why don't you ask Melvin to come?

 W : No, it's okay. I have something I need to discuss
  with him over lunch.

 M : Okay. See you later, then.

 Question : What's the woman going to do?

 A. She's not going to meet Melvin.

 B. She's going back home.

 C. She's meeting someone else for lunch.

 D. She's going back to the office.

21. (**C**) W: I think that our problem is that we haven't reengineered. But the fact is that the market has changed and we have new competition to face.

M: Each time I hear the word "reengineering," I get scared. I feel like there will be many layoffs and transfers. And people don't like change. Let's think of other ways.

W: If we can't make a profit, we go out of business and everyone becomes unemployed. Tough choice.

M: I'm still dubious about that concept. We'll work on it later.

Question: What does the woman want?

A. To operate on a large scale.

B. To transfer the man.

C. To become more competitive.

D. To lay off the man.

* reengineer〔,riɛndʒə'nɪr〕v. 重新策畫
competition〔,kampə'tɪʃən〕n. 競爭
scared〔skɛrd〕adj. 感到害怕的   layoff〔'le,ɔf〕n. 解雇
transfer〔'trænsfɝ〕n. 調任;〔træns'fɝ〕v. 調任
profit〔'prafɪt〕n. 利潤   *out of business* 停業
unemployed〔,ʌnɪm'plɔɪd〕adj. 失業的
tough〔tʌf〕adj. 困難的
dubious〔'djubɪəs〕adj. 半信半疑的
concept〔'kansɛpt〕n. 概念   operate〔'apə,ret〕v. 運轉
scale〔skel〕n. 規模   *on a large scale* 大規模地
competitive〔kəm'pɛtətɪv〕adj. 有競爭力的
lay off 解雇

22. (**B**) W: Please take a seat. I received your résumé last week and I have gone through it carefully. You surely have a very interesting background. I must mention that a lot of what you have done will be quite relevant to the kind of work you'll be doing here.

M: You might want to look at my other references from one of my former employers.

W: Well, we've seen enough. And we are very impressed with you.

M: Thank you for your compliment. I'm flattered.

W: Now, one last thing. When can you start?

Question: What is obvious in this conversation?

A. The woman is well qualified for the job.

B. The man will surely be hired for the job.

C. They don't seem to understand each other.

D. The man's documents are insufficient.

* résumé (ˈrɛzuˌme) n. 履歷表　*go through* 詳細查看
background (ˈbækˌgraʊnd) n. 背景
relevant (ˈrɛləvənt) adj. 有關的
reference (ˈrɛfərəns) n. 推薦函
former (ˈfɔrmə) adj. 以前的
employer (ɪmˈplɔɪə) n. 雇主
impressed (ɪmˈprɛst) adj. 對～印象深刻的
compliment (ˈkɑmpləmənt) n. 恭維；讚揚
flattered (ˈflætəd) adj. 感到高興的
obvious (ˈɑbvɪəs) adj. 明顯的
qualified (ˈkwɑləˌfaɪd) adj. 能勝任的；夠資格的
document (ˈdɑkjəmənt) n. 文件
insufficient (ˌɪnsəˈfɪʃənt) adj. 不足的

23. (**C**)　W: Where are you going after the conference?

M: I haven't made any plans yet. What about you?

W: We are thinking of climbing Mt. Hood. Do you want to come with us?

M: That is some serious activity. I don't know if I can do it.

W: Oh, come on. It's really easy. In fact, Mt. Hood is the perfect place for beginners. Besides, we are all experienced climbers.

Question: What's the woman going to do?

A. She's returning to the office.

B. She's going to have a shower.

C. She may climb Mt. Hood.

D. She will go rock-climbing.

* conference〔'kɑnfərəns〕*n.* 會議

　Mt. 山（= *Mount*）　　***come on***　（作慫恿語）好啦

　experienced〔ɪk'spɪrɪənst〕*adj.* 有經驗的

　climber〔'klaɪmɚ〕*n.* 登山者

　shower〔'ʃaʊɚ〕*n.* 淋浴

　rock-climbing〔'rɑk͵klaɪmɪŋ〕*n.* 攀岩

24. (**A**) M：Did you remember to pick up my passport?

W：I arrived just in time to see the doors close. Definitely, tomorrow.

M：Well, you'd better make it the first thing in the morning.

W：I will. Don't worry about it. But you know, these visa officials are not very flexible. They could've let me pick up the passport, but they just wouldn't budge.

M：I know. That's why I told you to be there earlier.

Question：Where is the man's passport?

A. At the visa office.

B. The woman's house.

C. In the drawer.

D. It's lost.

* ***pick up*** 領取　　passport〔'pæs,port〕*n.* 護照

in time 及時　　definitely〔'dɛfənɪtlɪ〕*adv.* 一定

visa〔'vizə〕*n.* 簽證　　official〔ə'fɪʃəl〕*n.* 官員

visa official 簽證官

flexible〔'flɛksəbḷ〕*adj.* 有彈性的

budge〔bʌdʒ〕*v.* 讓步　　drawer〔drɔr〕*n.* 抽屜

25. (**D**) W: You are aware that the directors' meeting is on at two, aren't you?

M: Do you mean two o'clock today?

W: No, tomorrow.

M: Are you sure? I could've sworn that I heard it's today.

W: No. It's tomorrow. See, here it says on the e-mail.

Question: What are the man and the woman talking about?

A. The directors.

B. The day's plan.

C. The clock.

D. A meeting.

* aware〔ə'wɛr〕*adj.* 知道的

director〔də'rɛktə〕*n.* 主任；董事

swear〔swɛr〕*v.* 發誓（三態變化為：swear-swore-sworn）

26. (**D**) M: I want to know exactly when you are going to make the delivery.

W: It'll have to be sometime after the holidays.

M: Then I might go somewhere else. I need the order right away.

W: It's going to be pretty hard for you to find anyone else who can do it before the holidays, unless you can arrange to pick it up yourself.

M: That's all right. I'll try somewhere else.

Question: What does the man want?

A. He wants to deliver the order now.

B. He's going to get another job.

C. He's going on holiday.

D. He needs the order quickly.

* delivery〔dɪ'lɪvərɪ〕*n.* 遞送

 order〔'ɔrdə〕*n.* 訂貨 pretty〔'prɪtɪ〕*adv.* 相當地

 arrange〔ə'rendʒ〕*v.* 設法;安排 ***pick up*** 領取

27.（**B**）M: Whom did you send to the airport?

 W: Why? Is someone coming?

 M: Mr. Kiley is due to arrive at 1:30 this afternoon.

 W: Oh, no! I had completely forgotten about it. I didn't arrange for anyone to pick him up.

 M: You'd better do it soon or you'll have to go yourself.

Question: Why should someone go to the airport?

A. The manager is leaving for Japan.

B. A guest is arriving.

C. Mr. Kiley is leaving at 1:30.

D. There should always be someone going.

* due〔dju〕*adj.* 預定的

 completely〔kəm'plitlɪ〕*adv.* 完全地

 pick *sb*. ***up*** 開車去接某人 ***leave for*** 前往

28. (**B**) W: The car won't start. I don't know a thing about cars.

M: Maybe we should call a cab.

W: That's too far to go by cab.

M: We don't really have many options, do we?

W: I guess you're right.

Question: What's wrong with the car?

A. It has run out of gas.

B. It won't start.

C. It has a flat tire.

D. Its brakes don't work well.

* cab〔kæb〕*n.* 計程車　　start〔stɑrt〕*v.* 發動
option〔'ɑpʃən〕*n.* 選擇　　***run out of*** 用完
gas〔gæs〕*n.* 汽油　　***flat tire*** 爆胎
brake〔brek〕*n.* 煞車

29. (**D**) W: Frank, have you finished printing yet?

M: No, not yet.

W: Sorry, I have to use the printer now.

M: I'll be done in a few more minutes. Can you wait that long?

W: Okay.

Question: What seems to be the problem?

A. The printer is jammed.

B. The woman doesn't know how to use it.

C. The printer is broken.

D. They don't have enough printers.

* print〔prɪnt〕*v.* 列印　　printer〔'prɪntɚ〕*n.* 印表機
jam〔dʒæm〕*v.* 卡住

30. (**D**)　W: It's not one of those time-consuming jobs, is it?

　　　　　M: No.　You'll be done in no time.

　　　　　W: I don't want to be stuck working on Saturdays.

　　　　　M: I promise you it's a quickie.　You'll be done with it by the time you know it.

　　　　　W: Ok.　I'll take your word for it.

　　　　　Question: What does the woman want?

　　　　　A.　To work on Saturday.

　　　　　B.　To find a new job.

　　　　　C.　To take Saturday off.

　　　　　D.　To finish work early.

　　　　　* time-consuming〔'taɪmkənˌsjumɪŋ〕 adj. 費時的
　　　　　in no time 立刻　　***be stuck*** 被困住
　　　　　quickie〔'kwɪkɪ〕 n. 速成的研究或計畫
　　　　　take one's ***word for it*** 相信某人的話
　　　　　take off 休假

Part C

Questions 31-33 are based on the following passage.

> You have reached the Hilltop Movie-Line. Located at 1532 Marvin Rd., the Hilltop Cinema is open seven days a week. This month's features include *Time Bomb*, a thriller starring Bobby Chang, *What Women Know*, a romantic comedy starring Barbara Streisberg, and *La Vida*, a Spanish tragedy starring Victor Marquez. All films are scheduled to run at noon, 3, 6, and at 9 p.m. Monday through Friday; and at 2, 4, 6, 8, and at 10 p.m. during the weekend. Thank you for calling the Hilltop Movie-Line. This is a recording.

** hilltop〔ˈhɪlˌtɑp〕*n.* 山頂　　locate〔loˈket〕*v.* 使位於
cinema〔ˈsɪnəmə〕*n.* 電影院
feature〔ˈfitʃɚ〕*n.* 上映電影　　***time bomb*** 定時炸彈
thriller〔ˈθrɪlɚ〕*n.* 驚悚片　　star〔stɑr〕*v.* 由～主演
comedy〔ˈkɑmədɪ〕*n.* 喜劇
romantic comedy 浪漫愛情喜劇
tragedy〔ˈtrædʒədɪ〕*n.* 悲劇
schedule〔ˈskɛdʒʊl〕*v.* 預定
run〔rʌn〕*v.*（電影）播映
recording〔rɪˈkɔrdɪŋ〕*n.* 錄音

31. (**C**) How is this message being transmitted?

    A. By radio.

    B. By television.

    C. By telephone.

    D. By satellite.

    * transmit〔træns'mɪt〕v. 傳達

      radio〔'redɪ͵o〕n. 無線電通訊

      satellite〔'sætḷ͵aɪt〕n. 人造衛星

32. (**A**) How many movies are showing this month?

    A. Three.

    B. Two.

    C. One.

    D. Four.

    * show〔ʃo〕v.（影片）上映

33. (**C**) How many times does a feature film run on a weekday?

    A. Once.

    B. Twice.

    C. Four times.

    D. Nine times.

    * weekday〔'wik͵de〕n. 平日

Questions 34-35 are based on the following speech.

What this city needs is a mayor who is not afraid to make the difficult choices. If I am elected mayor, I will not hesitate to eliminate unnecessary bureaucracy. No matter how many jobs are lost by my cuts, if the job is not necessary, then taxpayers shouldn't have to pay out of their own hard-earned income to support it. Elect me, Peter Synder, as your mayor and this city will have a leaner, more efficient government that will serve you better for less.

** mayor〔ˋmeɚ〕*n.* 市長

elect〔ɪˋlɛkt〕*v.* 選舉

hesitate〔ˋhɛzəˌtet〕*v.* 猶豫

eliminate〔ɪˋlɪməˌnet〕*v.* 消除

bureaucracy〔bjʊˋrɑkrəsɪ〕*n.* 官僚政治

cut〔kʌt〕*n.* 削減   taxpayer〔ˋtæksˌpeɚ〕*n.* 納稅人

out of 從～當中   hard-earned〔ˋhɑrdˋɝnd〕*adj.* 辛苦賺的

income〔ˋɪnˌkʌm〕*n.* 所得

elect〔ɪˋlɛkt〕*v.* 選擇   lean〔lin〕*adj.* 精瘦的

efficient〔ɪˋfɪʃənt〕*adj.* 有效率的

serve sb. better for less 使人感到物超所值（此指得到一個
勤政廉能的政府）

34. (**A**) What position is Mr. Synder running for?

    A. Mayor.

    B. Congressman.

    C. President.

    D. Governor.

    * position〔pə'zɪʃən〕n. 職務

      run〔rʌn〕v. 競選 < *for* >

      Congressman〔'kɑŋgrəsmən〕n. 美國國會議員

      governor〔'gʌvənə〕n. 州長

35. (**B**) What has Mr. Synder promised to do if elected?

    A. Cut income and property taxes.

    B. Reduce the size of government.

    C. Increase job opportunities.

    D. Fight crime in the city.

    * property〔'prɑpətɪ〕n. 財產

      tax〔tæks〕n. 稅   reduce〔rɪ'djus〕v. 縮小

      opportunity〔ˏɑpə'tjunətɪ〕n. 機會

      fight〔faɪt〕v. 打擊   crime〔kraɪm〕n. 犯罪

<u>Questions 36-37</u> *are based on the following talk.*

> We have quite a lot of information on imports and exports. We have available data on population, production, consumption, and foreign exchange reserves. We can also give you figures on incomes of your possible customers. We have the fullest and most recent information from the most reliable sources. We also give legal advice.

** import〔'ɪmport〕*n.* 進口

export〔'ɛksport〕*n.* 出口

available〔ə'veləbḷ〕*adj.* 可獲得的

data〔'detə〕*n. pl.* 資料

population〔͵pɑpjə'leʃən〕*n.* 人口

production〔prə'dʌkʃən〕*n.* 生產

consumption〔kən'sʌmpʃən〕*n.* 消費

reserve〔rɪ'zɝv〕*n.* 儲備金

foreign exchange reserves 外匯存底

figure〔'fɪgjɚ〕*n.* 數字　　recent〔'risn̩t〕*adj.* 最近的

reliable〔rɪ'laɪəbḷ〕*adj.* 可靠的

source〔sors〕*n.* 消息來源　　legal〔'ligḷ〕*adj.* 法律上的

36. (**A**) Who is talking?

    A. A consultant.

    B. An immigration officer.

    C. A travel agent.

    D. A bank clerk.

    * consultant〔kən'sʌltənt〕n. 顧問

    immigration〔ˏɪmə'greʃən〕n. 移民

    immigration officer 移民官

    travel agent 旅遊代辦人   clerk〔klɝk〕n. 職員

37. (**C**) Which of the following statements is true?

    A. The data is incomplete.

    B. They don't have data on incomes.

    C. The information is dependable.

    D. The information covers the domestic market.

    * incomplete〔ˏɪnkəm'plit〕adj. 不充足的

    dependable〔dɪ'pɛndəbḷ〕adj. 可靠的

    cover〔'kʌvɚ〕v. 包含

    domestic〔də'mɛstɪk〕adj. 國內的

Questions 38-40 are based on the following advertisement.

> The proofs of the new instruction book have arrived. We would like four volunteers to proofread. Since the proofs have to be returned to the publisher by the 16th of next month, we have just twenty-four days. There are several points to note; since the instructor's books went to the publisher's, there have been some modifications, notably the portion of the off/on button, which is now on the left, not the right side and now red, not blue as stated in the book. Further, the wiring is slightly different, to allow for an extra jack socket. The wires marked F in the instructor's book should read F plus S going side by side.

** proof〔pruf〕*n.* 打樣　*v.* 校對

instruction〔ɪnˈstrʌkʃən〕*n.* 說明

instruction book 說明書（ = *instructor's book* ）

volunteer〔͵vɑlənˈtɪr〕*n.* 志願者　　proofread〔ˈprufˏrid〕*v.* 校對

publisher〔ˈpʌblɪʃɚ〕*n.* 出版者　　note〔not〕*v.* 注意

instructor〔ɪnˈstrʌktɚ〕*n.* 指導者

modification〔͵mɑdəfəˈkeʃən〕*n.* 修正

notably〔ˈnotəblɪ〕*adv.* 值得注意地　　portion〔ˈporʃən〕*n.* 部分

button〔ˈbʌtn̩〕*n.* 按鈕　　state〔stet〕*v.* 陳述

further〔ˈfɝðɚ〕*adv.* 此外　　wiring〔ˈwaɪrɪŋ〕*n.* 配線

slightly〔ˈslaɪtlɪ〕*adv.* 稍微　　***allow for*** 考慮到

jack〔dʒæk〕*n.* 起重機　　socket〔ˈsɑkɪt〕*n.* 插座

wire〔waɪr〕*n.* 電線　　mark〔mɑrk〕*v.* 標明

plus〔plʌs〕*prep.* 加上　　***side by side*** 並列

38. (**C**) When do the proofs have to be returned?

    A. At six o'clock.

    B. On the 6th.

    C. On the 16th.

    D. Anytime.

39. (**B**) How many volunteers are needed?

    A. 16.

    B. 4.

    C. 24.

    D. 6.

40. (**B**) What sort of book is being written?

    A. A book about mathematical proofs.

    B. An instruction manual.

    C. A historical periodical.

    D. A novel.

* sort〔sɔrt〕*n.* 種類

  mathematical〔͵mæθə'mætɪkḷ〕*adj.* 數學的（= *mathematic*）

  proof〔pruf〕*n.* 證明

  instruction〔ɪn'strʌkʃən〕*n.* 教導

  manual〔'mænjʊəl〕*n.* 說明書；手冊

  historical〔hɪs'tɔrɪkḷ〕*adj.* 歷史的

  periodical〔͵pɪrɪ'ɑdɪkḷ〕*n.* 期刊

Questions 41-43 are based on the following statement.

> I've just been in the meeting. I have to tell you there has been no progress yet. And there is a strong possibility that an arbitrator will be called in. If this happens it will be the first time in the history of this company that we have been unable to settle a dispute by ourselves. We feel this is a sad position; however, the disruption to production cannot be allowed to continue. Therefore, I should warn you that the next communiqué from the meeting will probably be a call for arbitration. I do hope we can reach a compromise. In spite of the difficulty, I'm confident that we will agree on a 7 % pay raise.

** progress〔'prɑgrɛs〕*n.* 進展

   possibility〔,pɑsə'bɪlətɪ〕*n.* 可能性

   arbitrator〔'ɑrbə,tretɚ〕*n.* 仲裁者　***call in*** 延請

   settle〔'sɛtḷ〕*v.* 解決　　dispute〔dɪ'spjut〕*n.* 爭論

   by *oneself* 獨自　　position〔pə'zɪʃən〕*n.* 情形

   disruption〔dɪs'rʌpʃən〕*n.* 中斷

   warn〔wɔrn〕*v.* 預先通知

   communiqué〔kə,mjunə'ke〕*n.* 公報

   arbitration〔,ɑrbə'treʃən〕*n.* 仲裁

   compromise〔'kɑmprə,maɪz〕*n.* 和解

   reach a compromise 達成和解　　***in spite of*** 儘管

   confident〔'kɑnfədənt〕*adj.* 確信的

   agree on 對～看法一致　　raise〔rez〕*n.* 加薪

41. (**A**)   What's the problem?

A. There is a strike.

B. There is a problem with production.

C. Some workers have been declared redundant.

D. The factory is unsafe to work.

* strike〔straɪk〕n. 罷工

declare〔dɪˈklɛr〕v. 宣布

redundant〔rɪˈdʌndənt〕adj. 多餘的

42. (**A**)   What do the workers want?

A. They want a pay raise.

B. They want the CEO fired.

C. They want shorter working hours.

D. They want to take over the company.

* **CEO** 總裁 (= *Chief Executive Officer*)

working hours 工時   **take over** 接管

43. (**C**)   When will the negotiations finish?

A. Tomorrow afternoon.

B. It's already finished.

C. It's difficult to tell.

D. After the next communiqué.

* negotiation〔nɪ͵goʃɪˈeʃən〕n. 談判

tell〔tɛl〕v. 知道

Questions 44-45 are based on the following announcement.

> Sunday at 1:30, CBS Sports takes you live to Houston where the Oilers will take on the Cleveland Browns in a game that will determine who will lead the AFC Central division. Then at 5:00 o'clock, it's more football action as Chicago and Green Bay revive their decades-old rivalry. Don't miss all the hard-hitting action of the National Football League and the in-depth commentaries of the CBS half-time reports. CBS, your sports connection.

** live〔laɪv〕*adv.* 在現場　　***take on*** 與～較量
determine〔dɪ'tɜmɪn〕*v.* 決定　　division〔də'vɪʒən〕*n.* 區域
action〔'ækʃən〕*n.* 戰鬥；動作　　revive〔rɪ'vaɪv〕*v.* 使復甦
decade〔'dɛked〕*n.* 十年　　rivalry〔'raɪvḷrɪ〕*n.* 對抗
hard-hitting〔'hɑrd'hɪtɪŋ〕*adj.* 用力打擊的
league〔lig〕*n.* 聯盟　　in-depth〔'ɪn'dɛpθ〕*adj.* 深入的
commentary〔'kɑmən,tɛrɪ〕*n.* 實況報導
half-time〔'hæf'taɪm〕*adj.* (比賽) 中場休息的
connection〔kə'nɛkʃən〕*n.* 連接；聯絡工具

44. (**D**) What sport is the announcer talking about?
　　A. Baseball.　　　　　B. Basketball.
　　C. Hockey.　　　　　D. Football.

　　* announcer〔ə'naʊnsɚ〕*n.* 廣播員
　　 hockey〔'hɑkɪ〕*n.* 曲棍球

45. (**A**) Which game will determine the leader of the AFC Central division?
　　A. Houston and Cleveland.　　B. Cleveland and Chicago.
　　C. Chicago and Green Bay.　　D. Houston and Green Bay.

High-Intermediate Level
Listening Comprehension Test

This listening comprehension test will test your ability to understand spoken English. In this test, each conversation, short talk and question will be spoken JUST ONE TIME. They will not be written out for you. There are three parts to this test. Special instructions will be given to you at the beginning of each part.

Part A

In part A, you will hear 15 questions. After you hear a question, read the four choices in your test book and decide which one is the best answer to the question you have heard.

Example:

You will hear: Mary, can you tell me what time it is?

You will read: A. About two hours ago.
B. I used to be able to, but not now.
C. Sure, it's half past nine.
D. Today is October 22.

The best answer to the question "Mary, can you tell me what time it is?" is C: "Sure, it's half past nine." Therefore, you should choose answer C.

1. A. It was yesterday's news.
   B. I don't know. The temperature dropped abruptly.
   C. There are some bugs in the machine.
   D. There's a great demand of vegetables with the approach of the typhoon.

2. A. Give them to Frank.
   B. Post my letters, please.
   C. Who is over there?
   D. No, I can't stay away long.

3. A. No, as often as I can.
   B. No, people can dress casually.
   C. No, I dislike shopping.
   D. Yes, whenever you want.

4. A. I'll do it right away.
   B. I have no plans after work.
   C. We have three copiers in this office.
   D. But I don't have the negatives.

5. A. Yes, I'm running late.
   B. Yes, take the next left.
   C. Yes, my ticket was expensive.
   D. Yes, would you pick me up?

6. A. Are these the keys for her desk?
   B. How many words can you type in one minute?
   C. Have you checked the cable connections?
   D. Because all these lockers are brand-new.

7. A. The piano was tuned just last week.
   B. He made 15 copies of the report.
   C. We used up the last bottle a week ago.
   D. I can't believe it is on the blink again.

8. A. Either a Master's degree or 2 years experience.
   B. You need to use either blue or black ink.
   C. We don't accept credit cards here.
   D. Please tell me your social security number.

9. A. No, I don't think I heard that before.
   B. Yes, it's what I do now.
   C. Why not use a telescope?
   D. Yes, he persuaded me to buy a coffee machine.

10. A. I overslept this morning, but I was only 5 minutes late.
    B. I hope it works this time.
    C. You have to learn to manage your time.
    D. Because the deadline is next Friday.

11. A. There are buses from downtown.
    B. There won't be much time.
    C. We can play some golf instead.
    D. Let's go aboard right now.

12. A. Can I borrow it from the library?
    B. You are right. It was here.
    C. I don't have a clue.
    D. The main characters are all dead in the end.

13. A. Gee, I really don't think I can borrow anything today.
    B. You mean you lost your wallet again?
    C. I don't mind waiting if I can see you then.
    D Yes, five for one hundred and one for five hundred.

14. A. Who are you calling a crook?
    B. Olive oil is good for your health.
    C. But I thought Mr. Johnson did all the cooking.
    D. Thank you. Can I get you some more potatoes?

15. A. Golf is quite a difficult game.
    B. I didn't say that.
    C. I prefer bowling to watching a game of golf.
    D. Actually, I don't think we have the time.

Part B

In part B, you will hear 15 conversations between a man and a woman. After each conversation, you will hear a question about the conversation. After you hear the question, read the four choices in your test book and choose the best answer to the question you have heard.

Example:

You will hear: (Man)   May I see your driver's license?
                (Woman)   Yes, officer. Here it is. Was I speeding?
                (Man)   Yes, ma'am. You were doing sixty in a forty-five mile an hour zone.
                (Woman)   No way! I don't believe you.
                (Man)   Well, it is true and here is your ticket.

                Question: Why does the man ask for the woman's driver's license?

You will read: A. She was going too fast.
                B. To check its limitations.
                C. To check her age.
                D. She entered a restricted zone.

The best answer to the question "Why does the man ask for the woman's driver's license?" is A: "She was going too fast." Therefore, you should choose answer A.

16. A. Airlines are speculating.
    B. Some may have been hijacked.
    C. It's a holiday.
    D. Flying is scary.

17. A. see a movie.
    B. to dinner.
    C. a lab.
    D. go shopping.

18. A. She has no special skills.
    B. She is negotiating for a raise.
    C. She thinks nobody likes her.
    D. She hates translating.

19. A. He was out for the weekend.
    B. He went for his honeymoon.
    C. He attended an educational program.
    D. He went for a competition.

20. A. He wants to go to American Express.
    B. He wants to get a credit card.
    C. He wants to buy an air ticket.
    D. He needs to get a card by three o'clock.

21. A. The driver.
    B. The CEO.
    C. The woman.
    D. The cashier.

22. A. The secretary is inefficient.
    B. They have more legal problems now.
    C. The company is expanding.
    D. The secretary is taking some time off.

23. A. How to use maps.
    B. How to increase the profit margin.
    C. Improving company image.
    D. Freight charge decision.

24. A. A man in Indonesia.
    B. Grace.
    C. A tourist.
    D. An Indian businessman.

25. A. It dealt with a legal problem.
    B. Difficult to tell due to bad English.
    C. It was an overseas order.
    D. Difficult to tell because some parts were hard to read.

26. A. Can he bring a computer through customs?
    B. He wants to know the customs of the States.
    C. Can he bring a lot of books into the country?
    D. He would like some stamps to mail his passport.

27. A. By cab.
    B. He'll fly.
    C. He'll walk.
    D. By train.

28. A. Good fringe benefits.
    B. Free housing.
    C. Conditions are negotiable.
    D. The salary is very good.

29. A. She got a promotion.
    B. She started a new company.
    C. She left the company.
    D. She started to work for AT&T.

30. A. Some jelly.
    B. Nothing.
    C. Pizza.
    D. Chicken.

Part C

In part C, you will hear several short talks. After each talk, you will hear 2 to 3 questions about the talk. After you hear each question, read the four choices in your test book and choose the best answer to the question you have heard.

Example:

<u>You will hear:</u>

> Thank you for coming to this, the first in a series of seminars on the use of computers in the classroom. As the brochure informed you, there will be a total of five seminars given in this room every Monday morning from 6:00 to 7:30. Our goal will be to show you, the teachers of our school children, how the changing technology of today can be applied to the unchanging lessons of yesterday to make your students' learning experience more interesting and relevant to the world they live in. By the end of the last seminar, you will not be computer literate, but you will be able to make sense of the hundreds of complex words and technical terms related to the field and be aware of the programs available for use in the classroom.

Question number 1: What is the subject of this seminar series?

You will read: A. Self-improvement.
B. Using computers to teach.
C. Technology.
D. Study habits of today's students.

The best answer to the question "What is the subject of this seminar series?" is B: "Using computers to teach." Therefore, you should choose answer B.

Now listen to another question based on the same talk.

You will hear:
Question number 2: What does the speaker say participants will be able to do after attending the seminars?

You will read: A. Understand today's students.
B. Understand computer terminology.
C. Motivate students.
D. Deal more confidently with people.

The best answer to the question "What does the speaker say participants will be able to do after attending the seminars?" is B: "Understand computer terminology." Therefore, you should choose answer B.

31. A. To tell callers that the number is not in service.

    B. To tell callers that nobody is available.

    C. To tell callers that they have dialed the wrong number.

    D. To tell callers that they are not wanted.

32. A. He should record his name and phone number at the beep.

    B. He should call back later when someone arrives.

    C. He should disconnect the line and try again.

    D. He should page the wanted person at work.

33. A. Its sales have been decreasing.

    B. The company is being sued.

    C. Its cargo ship has been pirated.

    D. It has been accused of stealing.

34. A. Clothing.

    B. Software.

    C. Shipping.

    D. Pirate control.

35. A. The market relies on imports only.

    B. Demand is declining.

    C. Prices are declining.

    D. There are some illegal dealers.

36. A. It is a public park.

    B. It is a private club.

    C. It is a billiards hall.

    D. It is a hotel recreation center.

37. A. Lunch will be served.
    B. The facility will close early.
    C. There will be a performance.
    D. The swimming pool will open.

38. A. Traveling time.
    B. Distance.
    C. An outing.
    D. Admission fee.

39. A. Too many people came.
    B. There was too much to eat.
    C. The manager didn't show up.
    D. The program was too long.

40. A. Make a list of organizers.
    B. Choose the place for the event.
    C. Reschedule the event.
    D. Plan the program.

41. A. Friday.
    B. Tuesday.
    C. Yesterday.
    D. Thursday.

42. A. To shorten the work week.
    B. To introduce an afternoon break.
    C. To increase salaries.
    D. To hire more workers.

43. A. To make a registration.
    B. To negotiate the break time.
    C. To fill out the forms.
    D. To listen to the president's speech.

44. A. Italian pasta.
    B. Fish and beef.
    C. Steak dinner.
    D. Vegetarian dinner.

45. A. $19.00.
    B. $24.99.
    C. $12.00.
    D. $9.00.

中高級聽力測驗詳解 ⑥

Part A

1. (**D**) Why are the prices going up so fast?
   A. It was yesterday's news.
   B. I don't know. The temperature dropped abruptly.
   C. There are some bugs in the machine.
   D. There's a great demand for vegetables with the approach of the typhoon.

   * **go up** 上升　　temperature〔'tɛmprətʃə〕 n. 溫度
   drop〔drɑp〕 v. 降低　　abruptly〔ə'brʌptlɪ〕 adv. 突然地
   bug〔bʌg〕 n. 毛病　　demand〔dɪ'mænd〕 n. 需求
   approach〔ə'protʃ〕 n. 接近　　typhoon〔taɪ'fun〕 n. 颱風

2. (**A**) Can I leave the keys with you?
   A. Give them to Frank.
   B. Post my letters, please.
   C. Who is over there?
   D. No, I can't stay away long.

   * post〔post〕 v. 郵寄　　away〔ə'we〕 adv. 離開

3. (**B**) Is there a dress code at your office?
   A. No, as often as I can.
   B. No, people can dress casually.
   C. No, I dislike shopping.
   D. Yes, whenever you want.

   * **dress code** 服裝規定　　casually〔'kæʒʊəlɪ〕 adv. 隨意地

4. (**A**) Would you make a photocopy of this report?

    A. I'll do it right away.

    B. I have no plans after work.

    C. We have three copiers in this office.

    D. But I don't have the negatives.

    * photocopy〔'fotə,kɑpɪ〕*n.* 影印

    copier〔'kɑpɪɚ〕*n.* 影印機　　negative〔'nɛgətɪv〕*n.* 底片

5. (**A**) Shouldn't you have already left for the airport?

    A. Yes, I'm running late.

    B. Yes, take the next left.

    C. Yes, my ticket was expensive.

    D. Yes, would you pick me up?

    * ***leave for*** 前往　　run〔rʌn〕*v.* 變得 (= *become*)

    I'm running late. 我快來不及了。

    pick *sb.* ***up*** 搭載某人

6. (**C**) I don't understand why my computer is locked up!

    A. Are these the keys for her desk?

    B. How many words can you type in one minute?

    C. Have you checked the cable connections?

    D. Because all these lockers are brand-new.

    * ***My computer is locked up.*** 我的電腦當機了。

    type〔taɪp〕*n.* 打 (字)　　cable〔'kebḷ〕*n.* 纜線

    connection〔kə'nɛkʃən〕*n.* 連接

    locker〔'lɑkɚ〕*n.* 置物櫃

    brand-new〔'brænd'nju〕*adj.* 全新的

7. (**C**) Don't we have anymore toner for the copier machine?

    A. The piano was tuned just last week.

    B. He made 15 copies of the report.

    C. We used up the last bottle a week ago.

    D. I can't believe it is on the blink again.

    * toner〔'tonɚ〕*n.* 碳粉　　copier〔'kɑpɪɚ〕*n.* 影印機

    tune〔tjun〕*v.* 調音　　copy〔'kɑpɪ〕*n.* 副本；影本

    use up 用完　　blink〔blɪŋk〕*n.* 眨眼

    on the blink 故障的（ = *out of order*）

8. (**A**) What kind of credentials do I need for the job?

    A. Either a Master's degree or 2 years experience.

    B. You need to use either blue or black ink.

    C. We don't accept credit cards here.

    D. Please tell me your social security number.

    * credential〔krɪ'dɛnʃəl〕*n.*（學歷、資格）背景

    Master〔'mæstɚ〕*n.* 碩士

    degree〔dɪ'gri〕*n.* 學位　　ink〔ɪŋk〕*n.* 墨水

    security〔sɪ'kjʊrətɪ〕*n.* 安全

    social security number 社會安全碼

9. (**B**) Have you ever worked as a telemarketer before?

    A. No, I don't think I heard that before.

    B. Yes, it's what I do now.

    C. Why not use a telescope?

    D. Yes, he persuaded me to buy a coffee machine.

    * telemarketer〔'tɛlə'mɑrkɪtɚ〕*n.* 電話推銷員

    telescope〔'tɛlə,skop〕*n.* 望遠鏡

    persuade〔pɚ'swed〕*v.* 說服　　***coffee machine*** 煮咖啡機

10. (**D**) How come you have to work late all next week?

    A. I overslept this morning, but I was only 5 minutes late.

    B. I hope it works this time.

    C. You have to learn to manage your time.

    D. Because the deadline is next Friday.

    * *How come* ~ ? 為什麼~？
    oversleep〔'ovɚ'slip〕v. 睡過頭
    manage〔'mænɪdʒ〕v. 管理
    deadline〔'dɛd,laɪn〕n. 截止日期

11. (**A**) How are we going to travel to the resort?

    A. There are buses from downtown.

    B. There won't be much time.

    C. We can play some golf instead.

    D. Let's go aboard right now.

    * resort〔rɪ'zɔrt〕n. 名勝；度假中心
    golf〔gɔlf〕n. 高爾夫球　　instead〔ɪn'stɛd〕adv. 作為代替
    aboard〔ə'bord〕adv. 在船（飛機、車）上
    go aboard 上船（飛機、車）

12. (**C**) What happened to the book I left here?

    A. Can I borrow it from the library?

    B. You are right. It was here.

    C. I don't have a clue.

    D. The main characters are all dead in the end.

    * clue〔klu〕n. 線索　　*I don't have a clue.* 我不知道。
    character〔'kærɪktɚ〕n. 角色　　*in the end* 最後

13. (**B**)　Would you mind lending me just a little to see me
through the day?

    A.　Gee, I really don't think I can borrow anything today.

    B.　You mean you lost your wallet again?

    C.　I don't mind waiting if I can see you then.

    D.　Yes, five for one hundred and one for five hundred.

    * **see through**　幫助～度過
       gee〔dʒi〕*interj.* 唉呀（表示驚訝的語氣）
       wallet〔ˈwɑlɪt〕*n.* 皮夾

14. (**D**)　Your wife certainly is a wonderful cook, Mr. Johnson.

    A.　Who are you calling a crook?

    B.　Olive oil is good for your health.

    C.　But I thought Mr. Johnson did all the cooking.

    D.　Thank you.　Can I get you some more potatoes?

    * cook〔kʊk〕*n.* 廚師　　　crook〔krʊk〕*n.* 騙子
       olive〔ˈɑlɪv〕*n.* 橄欖　　*olive oil* 橄欖油
       do the cooking 煮菜　　potato〔pəˈteto〕*n.* 馬鈴薯

15. (**D**)　What do you say to a game of golf?

    A.　Golf is quite a difficult game.

    B.　I didn't say that.

    C.　I prefer bowling to watching a game of golf.

    D.　Actually, I don't think we have the time.

    * **What do you say to～?** 你認為～如何？（= *What about～?*）
       prefer…to～ 比較喜歡…比較不喜歡～
       bowling〔ˈbolɪŋ〕*n.* 打保齡球

Part B

16. (**B**) M : I understand all flights have been cancelled. Any explanation?

   W : I think there is speculation that there are several groups of hijackers on some of the flights.

   M : Oh my! That's scary!

   W : It is scary. But we are very serious about flight security and we are currently investigating it.

   M : I sure hope you people catch them soon.

   Question : Why have the flights been canceled?

   A. Airlines are speculating.

   B. Some may have been hijacked.

   C. It's a holiday.

   D. Flying is scary.

* flight〔flaɪt〕*n.* 班機

   explanation〔͵ɛksplə'neʃən〕*n.* 解釋；說明

   speculation〔͵spɛkjə'leʃən〕*n.* 推測

   hijacker〔'haɪ͵dʒækə〕*n.* 劫機犯

   Oh my! 哦，我的天啊！　　scary〔'skærɪ〕*adj.* 可怕的

   flight security 飛航安全

   currently〔'kɝəntlɪ〕*adv.* 現在

   investigate〔ɪn'vɛstə͵get〕*v.* 調查

   airline〔'ɛr͵laɪn〕*n.* 航空公司

   speculate〔'spɛkjə͵let〕*v.* 推測

   hijack〔'haɪ͵dʒæk〕*v.* 劫機

17. (**C**)　M: Are you staying longer after the conference?

W: I'm not sure yet.

M: If you are, we would like you to come to our laboratory to look at the new equipment we just bought.

W: That will be great.　I've always wanted to see your facility.

Question: The woman has been invited to

A. see a movie.

B. to dinner.

C. a lab.

D. go shopping.

* conference〔'kɑnfərəns〕 *n.* 會議
  laboratory〔'læbrəˌtorɪ〕 *n.* 實驗室（ = *lab* ）
  equipment〔ɪ'kwɪpmənt〕 *n.* 設備
  facility〔fə'sɪlətɪ〕 *n.* 設施；設備

18. (**D**)　M: So, what are your new responsibilities?

W: They want me to do everything.　I really don't want to do any translation work.

M: I guess they appreciate your skills.

W: Ha!　That's because I'm the only person who can do it.　It will be so much easier if they get a professional translator.

M: Professional translators cost a lot of money and I don't think the company is ready to spend that kind of money.

Question: What's the woman's problem?

A. She has no special skills.

B. She is negotiating for a raise.

C. She thinks nobody likes her.

D. She hates translating.

* responsibilities (rɪˌspɑnsə'bɪlətɪz) n. pl. 職責；任務
  translation (træns'leʃən) n. 翻譯
  appreciate (ə'priʃɪˌet) v. 欣賞
  professional (prə'fɛʃənḷ) adj. 專業的
  translator (træns'letɚ) n. 翻譯者
  negotiate (nɪ'goʃɪˌet) v. 磋商　　raise (rez) n. 加薪

19. (**C**) M: It's nice to be back.

W: How was the training? We missed you.

M: The training was a great challenge. I learned a lot.

W: I'm glad you see it that way. Not a lot of people take a positive attitude towards training.

M: Anyway, I'm glad I went.

Question: Where was the man?

A. He was out for the weekend.

B. He went for his honeymoon.

C. He attended an educational program.

D. He went for a competition.

* training ('trenɪŋ) n. 訓練　　challenge ('tʃælɪndʒ) n. 挑戰
  positive ('pɑzətɪv) adj. 積極的
  attitude ('ætəˌtjud) n. 態度
  honeymoon ('hʌnɪˌmun) n. 蜜月
  competition (ˌkɑmpə'tɪʃən) n. 比賽

20. (**B**) M : Can you call American Express and inquire about how to get a credit card?

W : Okay.

M : I need to know before three o'clock. No. Before noon.

W : What's the rush? It takes a few weeks to process the application anyway.

M : I won't be here this afternoon so I need the information soon.

Question : What does the man want?

A. He wants to go to American Express.

B. He wants to get a credit card.

C. He wants to buy an air ticket.

D. He needs to get a card by three o'clock.

* ***American Express*** 美國運通公司

inquire〔ɪn'kwaɪr〕v. 訊問   rush〔rʌʃ〕n. 匆忙

What's the rush? 急什麼 ?   process〔'prɑsɛs〕v. 處理

application〔,æplə'keʃən〕n. 申請   ***air ticket*** 機票

21. (**B**) M : Did the CEO come in yet?

W : I wasn't paying attention, but I think I saw the driver around. He should be in the building.

M : Is there any way you can page him or check his office? I got something important to go over with him.

W : Sure thing.

Question : Who is the man looking for?

A. The driver.   B. The CEO.
C. The woman.   D. The cashier.

* page〔pedʒ〕*v.* 以呼叫器呼叫（某人）
go over 查看   ***Sure thing.*** 當然可以。
cashier〔kæˈʃɪr〕*n.* 收銀員

22. (**D**) M : We want to hire someone with experience in
handling legal documents.

W : But I thought that was Shannon's job.

M : Yeah, but she's taking leave starting next week.

W : Legal secretaries are not that easy to find.

M : That's why we require your expert recruiting
services.

Question : Why does the man want to hire another person?

A. The secretary is inefficient.

B. They have more legal problems now.

C. The company is expanding.

D. The secretary is taking some time off.

* handle〔ˈhændl̩〕*v.* 處理
legal〔ˈligl̩〕*adj.* 有關法律的；法務上的
document〔ˈdɑkjəmənt〕*n.* 文件   ***take leave*** 休長假
legal secretary 法務秘書
expert〔ˈɛkspɝt〕*adj.* 專業的
recruit〔rɪˈkrut〕*v.* 招收新成員；徵才
inefficient〔ɪnəˈfɪʃənt〕*adj.* 無效率的
expand〔ɪkˈspænd〕*v.* 擴張   ***take off*** 休假

23. (**B**) W: James, did you notice that suddenly freight charges are chewing up about 17 percent of the total price?

M: Yeah. That's one reason why our profit margin has declined.

W: We should hold a meeting and map out some strategies.

M: I've been saying that all along but no one seems to ever listen.

W: Well, I'm sure they will now.

Question: What will be the focus of the meeting?

A. How to use maps.

B. How to increase the profit margin.

C. Improving company image.

D. Freight charge decision.

* freight〔fret〕*n.* 貨運　　charge〔tʃɑrdʒ〕*n.* 費用
　chew up 用掉　　*profit margin* 利潤
　decline〔dɪ'klaɪn〕*v.* 減少
　map out 安排　　strategy〔'strætədʒɪ〕*n.* 策略
　all along 一直　　focus〔'fokəs〕*n.* 重點
　image〔'ɪmɪdʒ〕*n.* 形象

24. (**A**) M: Has there been any response from the Indonesian businessman we met three weeks ago?

W: I'm not sure, but I heard Grace talk about an overseas phone call. You were not in then.

M: O.K. I want you to contact him as soon as possible.

W: I don't have his business card, do you?

M: Oh… Here it is. Contact him and let me know.

Question : Whom are they talking about?

A. A man in Indonesia.   B. Grace.

C. A tourist.   D. An Indian businessman.

* Indonesian〔͵ɪndo'niʒən〕*adj.* 印尼的
    overseas〔'ovɚ'siz〕*adj.* 國外的
    contact〔'kɑntækt〕*v.* 聯繫   *as soon as possible* 儘快
    business card 名片   tourist〔'tʊrɪst〕*n.* 觀光客
    Indonesia〔͵ɪndo'niʒə〕*n.* 印尼
    Indian〔'ɪndɪən〕*adj.* 印度的

25. (**D**)   M : Good morning, Sue.

W : Good morning, Steve. Did you receive your fax
       yesterday?

M : Yes, but it was partially illegible.

W : It must have been something on the other end.
       Maybe a paper jam or something.

M : Probably. I'll call them to have them resend it.

Question : What was the content of the fax?

A. It dealt with a legal problem.

B. Difficult to tell due to bad English.

C. It was an overseas order.

D. Difficult to tell because some parts were hard to read.

* partially〔'pɑrʃəlɪ〕*adv.* 部分地
    illegible〔ɪ'lɛdʒəbḷ〕*adj.* 難辨認的   *the other end* 對方
    jam〔dʒæm〕*n.* 堵塞   *paper jam* 卡紙
    or something 或什麼的   resend〔ri'sɛnd〕*v.* 再傳送
    content〔'kɑntɛnt〕*n.* 內容   *deal with* 和~有關
    legal〔'ligḷ〕*adj.* 法律的   *due to* 由於
    order〔'ɔrdɚ〕*n.* 訂單

26. (**A**) M : I'm thinking of bringing a notebook from the States. Do you think it's going to cause a problem?

W : They might stamp it in your passport and if that happens, you have to carry it with you each time you leave the country.

M : Is there any way I can check with customs before I leave?

W : I'm sure there is. You can go on to the government website and search for customs regulations.

M : Thanks.

Question : What's the man concerned about?

A. Can he bring a computer through customs?

B. He wants to know the customs of the States.

C. Can he bring a lot of books into the country?

D. He would like some stamps to mail his passport.

* notebook〔'not͵bʊk〕 n. 筆記型電腦

stamp〔stæmp〕 v. 蓋章於　 n. 郵票

customs〔'kʌstəmz〕 n. pl. 海關（為複數形）；風俗

website〔'wɛb͵saɪt〕 n. 網站　 *search for* 尋找

regulation〔͵rɛgjə'leʃən〕 n. 規則

be concerned about 關心

27. (**D**) M : Is there a train back after midnight?

W : There's one at 12:27, but even if you miss it, you can always get a cab.

M : I prefer to take the train.

W : Okay. Then try not to miss the train.

Question：How is the man going to travel?

A. By cab.　　　　　B. He'll fly.
C. He'll walk.　　　 D. By train.

* cab〔kæb〕n. 計程車　　fly〔flaɪ〕v. 搭飛機（旅行）

28.（ **C** ）W：Put an ad in the papers. We've got to find a person
　　　　　　 for this job.

M：Can you give me an idea about what sort of
　　conditions we are offering?

W：Just say salary negotiable based on qualification and
　　experience.

M：No other details, then?

W：Nope.

Question：What conditions is the company offering?

A. Good fringe benefits.

B. Free housing.

C. Conditions are negotiable.

D. The salary is very good.

* ad〔æd〕n. 廣告（= *advertisement* ）
　sort〔sɔrt〕n. 種類　　condition〔kən'dɪʃən〕n. 條件
　salary〔'sælərɪ〕n. 薪水
　negotiable〔nɪ'goʃɪəbḷ〕adj. 可協議的
　based on 根據　　qualification〔ˌkwɑləfə'keʃən〕n. 資格
　detail〔'ditel〕n. 細節　　nope〔nop〕adv. 沒有（= *no* ）
　fringe〔frɪndʒ〕n. 周邊
　fringe benefit 員工福利；附加福利
　housing〔'haʊzɪŋ〕n. 供給住宅

29. (**C**)　M：Have you heard from Veronica yet?

　　　　　W：No, but there are rumors that she may start working for AT&T.

　　　　　M：Can you get in touch with her and mention that we are giving her a raise?

　　　　　W：If the rumors turn out to be true, it may be too late.

　　　　　M：Yeah.　Well, try it anyway.

　　　　Question：What happened to Veronica?

　　　　A.　She got a promotion.

　　　　B.　She started a new company.

　　　　C.　She left the company.

　　　　D.　She started to work for AT&T.

　　　　＊ ***hear from*** 得到消息　　　rumor〔ˋrumɚ〕n. 謠言
　　　　　AT&T 美國電話電報公司 (全名為 *American Telephone & Telegraph Company*)
　　　　　get in touch with 和～聯絡
　　　　　mention〔ˋmɛnʃən〕v. 提到　　　raise〔rez〕n. 加薪
　　　　　turn out 結果是　　　promotion〔prəˋmoʃən〕n. 升遷

30. (**D**)　M：Well, thanks for a pleasant evening.

　　　　　W：You're welcome.

　　　　　M：I really enjoyed the chicken.

　　　　　W：I'm glad you like it.　It's my mother's special recipe.

　　　　　M：I hope we can do this again soon.

　　　　Question：What did the man eat?

　　　　A.　Some jelly.　　　　　B.　Nothing.

　　　　C.　Pizza.　　　　　　　D.　Chicken.

　　　　＊ recipe〔ˋrɛsəpɪ〕n. 烹飪法　　　jelly〔ˋdʒɛlɪ〕n. 果凍

Part C

Questions 31-32 are based on the following message.

> Hi, you've reached 555-6875. No one's in right now, so if you'll leave your name and number at the beep, we'll be sure to get back to you. Thank you.

** reach〔ritʃ〕*v.* (用電話等) 與~連絡
beep〔bip〕*n.* 嗶嗶的聲音　　***get back to*** 再與~聯絡

31. (**B**)　What is the purpose of this message?
　　A. To tell callers that the number is not in service.
　　B. To tell callers that nobody is available.
　　C. To tell callers that they have dialed the wrong number.
　　D. To tell callers that they are not wanted.

　　* ***be not in service*** 暫停使用
　　available〔ə'veləbḷ〕*adj.* 有空的　　dial〔'daɪəl〕*v.* 撥 (號)

32. (**A**)　What should a person hearing this message do?
　　A. He should record his name and phone number at the beep.
　　B. He should call back later when someone arrives.
　　C. He should disconnect the line and try again.
　　D. He should page the wanted person at work.

　　* disconnect〔ˌdɪskə'nɛkt〕*v.* 切斷　　line〔laɪn〕*n.* 電話線
　　page〔pedʒ〕*v.* 用呼叫器呼叫 (某人)
　　wanted〔'wɑntɪd〕*adj.* 被需要的

Questions 33-35 are based on the following statement.

> We have just discovered why our market share has been pinched. There is a whole lot of pirates out there marketing unlicensed software. This can't continue. We've got to go out and get them. We are the only authorized dealer in this city. We can't just sit and let these people go on stealing. We've got to take action.

** share〔ʃɛr〕*n.*（市場）佔有率　　*market share* 市場佔有率
pinch〔pɪntʃ〕*v.* 使縮小
pirate〔'paɪrət〕*n.* 非法翻印者；海盜　*v.* 掠奪
market〔'markɪt〕*v.* 銷售
unlicensed〔ʌn'laɪsənst〕*adj.* 沒有執照的
software〔'sɔft,wɛr〕*n.* 軟體　　*have got to* 必須（= have to）
authorized〔'ɔθə,raɪzd〕*adj.* 經授權的
dealer〔'dilɚ〕*n.* 代理商　　*go on* 繼續
take action 採取行動

33. (**A**) What is the company's problem?

    A. Its sales have been decreasing.

    B. The company is being sued.

    C. Its cargo ship has been pirated.

    D. It has been accused of stealing.

    * sue 〔 su 〕 v. 控告　　cargo 〔'kɑrgo 〕 n. 貨物
    be accused of 被指控

34. (**B**) What line of business is the company involved in?

    A. Clothing.

    B. Software.

    C. Shipping.

    D. Pirate control.

    * line 〔 laɪn 〕 n. 行業　　***be involved in***　和～有關
    shipping 〔'ʃɪpɪŋ 〕 n. 運輸
    pirate control　防制海上掠奪行為

35. (**D**) What is happening in this market?

    A. The market relies on imports only.

    B. Demand is declining.

    C. Prices are declining.

    D. There are some illegal dealers.

    * ***rely on*** 依靠　　demand 〔 dɪ'mænd 〕 n. 需求
    decline 〔 dɪ'klaɪn 〕 v. 衰退；下降
    illegal 〔 ɪ'ligl̩ 〕 adj. 非法的

Questions 36-37 refer to the following announcement.

The swimming pool will open in fifteen minutes. Guests wishing to use the pool facilities will need to show their guest pass and be accompanied by a club member. Members are responsible for guests' dress and behavior during their visit. Please make sure your guests are aware of the rules of the pool, and especially that they are dressed appropriately. At two o'clock today, we will be serving a poolside lunch for everybody to celebrate the Independence Day holiday. If you plan to take part in the festivities, please sign up for a table at the lifeguard's office. Finally, we will close at 6:00 PM today instead of 9:00, so that our staff may spend the evening with their families. We're sure you'll want to do so, too. Thank you and have a good day.

** pool 〔 pul 〕 *n.* 游泳池　　guest 〔 gɛst 〕 *n.* 來賓
facility 〔 fəˈsɪlətɪ 〕 *n.* 設施；場所　　pass 〔 pæs 〕 *n.* 通行證
accompany 〔 əˈkʌmpənɪ 〕 *v.* 陪同
behavior 〔 bɪˈhevjɚ 〕 *n.* 行為　　***be aware of*** 知道
appropriately 〔 əˈpropriɪtlɪ 〕 *adv.* 適當地
serve 〔 sɝv 〕 *v.* 供應　　celebrate 〔ˈsɛləˌbret 〕 *v.* 慶祝
independence 〔ˌɪndɪˈpɛndəns 〕 *n.* 獨立
Independence Day 美國獨立紀念日（七月四日）
take part in 參加　　festivity 〔 fɛsˈtɪvətɪ 〕 *n.* 慶祝活動
sign up 報名　　lifeguard 〔ˈlaɪfˌgɑrd 〕 *n.* 救生員
staff 〔 stæf 〕 *n.* （全體）工作人員

36. (**B**) What is the nature of the facility?

    A. It is a public park.

    B. It is a private club.

    C. It is a billiards hall.

    D. It is a hotel recreation center.

    * nature〔'netʃɚ〕*n.* 性質　　public〔'pʌblɪk〕*adj.* 公共的
    private〔'praɪvɪt〕*adj.* 私人的
    billiards〔'bɪljɚdz〕*n.* 撞球
    hall〔hɔl〕*n.* 會館
    recreation〔,rɛkrɪ'eʃən〕*n.* 休閒；娛樂

37. (**A**) What will happen at two o'clock?

    A. Lunch will be served.

    B. The facility will close early.

    C. There will be a performance.

    D. The swimming pool will open.

    * performance〔pɚ'fɔrməns〕*n.* 表演

Questions 38-40 are based on the following talk.

Today we have to discuss the plans for our annual outing. Last year, if you remember, we had a serious problem, well two serious problems, really. One was too much food and the other, too little time. Everyone complained that we drove too far, and the traveling time was too long. We spent four hours on the road, to and fro. So this year we have chosen Yard Way as the destination. It should only take about 45 minutes to get there. I suggest we take this time to select people who will be the main organizers of the event.

** annual〔ˈænjʊəl〕*adj.* 年度的　　outing〔ˈaʊtɪŋ〕*n.* 出遊
complain〔kəmˈplen〕*v.* 抱怨　　***traveling time*** 通車時間
to and fro 來回地　　destination〔ˌdɛstəˈneʃən〕*n.* 目的地
time〔taɪm〕*n.* 時機　　select〔səˈlɛkt〕*v.* 選拔
organizer〔ˈɔrgənˌaɪzɚ〕*n.* 組織者
event〔ɪˈvɛnt〕*n.* 事情；（大型）活動

38. (**C**) What is this meeting about?

A. Traveling time.

B. Distance.

C. An outing.

D. Admission fee.

* distance〔'dɪstəns〕*n.* 距離

admission〔əd'mɪʃən〕*n.* 入場　fee〔fi〕*n.* 費用

39. (**B**) What was the problem last year?

A. Too many people came.

B. There was too much to eat.

C. The manager didn't show up.

D. The program was too long.

* **show up** 出現　program〔'progræm〕*n.* 節目

40. (**A**) What are they going to do during this meeting?

A. Make a list of organizers.

B. Choose the place for the event.

C. Reschedule the event.

D. Plan the program.

* list〔lɪst〕*n.* 名單

reschedule〔,ri'skɛdʒʊl〕*v.* 重新安排～的時間

Questions 41-43 are based on the following announcement.

　　As of October 1st, the company will introduce a special afternoon break. In your mailbox you will find a form. Please fill it out and submit it by Friday. Please read each question very carefully before answering. There will possibly be some need for negotiation about times. Therefore, a special staff meeting has been arranged for Friday the 16th at 6:30. Please bear in mind that for this system to be successful there must be full cooperation between staff and management. The management has set up a special extension number 0046. Any questions you have will be dealt with by Ms. Hue from 10-4, Monday through Friday.

** ***as of*** 從～開始　　introduce〔͵ɪntrə'djus〕v. 採用
　　break〔brek〕n. 休息　　form〔fɔrm〕n. 表格
　　fill out 填寫（表格）　　submit〔səb'mɪt〕v. 繳交
　　negotiation〔nɪ͵goʃɪ'eʃən〕n. 磋商
　　staff〔stæf〕n.（全體）工作人員
　　arrange〔ə'rendʒ〕v. 安排　　***bear in mind*** 記住
　　cooperation〔ko͵ɑpə'reʃən〕n. 合作
　　management〔'mænɪdʒmənt〕n. 主管
　　set up 設立　　extension〔ɪk'stɛnʃən〕n. 電話分機
　　deal with 討論

41. (**A**) What is the deadline for the form?

      A. Friday.

      B. Tuesday.

      C. Yesterday.

      D. Thursday.

      * deadline (ˈdɛdˌlaɪn) *n.* 截止日期

42. (**B**) What does the company want to do?

      A. To shorten the work week.

      B. To introduce an afternoon break.

      C. To increase salaries.

      D. To hire more workers.

      * shorten (ˈʃɔrtn̩) *v.* 縮短   ***work week*** 工作時數

        salary (ˈsælərɪ) *n.* 薪水   hire (haɪr) *v.* 雇用

43. (**B**) Why is a meeting needed?

      A. To make a registration.

      B. To negotiate the break time.

      C. To fill out the forms.

      D. To listen to the president's speech.

      * registration (ˌrɛdʒɪˈstreʃən) *n.* 登記

        negotiate (nɪˈgoʃɪˌet) *v.* 協商

        president (ˈprɛzədənt) *n.* 總裁

Questions 44-45 are based on the following statement.

Good evening, gentlemen. My name is Linda and I'll be your waitress. Tonight's dinner special is called Surf and Turf. It is a selected combination of the finest seafood and choice beef. It comes with a baked potato, a salad and a drink of your choice—all for just $24.99. If that doesn't fit your appetite, our menu features over 120 different dishes from around the world. We also have an all-you-can-eat buffet dinner for just $19.00 per person. I'll give you a few minutes to think about it and I'll be back to take your order. Okay?

** special〔'spɛʃəl〕 n. 特餐　　*surf and turf* 海陸大餐
selected〔sə'lɛktɪd〕 adj. 精選的
combination〔ˏkɑmbə'neʃən〕 n. 結合
baked〔bekt〕 adj. 烘烤的　　choice〔tʃɔɪs〕 adj. 精選的
fit〔fɪt〕 v. 適合　　appetite〔'æpəˏtaɪt〕 n. 胃口
feature〔'fitʃə〕 v. 以~為特色　　dish〔dɪʃ〕 n. 菜餚
all-you-can-eat 吃到飽的　　buffet〔bʊ'fe〕 n. 自助餐
take one's *order* 接受點菜

44. (**B**)　What is the special for the evening?
　　　　A. Italian pasta.　　　B. Fish and beef.
　　　　C. Steak dinner.　　　D. Vegetarian dinner.

　　* pasta〔'pɑstə〕 n. 義大利通心粉
　　vegetarian〔ˏvɛdʒə'tɛrɪən〕 adj. 素食的

45. (**A**)　How much is the buffet dinner?
　　　　A. $19.00.　　　　B. $24.99.
　　　　C. $12.00.　　　　D. $9.00.

High-Intermediate Level
Listening Comprehension Test

This listening comprehension test will test your ability to understand spoken English. In this test, each conversation, short talk and question will be spoken JUST ONE TIME. They will not be written out for you. There are three parts to this test. Special instructions will be given to you at the beginning of each part.

Part A

In part A, you will hear 15 questions. After you hear a question, read the four choices in your test book and decide which one is the best answer to the question you have heard.

Example:

<u>You will hear</u>: Mary, can you tell me what time it is?

<u>You will read</u>: A. About two hours ago.
B. I used to be able to, but not now.
C. Sure, it's half past nine.
D. Today is October 22.

The best answer to the question "Mary, can you tell me what time it is?" is C: "Sure, it's half past nine." Therefore, you should choose answer C.

1. A. Any minute now.
   B. Yesterday, around noon.
   C. The latest model will come out this month.
   D. The bus is due for a check-up.

2. A. We discourage any form of manual labor.
   B. Generally, management frowns on any such organization.
   C. Management plans to cut the company's labor force.
   D. Labor unions don't make company policies.

3. A. I don't have a watch.
   B. Yes, philanthropy is a virtue.
   C. No thanks, I'm full.
   D. I can't help you for a second time.

4. A. My brother will.
   B. I'll go by car.
   C. I'm leaving at six.
   D. I'm going to pick up the car.

5. A. Sorry, I don't know anything about personnel.
   B. The questions can be personal.
   C. I'm sorry I haven't been around.
   D. I'd rather you don't.

6. A. Why should I be? I haven't invested a single cent.
   B. Yes. That's why I wear a seat belt.
   C. No. I already got my wife to overstock on necessities.
   D. No. I was not hurt during the crash.

7. A. No, but I'm going to
      mull over your advice.
   B. Yes, I sent it by express
      mail yesterday.
   C. No, I didn't feel like
      shopping.
   D. Yes, the mall was
      closed yesterday.

8. A. No, I don't usually get
      angry.
   B. Every chance I get.
   C. I think I'm a reticent
      person.
   D. I go to the bookstore
      once a week.

9. A. It was terrible, only a
      few people showed up.
   B. That's fine with me.
   C. We went there by bus.
   D. The conference didn't
      go until the next day.

10. A. He couldn't hold on
       anymore.
    B. He was doing a
       fantastic job.
    C. He wanted to go home
       early.
    D. He was negligent on
       the job.

11. A. Yes, I still have
       outstanding debts.
    B. No, I'll be making
       monthly payments for
       another year or so.
    C. Yes. The gauge is
       working quite nicely
       now.
    D. No, I made my last
       payment yesterday.

12. A. No, it's very durable.
　　B. No, I catch cold quite easily.
　　C. Yes, your scarf really has warm colors.
　　D. Scarves are for cold weather.

13. A. Are you kidding? How on earth can I desert my family?
　　B. That would be nice. Can I have ice cream?
　　C. I'm apathetic towards deserters.
　　D. I'm not too fond of sand.

14. A. I fell down the stairs last night.
　　B. I don't feel like going to sleep.
　　C. I'm careful when I'm walking.
　　D. Maybe next month.

15. A. Not really. I'm finding it harder to make ends meet.
　　B. Well, the government is very concerned about an inflationary spiral.
　　C. No. I haven't received a bad check yet.
　　D. I don't like inflatable toys.

Part B

In part B, you will hear 15 conversations between a man and a woman. After each conversation, you will hear a question about the conversation. After you hear the question, read the four choices in your test book and choose the best answer to the question you have heard.

Example:

You will hear: (Man)   May I see your driver's license?

(Woman) Yes, officer. Here it is. Was I speeding?

(Man)   Yes, ma'am. You were doing sixty in a forty-five mile an hour zone.

(Woman) No way! I don't believe you.

(Man)   Well, it is true and here is your ticket.

Question: Why does the man ask for the woman's driver's license?

You will read: A. She was going too fast.

B. To check its limitations.

C. To check her age.

D. She entered a restricted zone.

The best answer to the question "Why does the man ask for the woman's driver's license?" is A: "She was going too fast." Therefore, you should choose answer A.

16. A. It has risen.
    B. It has fallen.
    C. It's stable.
    D. It shot up.

17. A. Fix it himself.
    B. Exchange it.
    C. Take it in for repairs.
    D. Ask for his money
       back.

18. A. Reduce import taxes.
    B. Import more raw
       materials.
    C. Increase export taxes.
    D. Control exports.

19. A. The woman just had
       a blackout.
    B. They just got a new
       file.
    C. The woman lost a file.
    D. The woman saved a
       file.

20. A. To buy a travel ticket.
    B. To leave a bit later.
    C. To go with the
       woman.
    D. To leave early.

21. A. In a taxi.
    B. At customs.
    C. In a hotel.
    D. In a bank.

22. A. She doesn't need it.
    B. She must fill it out.
    C. She must submit it.
    D. She must post it.

23. A. for sale in the
       domestic market.
    B. produced by the man's
       company.
    C. a sample to be
       imported by the man.
    D. produced for export
       only.

24. A. He will draw some
     money.
    B. He will open the banks.
    C. He is leaving at 11:30.
    D. He will stay in the
     office all day.

25. A. Page 4 is missing.
    B. It has been dumped.
    C. It's binding.
    D. We can't tell.

26. A. He has no opinion.
    B. The client was
     unreasonable.
    C. He thinks they should
     be responsible.
    D. The client should be
     more responsible.

27. A. A night at the Hilton.
    B. Anniversary plan.
    C. Dinner schedule.
    D. Work schedule for
     the day.

28. A. The date of the
     meeting.
    B. Being in control of
     the situation.
    C. Reducing the price
     of the product.
    D. Going on contract.

29. A. In the evening.
    B. At 6 pm.
    C. At night.
    D. In the morning.

30. A. The man and the
     woman have different
     views.
    B. The woman is
     obviously from
     Bosnia.
    C. Mrs. Douglas is not
     interested in market
     expansion.
    D. The man is not too
     excited about Bosnia.

Part C

In part C, you will hear several short talks. After each talk, you will hear 2 to 3 questions about the talk. After you hear each question, read the four choices in your test book and choose the best answer to the question you have heard.

Example:

<u>You will hear</u>:

> Thank you for coming to this, the first in a series of seminars on the use of computers in the classroom. As the brochure informed you, there will be a total of five seminars given in this room every Monday morning from 6:00 to 7:30. Our goal will be to show you, the teachers of our school children, how the changing technology of today can be applied to the unchanging lessons of yesterday to make your students' learning experience more interesting and relevant to the world they live in. By the end of the last seminar, you will not be computer literate, but you will be able to make sense of the hundreds of complex words and technical terms related to the field and be aware of the programs available for use in the classroom.

Question number 1: What is the subject of this seminar series?

You will read: A. Self-improvement.
B. Using computers to teach.
C. Technology.
D. Study habits of today's students.

The best answer to the question "What is the subject of this seminar series?" is B: "Using computers to teach." Therefore, you should choose answer B.

Now listen to another question based on the same talk.

You will hear:

Question number 2: What does the speaker say participants will be able to do after attending the seminars?

You will read: A. Understand today's students.
B. Understand computer terminology.
C. Motivate students.
D. Deal more confidently with people.

The best answer to the question "What does the speaker say participants will be able to do after attending the seminars?" is B: "Understand computer terminology." Therefore, you should choose answer B.

31. A. Hillfield.
    B. Murryfield.
    C. Wendesburg.
    D. Marksfield.

32. A. The staff are rude.
    B. The switchboard was
       closed.
    C. The staff were late.
    D. The switchboard was
       out of order.

33. A. Corporate management.
    B. Corporate behavior.
    C. Corporate accounting.
    D. Corporate financing.

34. A. Janet McDouglas.
    B. John Grant.
    C. Phillip Krowsky.
    D. Walter Peabody.

35. A. Governor.
    B. Mayor.
    C. Congressman.
    D. President.

36. A. The company's
       Field Day.
    B. 10th anniversary
       celebration.
    C. The company is
       holding a seminar.
    D. A weekend party.

37. A. The employees will
       go out to have a big
       feast.
    B. They will have a
       dance competition.
    C. They'll have indoor
       entertainment.
    D. They will see a play
       called "Wait for it."

38. A. Window 22.
    B. Window 36.
    C. Window 26.
    D. Window 32.

39. A. Leave luggage in the waiting area.
　　B. Have their money out and ready.
　　C. Send only one person to buy for their group.
　　D. Keep a neat and orderly single file line.

40. A. It will create many jobs.
　　B. It will cost less than expected.
　　C. It's not mentioned.
　　D. It is environmental friendly.

41. A. She would like to meet the investors.
　　B. She would like to invest in the project.
　　C. She is not interested in the type of business.
　　D. She wants to know the safety level of the project.

42. A. Dissatisfaction.
　　B. Her pride.
　　C. Satisfaction.
　　D. Anger.

43. A. Company president.
　　B. A student.
　　C. Stewart's friend.
　　D. Program manager.

44. A. To give a briefing on a new study program.
　　B. To join a new management program.
　　C. To select the next batch of trainees.
　　D. He is looking for work.

45. A. Frank manages the selection program.
　　B. Paul has been selected for training.
　　C. Frank and Paul are being introduced.
　　D. A new program has been introduced.

中高級聽力測驗詳解 ⑦

Part A

1. (**A**) When's the next bus due?

　　A. Any minute now.

　　B. Yesterday, around noon.

　　C. The latest model will come out this month.

　　D. The bus is due for a check-up.

　　* due〔dju〕*adj.* 預定到達的；應有的

　　　around〔ə'raʊnd〕*prep.* 大約（= *about*）

　　　model〔'mɑdḷ〕*n.* 型號

　　　come out 推出　　check-up〔'tʃɛk͵ʌp〕*n.* 檢查

2. (**B**) What's the company policy on labor unions?

　　A. We discourage any form of manual labor.

　　B. Generally, management frowns on any such
　　　organization.

　　C. Management plans to cut the company's labor force.

　　D. Labor unions don't make company policies.

　　* policy〔'pɑləsɪ〕*n.* 政策

　　　labor〔'lebɚ〕*n.* 勞工；勞動　　union〔'junjən〕*n.* 工會

　　　labor union 工會　　discourage〔dɪs'kɝɪdʒ〕*v.* 不允許

　　　form〔fɔrm〕*n.* 型式　　manual〔'mænjʊəl〕*adj.* 手工的

　　　manual labor 體力勞動

　　　management〔'mænɪdʒmənt〕*n.* 資方

　　　frown〔fraʊn〕*v.* 表示不滿＜*on*＞

　　　organization〔͵ɔrgənaɪ'zeʃən〕*n.* 組織

　　　labor force 勞工

3. (**C**) Care for a second helping?

    A. I don't have a watch.

    B. Yes, philanthropy is a virtue.

    C. No thanks, I'm full.

    D. I can't help you for a second time.

    * ***care for*** 想要

    helping〔'hɛlpɪŋ〕 *n.* 一份（食物）

    philanthropy〔fə'lænθrəpɪ〕 *n.* 慈善

    virtue〔'vɝtʃʊ〕 *n.* 美德   full〔fʊl〕 *adj.* 吃飽的

    for a second time 再一次地

4. (**A**) Who's coming to pick you up?

    A. My brother will.

    B. I'll go by car.

    C. I'm leaving at six.

    D. I'm going to pick up the car.

    * ***pick up*** 搭載（某人）；領取

5. (**D**) Could I ask you a personal question?

    A. Sorry, I don't know anything about personnel.

    B. The questions can be personal.

    C. I'm sorry I haven't been around.

    D. I'd rather you don't.

    * personal〔'pɝsn̩l̩〕 *adj.* 私人的

    personnel〔,pɝsn̩'ɛl〕 *n.* 人事

    around〔ə'raʊnd〕 *adv.* 在附近   ***would rather*** 寧願

6. (**A**) Aren't you worried that the stock market will crash?

    A. Why should I be? I haven't invested a single cent.

    B. Yes. That's why I wear a seat belt.

    C. No. I already got my wife to overstock on necessities.

    D. No. I was not hurt during the crash.

  * ***stock market*** 股市　　crash〔kræʃ〕*v.* 崩盤　*n.* 碰撞
    invest〔ɪn'vɛst〕*v.* 投資
    single〔'sɪŋgḷ〕*adj.* 連一個也（沒有）的（用於否定句）
    seat belt 安全帶（= *safety belt*）
    overstock〔'ovɚ'stɑk〕*v.* 進貨過多
    necessity〔nə'sɛsətɪ〕*n.* 必需品

7. (**C**) Did you go to the mall last night?

    A. No, but I'm going to mull over your advice.

    B. Yes, I sent it by express mail yesterday.

    C. No, I didn't feel like shopping.

    D. Yes, the mall was closed yesterday.

  * mall〔mɔl〕*n.* 購物中心　　mull〔mʌl〕*v.* 慎思熟慮
    mull over *sth.* 仔細考慮某事　　***express mail*** 限時郵件
    feel like + ***V-ing*** 想要

8. (**B**) How often do you buy books?

    A. No, I don't usually get angry.

    B. Every chance I get.

    C. I think I'm a reticent person.

    D. I go to the bookstore once a week.

  * reticent〔'rɛtəsṇt〕*adj.* 沈默寡言的

9. (**A**) How did the conference go?

    A. It was terrible, only a few people showed up.

    B. That's fine with me.

    C. We went there by bus.

    D. The conference didn't go until the next day.

    * conference〔'kɑnfərəns〕 n. 會議

      go〔go〕v. 進展；開始　　***show up*** 出現

10. (**D**) Why was Mr. Hansen let go?

    A. He couldn't hold on anymore.

    B. He was doing a fantastic job.

    C. He wanted to go home early.

    D. He was negligent on the job.

    * ***be let go*** 被開除　　***hold on*** 抓住

      fantastic〔fæn'tæstɪk〕 adj. 極好的

      negligent〔'nɛglədʒənt〕 adj. 怠忽職守的

11. (**B**) Has the mortgage been paid off yet?

    A. Yes, I still have outstanding debts.

    B. No, I'll be making monthly payments for another
       year or so.

    C. Yes. The gauge is working quite nicely now.

    D. No, I made my last payment yesterday.

    * mortgage〔'mɔrgɪdʒ〕 n. 抵押貸款　　***pay off*** 付清

      outstanding〔aʊt'stændɪŋ〕 adj. 未償付的

      debt〔dɛt〕 n. 借款　　***outstanding debt*** 未清欠款

      monthly〔'mʌnθlɪ〕 adj. 每月一次的

      payment〔'pemənt〕 n. 付款

      or so 大約　　gauge〔gedʒ〕 n. 儀錶

12. (**B**) Isn't it a bit warm for a scarf?

    A. No, it's very durable.

    B. No, I catch cold quite easily.

    C. Yes, your scarf really has warm colors.

    D. Scarves are for cold weather.

    * ***a bit*** 有點   scarf〔skɑrf〕*n.* 圍巾

      durable〔'djʊrəbḷ〕*adj.* 耐用的

      catch cold 感冒   ***warm colors*** 暖色調

13. (**B**) Would you like to have a little dessert?

    A. Are you kidding? How on earth can I desert my family?

    B. That would be nice. Can I have ice cream?

    C. I'm apathetic towards deserters.

    D. I'm not too fond of sand.

    * dessert〔dɪ'zɝt〕*n.* 甜點

      on earth 究竟（置於疑問詞之後）

      desert〔dɪ'zɝt〕*v.* 拋棄

      apathetic〔͵æpə'θɛtɪk〕*adj.* 冷淡的

      deserter〔dɪ'zɝtɚ〕*n.* 背叛者

      be fond of 喜歡

14. (**D**) When are you going on a trip?

    A. I fell down the stairs last night.

    B. I don't feel like going to sleep.

    C. I'm careful when I'm walking.

    D. Maybe next month.

    * ***go on a trip*** 去旅行   stair〔stɛr〕*n.* 樓梯

15. (**A**) Has your pay risen commensurate with the high inflation rate?

A. Not really. I'm finding it harder to make ends meet.

B. Well, the government is very concerned about an inflationary spiral.

C. No. I haven't received a bad check yet.

D. I don't like inflatable toys.

* commensurate〔kə'mɛnʃərɪt〕adj. 相稱的

inflation〔ɪn'fleʃən〕n. 通貨膨脹

rate〔ret〕n. 速度

make ends meet 使收支平衡

be concerned about 關心

inflationary〔ɪn'fleʃənˌɛrɪ〕adj. 通貨膨脹的

spiral〔'spaɪrəl〕n. 惡性循環

inflationary spiral 惡性通貨膨脹

bad check 空頭支票

inflatable〔ɪn'fletəbl̩〕adj. 可充氣的

Part B

16. (**C**) W：Has anyone figured out the exchange rate yet?

M：Yeah. It's the same as yesterday.

W：That's unusual!

M：These things do happen once in a while.

Question：What happened to the exchange rate?

A. It has risen.　　　B. It has fallen.

C. It's stable.　　　D. It shot up.

* ***figure out*** 知道　　***exchange rate*** 匯率

once in a while 偶爾　　stable〔'steblˌ〕*adj.* 穩定的

shoot up 巨幅上揚

17. (**B**) W：We can come to your office and fix it, or you can bring it in.

M：It's almost new and it doesn't work. I think I'd rather have it replaced.

W：Certainly, sir. We're open until 6:00 o'clock this evening.

M：Okay. I'll bring it back this afternoon.

Question：What has the man decided he will do?

A. Fix it himself.　　　B. Exchange it.

C. Take it in for repairs.

D. Ask for his money back.

* fix〔fɪks〕*v.* 修理　　replace〔rɪ'ples〕*v.* 替換

exchange〔ɪks'tʃendʒ〕*v.* 交換

repair〔rɪ'pɛr〕*n.* 修理

18. (**A**) W: I think the government should do something about the tariffs.

M: You have a point there. They are unnecessarily high.

W: Import tariffs on raw materials are making our products too expensive.

M: Maybe we can petition the Congressman and let him try to do something about it.

W: Why don't we start on that? With a couple of thousand constituents under our employment, he is surely to do something.

Question: What should the government do?

A. Reduce import taxes.

B. Import more raw materials.

C. Increase export taxes.

D. Control exports.

* tariff〔'tærɪf〕*n.* 關稅

You have a point. 你說得對。

unnecessarily〔ʌn'nɛsə,sɛrəlɪ〕*adv.* 不必要地

import〔'ɪmport〕*n.,v.* 進口　　raw〔rɔ〕*adj.* 未加工的

raw material 原料　　petition〔pə'tɪʃən〕*v.* 向～請願

Congressman〔'kɑŋgrəsmən〕*n.* 美國國會議員（尤指眾議院議員）

start on 開始進行　　***a couple of*** 幾個

constituent〔kən'stɪtʃuənt〕*n.* 選民

employment〔ɪm'plɔɪmənt〕*n.* 雇用

tax〔tɛks〕*n.* 稅　　export〔'ɛksport〕*n.,v.* 出口

19. (**C**) W: Oh gosh! It's a blackout again.

M: Did you save your file?

W: No. I was just about to.

M: The autosave feature probably saved some for you.

W: I hope so.

Question: What happened?

A. The woman just had a blackout.

B. They just got a new file. C. The woman lost a file.

D. The woman saved a file.

* gosh〔gɑʃ〕*interj.* 老天！（表示驚訝的語氣）

blackout〔'blæk‚aʊt〕*n.* 停電；失去知覺

be about to + *V.* 正要　　autosave〔'ɔto'sev〕*n.* 自動儲存

feature〔'fitʃɚ〕*n.* 特色

20. (**D**) M: I think I'll confirm my flight first.

W: Don't worry. I took care of that already.

M: Well, I have to change my flight. I'm leaving one day earlier.

W: Really? Why?

M: Something came up and I have to go back to take care of it.

W: Oh… That's too bad. We really wanted you to stay longer so we could show you around.

Question: What does the man want?

A. To buy a travel ticket. B. To leave a bit later.

C. To go with the woman. D. To leave early.

* confirm〔kən'fɝm〕*v.* 確認　　flight〔flaɪt〕*n.* 班機

take care of 處理　　*come up* 發生

show sb. around 帶某人到處參觀　　*a bit* 有點

21. (**B**)　W：Can I see your passport, please?

M：Here you are.

W：May I know where you've traveled in the last two weeks?

M：I was in Germany and Austria.

W：Do you have anything to declare?

M：No.

Question：Where is this conversation taking place?

A. In a taxi.　　　　　B. At customs.

C. In a hotel.　　　　　D. In a bank.

* passport〔'pæs,port〕*n.* 護照

Austria〔'ɔstrɪə〕*n.* 奧地利　　declare〔dɪ'klɛr〕*v.* 申報

take place 發生　　customs〔'kʌstəmz〕*n.* 海關

22. (**A**)　M：Yes, ma'am. What can I do for you?

W：Could you show me how to fill out this form?

M：You don't need to do that any more.

W：Really! I wasn't aware of that. What do I have to do then?

M：Just give me your name and social security number and I'll take care of it for you.

Question：What does the woman have to do with the form?

A. She doesn't need it.　　B. She must fill it out.

C. She must submit it.　　D. She must post it.

* *fill out* 填寫　　*be aware of* 知道

social security number 社會安全碼

take care of 處理　　*do with* 處理

submit〔səb'mɪt〕*v.* 繳交　　post〔post〕*v.* 張貼

23. (**D**)　M：I haven't seen anything like this before.

W：It's our new multi-function video camera.　It's not for sale in the domestic market.

M：I didn't think you were doing any exports at all.

W：In fact, a lot of our products are for export only.

Question：The video camera is

A. for sale in the domestic market.

B. produced by the man's company.

C. a sample to be imported by the man.

D. produced for export only.

* multi-function〔'mʌltɪ'fʌŋkʃən〕*adj.* 多功能的
video camera 攝影機　　***for sale*** 出售的
domestic〔də'mɛstɪk〕*adj.* 國內的
sample〔'sæmpḷ〕*n.* 樣品

24. (**A**)　M：Are the banks still open?

W：I should think so.　It's only 11:30.

M：I need some cash for the weekend.

W：Out of money already!　What did you do, go on a spending spree or something?

M：Not really.　I just need some cash.

Question：What will the man do?

A. He will draw some money.

B. He will open the banks.　　C. He is leaving at 11:30.

D. He will stay in the office all day.

* cash〔kæʃ〕*n.* 現金　　***out of*** 用完
spree〔spri〕*n.* 一段極其放縱的時間
spending spree 拼命花錢　　***or something*** 或什麼的
draw〔drɔ〕*v.* 領取

25. (**D**) W: I think this contract is self-contradictory. Check Page 3.

M: That's not the final copy, Mrs. Simpson. In fact, the final version does not include Page 3 and there's a new clause on fringe benefits.

W: So why was this dumped on my desk?

M: Somebody must have made a mistake. You were supposed to get the final draft.

W: All right. Get one to me as quickly as possible.

Question：What's the problem with the final draft of the contract?

A. Page 4 is missing.

B. It has been dumped.

C. It's binding.

D. We can't tell.

* contract〔ˈkɑntrækt〕*n.* 契約

self-contradictory〔ˈsɛlf͵kɑntrəˈdɪktərɪ〕*adj.* 自相矛盾的

final copy 定稿（*= final draft*）

version〔ˈvɝʒən〕*n.* 版本　　clause〔klɔz〕*n.* 條款

fringe benefits 員工福利

dump〔dʌmp〕*v.* 拋棄　　*be supposed to* 應該

draft〔dræft〕*n.* 草稿　　*as~as possible* 愈~愈好

missing〔ˈmɪsɪŋ〕*adj.* 遺失的

binding〔ˈbaɪndɪŋ〕*adj.* 有約束力的；有效力的

26. (**C**)　M：What did you think of the client's complaint?

W：I didn't think it was totally justifiable.　What did you think?

M：Well, I think we have to assume some responsibility.

W：I don't see it that way.　They knew the risk from the git go.

M：Yeah.　But if we don't do anything about it, it could cause trouble for us in the future.

Question：What does the man think?

A. He has no opinion.

B. The client was unreasonable.

C. He thinks they should be responsible.

D. The client should be more responsible.

* client〔'klaɪənt〕*n.* 顧客
  complaint〔kəm'plent〕*n.* 抱怨
  totally〔'totḷɪ〕*adv.* 完全地
  justifiable〔'dʒʌstə,faɪəbḷ〕*adj.* 合理的
  assume〔ə'sjum〕*v.* 承擔
  I don't see it that way. 我不那樣認為。
  risk〔rɪsk〕*n.* 風險　　***from the git go*** 一開始
  unreasonable〔ʌn'riznəbḷ〕*adj.* 過分的；不講理的

27. (**B**)　W：What plans have you made for our anniversary?

M：We are going to the Hilton for dinner.

W：Is that all?

M：Of course not, honey.　You're getting the royal treatment.

W：Oh…. Don't tell me.　I want to be surprised.

Question: What are the man and the woman talking about?

A. A night at the Hilton.

B. Anniversary plan.

C. Dinner schedule.

D. Work schedule for the day.

* anniversary〔͵ænəˋvɝsərɪ〕 *n.* 週年紀念

　royal〔ˋrɔɪəl〕 *adj.* 皇室般的；尊榮的

　treatment〔ˋtritmənt〕 *n.* 待遇

　schedule〔ˋskɛdʒul〕 *n.* 計劃表；行程表

28. (**B**) W: What was the result of your meeting yesterday?

M: Basically, we agreed on reducing the per unit price of our products so long as they agree to go on contract with us.

W: But we are on top of the situation. Right?

M: We sure are.

Question: What is the woman concerned about?

A. The date of the meeting.

B. Being in control of the situation.

C. Reducing the price of the product.

D. Going on contract.

* basically〔ˋbesɪkḷɪ〕 *adv.* 基本上

　agree on 對～意見一致　　unit〔ˋjunɪt〕 *n.* 單位

　unit price 單價　　*so long as* 只要 (= *as long as*)

　go on 繼續　　contract〔ˋkɑntrækt〕 *n.* 契約

　on top of 完全控制　　*in control of* 控制

29. (**D**) W: I appreciate your inviting me to breakfast.

M: I am glad you could make it. I have something very important to discuss with you.

W: Is this about the pharmaceutical plant you are starting in Mexico?

M: You read my mind. So… Are you interested?

W: I want full management authority and no micromanagement from corporate.

M: It's a deal.

Question: At what time is this conversation taking place?

A. In the evening.

B. At 6 pm.

C. At night.

D. In the morning.

* appreciate〔ə'priʃɪˌet〕v. 感謝   ***make it*** 及時趕到

pharmaceutical〔ˌfɑrmə'sjutɪkl̩〕adj. 製藥的

plant〔plænt〕n. 工廠   start〔stɑrt〕v. 創辦

You read my mind. 你看穿我的心思。

management〔'mænɪdʒmənt〕n. 管理

authority〔ə'θɔrətɪ〕n. 權力

micromanagement〔'maɪkro'mænɪdʒmənt〕n. 緊迫盯人的 管理方式

corporate〔'kɔrpərɪt〕n. 總公司

deal〔dil〕n. 約定   ***It's a deal.*** 一言為定。

30. (**A**) W: It's a lot easier for us to export to English-speaking countries. I'm not too excited about Bosnia.

M: But Mrs. Douglas, we can make money there.

W: There're still a lot of marketing opportunities in English-speaking countries. Besides, we don't have to hire translators and we are familiar with their legal systems. I think we are making a very big mistake.

M: The market in English-speaking countries is already too saturated for us to do well.

Question: Which of the following statements is true?

A. The man and the woman have different views.

B. The woman is obviously from Bosnia.

C. Mrs. Douglas is not interested in market expansion.

D. The man is not too excited about Bosnia.

* Bosnia〔'bɑznɪə〕n. 波士尼亞（南斯拉夫原六個組成共和國之一，1991 年獨立）

marketing〔'mɑrkɪtɪŋ〕n. 買賣；行銷

translator〔træns'letɚ〕n. 翻譯者

legal〔'ligḷ〕adj. 法律的　　*legal system* 法律制度

saturated〔'sætʃə,retɪd〕adj. 飽和的

view〔vju〕n. 觀點

obviously〔'ɑbvɪəslɪ〕adv. 明顯地

expansion〔ɪk'spænʃən〕n. 擴張

Part C

Questions 31-33 are based on the following talk.

I have visited four of our branch offices in the last month. I regret to say that I found the level of efficiency very low in three of them. The office in Wendesburg was the exception. Marksfield was a disgrace — some workers arrived more than an hour late, without ever feeling uncomfortable. I guess that must be the practice there. Murryfield was no better, either; there was no one to answer the telephone from 12:15 to 1:45 — the excuse being, it was lunch hour. This company expects all calls to be answered from 9 to 5. We must be available to our customers at all times during business hours. Hillfield's staff will have to be given a course in corporate behavior. The secretaries there are very rude to customers.

** **branch office** 分公司　　regret〔rɪˈgrɛt〕v. 遺憾
level〔ˈlɛvḷ〕n. 程度　　efficiency〔ɪˈfɪʃənsɪ〕n. 效率
exception〔ɪkˈsɛpʃən〕n. 例外
disgrace〔dɪsˈgres〕n. 恥辱；丟臉的事
practice〔ˈpræktɪs〕n. 習慣　　excuse〔ɪkˈskjus〕n. 理由
expect〔ɪkˈspɛkt〕v. 要求
at all times 一直　　**business hours** 營業時間
staff〔stæf〕n.（全體）職員　　course〔kors〕n. 課程
corporate〔ˈkɔrpərɪt〕adj. 團體的；公司的
corporate behavior 企業專職訓練　　rude〔rud〕adj. 無禮的

31. (**C**) Which office seems to be doing well?
    A. Hillfield.
    B. Murryfield.
    C. Wendesburg.
    D. Marksfield.

32. (**A**) What was the complaint about Hillfield?
    A. The staff are rude.
    B. The switchboard was closed.
    C. The staff were late.
    D. The switchboard was out of order.

    * switchboard〔'swɪtʃ,bord〕*n.*（電話）總機
    out of order 故障的

33. (**B**) What course is the woman thinking to introduce?
    A. Corporate management.
    B. Corporate behavior.
    C. Corporate accounting.
    D. Corporate financing.

    * introduce〔,ɪntrə'djus〕*v.* 採用
    accounting〔ə'kaʊntɪŋ〕*n.* 記帳；會計
    financing〔faɪ'nænsɪŋ〕*n.* 融資

Questions 34-35 are based on the following report.

This just in to the Election Watch Center: In Texas, Democrat Janet McDouglas has conceded the governorship to her Republican rival, John Grant. Early results from the polls, which closed only two hours ago, show Grant leading McDouglas 68 percent to 29 percent, with the remaining 3 percent going to independent candidate, Phillip Krowsky. While a Republican victory was expected, the magnitude of this victory is certainly coming as a surprise to all. Now, for a live report from the Texas state capital, let's go to Walter Peabody who is with the Lone Star State's apparent governor-elect at his campaign headquarters in Austin.

** ***This just in~*** ～的最新消息　　election〔ɪˋlɛkʃən〕*n.* 選舉

election watch center 選情分析中心

Democrat〔ˋdɛməˏkræt〕*n.*（美國）民主黨員

concede〔kənˋsid〕*v.* 承認失敗

governorship〔ˋgʌvənəˏʃɪp〕*n.* 州長的職位

Republican〔rɪˋpʌblɪkən〕*n.*（美國）共和黨員

rival〔ˋraɪvl̩〕*n.* 對手　　poll〔pol〕*n.* 投票結果

lead〔lid〕*v.* 領先　　remaining〔rɪˋmenɪŋ〕*adj.* 剩下的

independent〔ˏɪndɪˋpɛndənt〕*n.* 無黨派人士

candidate〔ˋkændədet〕*n.* 候選人

victory〔ˋvɪktərɪ〕*n.* 勝利

magnitude〔ˋmægnəˏtjud〕*n.* 巨大

live〔laɪv〕*adj.* 現場的　　capital〔ˋkæpətl̩〕*n.* 首府

Lone Star State（美國）德州的別稱

apparent〔əˋpærənt〕*adj.* 篤定的；明顯的

governor〔ˋgʌvənə〕*n.* 州長　　elect〔ɪˋlɛkt〕*n.* 當選人

campaign〔kæmˋpen〕*n.* 競選活動

headquarters〔ˋhɛdˋkwɔrtəz〕*n. pl.* 總部

34. (**B**)　Who has apparently won the election?

　　　A. Janet McDouglas.　　　B. John Grant.

　　　C. Phillip Krowsky.　　　D. Walter Peabody.

35. (**A**)　To what office will the winner be elected?

　　　A. Governor.　　　B. Mayor.

　　　C. Congressman.　　　D. President.

　　　* office〔ˋɔfɪs〕*n.* 官職　　mayor〔ˋmeə〕*n.* 市長

　　　Congressman〔ˋkɑŋgrəsmən〕*n.* 美國國會議員

　　　president〔ˋprɛzədənt〕*n.* 總統

Questions 36-37 are based on the following memo.

> Attention everyone. On the occasion of the 10th anniversary of the organization, the general affairs department has arranged a grand showing of "*Wait for it*" this Saturday in the main auditorium. It's a three-hour-show starting at 2:30. After the movie, light refreshments will be served in the cafeteria.

** occasion〔ə'keʒən〕*n.* 特殊場合

on the occasion of 在～的時候

anniversary〔͵ænə'vɜsərɪ〕*n.* 週年紀念

organization〔͵ɔrgənaɪ'zeʃən〕*n.* 組織

general affairs 總務

department〔dɪ'partmənt〕*n.* 部門

arrange〔ə'rendʒ〕*v.* 安排

grand〔grænd〕*adj.* 盛大的   showing〔'ʃoɪŋ〕*n.* 放映

auditorium〔͵ɔdə'torɪəm〕*n.* 禮堂

light〔laɪt〕*adj.* 清淡的

refreshments〔rɪ'frɛʃmənts〕*n. pl.* 茶點

serve〔sɜv〕*v.* 供應

cafeteria〔͵kæfə'tɪrɪə〕*n.* 自助餐廳

36. (**B**) What occasion is this?

    A. The company's Field Day.

    B. 10th anniversary celebration.

    C. The company is holding a seminar.

    D. A weekend party.

    * ***field day*** 出遊日；遠足日

      celebration〔‚sɛlə'breʃən〕 *n.* 慶祝活動

      seminar〔'sɛmə‚nɑr〕 *n.* 研討會

37. (**C**) How will the occasion be celebrated?

    A. The employees will go out to have a big feast.

    B. They will have a dance competition.

    C. They'll have indoor entertainment.

    D. They will see a play called "*Wait for it*."

    * feast〔fist〕 *n.* 盛宴

      competition〔‚kɑmpə'tɪʃən〕 *n.* 比賽

      indoor〔'ɪn‚dor〕 *adj.* 室內的

      entertainment〔‚ɛntɚ'tenmənt〕 *n.* 娛樂

      play〔ple〕 *n.* 戲劇

Questions 38-39 are based on the following announcement.

> Attention passengers going to Mansfield. Window 36 is now selling tickets to Mansfield. This is in addition to Window 22. If you are traveling with family or friends, be sure to purchase your tickets at the same window, as the tickets are for two different buses. I repeat, the tickets at Windows 22 and 36 are for different buses bound for Mansfield. Also, to minimize congestion at the ticket counters, we ask that groups or families send only one person to the ticket window to purchase tickets for all. Thank you for choosing Green Line Coaches.

** ***in addition to*** 除~外（還有）　　***be sure to*** 務必
purchase〔'pɝtʃəs〕v. 購買　　repeat〔rɪ'pit〕v. 重覆
bound〔baʊnd〕adj. 前往的 <*for*>
minimize〔'mɪnə,maɪz〕v. 使減到最少
congestion〔kən'dʒɛstʃən〕n. 擁擠；阻塞
counter〔'kaʊntɚ〕n. 櫃台　　coach〔kotʃ〕n. 巴士

38. (**B**) Which window has just opened for Mansfield passengers?

    A. Window 22.

    B. Window 36.

    C. Window 26.

    D. Window 32.

39. (**C**) How can passengers reduce congestion at the ticket counters?

    A. Leave luggage in the waiting area.

    B. Have their money out and ready.

    C. Send only one person to buy for their group.

    D. Keep a neat and orderly single file line.

   * reduce〔rɪ'djus〕v. 減少　　luggage〔'lʌgɪdʒ〕n. 行李
    waiting area 候車區　　neat〔nit〕adj. 整齊的
    orderly〔'ɔrdəlɪ〕adj. 整齊的
    single file 一列縱隊

Questions 40-42 are based on the following talk.

> Frankly, I didn't think he had any significant points. He wobbled back and forth. I still don't know the specifics. Perhaps we should have him answer questions. How much is the project going to cost? How many jobs are going to be created? Then we should challenge him on the negatives: Is it a safe project? We don't want workers working in a high risk environment. And of course, what are the long-term effects on the environment?

** frankly〔'fræŋklɪ〕*adv.* 坦白說（後省略 speaking）

significant〔sɪg'nɪfəkənt〕*adj.* 重要的

point〔pɔɪnt〕*n.* 觀點　　wobble〔'wɑbḷ〕*v.* 意見游移不定

back and forth 來回地　　specific〔spɪ'sɪfɪk〕*n.* 詳情

project〔'prɑdʒɛkt〕*n.* 計劃；工程

challenge〔'tʃælɪndʒ〕*v.* 質疑

negative〔'nɛgətɪv〕*n.* 負面的觀點

risk〔rɪsk〕*n.* 危險　　long-term〔'lɔŋ'tɝm〕*adj.* 長期的

effect〔ɪ'fɛkt〕*n.* 影響

40. (**C**) What will the benefits of the project be?

    A. It will create many jobs.

    B. It will cost less than expected.

    C. It's not mentioned.

    D. It is environmental friendly.

    * benefit〔'bɛnəfɪt〕 *n.* 好處

      mention〔'mɛnʃən〕 *n.* 提到

      environmental〔ɪnˏvaɪrən'mɛntḷ〕 *adj.* 環境的

      friendly〔'frɛndlɪ〕 *adj.* 有利的

41. (**D**) Which one of the following is of concern to the woman?

    A. She would like to meet the investors.

    B. She would like to invest in the project.

    C. She is not interested in the type of business.

    D. She wants to know the safety level of the project.

    * concern〔kən's3n〕 *n.* 關心

      investor〔ɪn'vɛstə〕 *n.* 投資者

      level〔'lɛvḷ〕 *n.* 程度   type〔taɪp〕 *n.* 類型

42. (**A**) What is the speaker expressing?

    A. Dissatisfaction.   B. Her pride.

    C. Satisfaction.   D. Anger.

    * express〔ɪk'sprɛs〕 *v.* 表達

      dissatisfaction〔ˏdɪssætɪs'fækʃən〕 *n.* 不滿

      pride〔praɪd〕 *n.* 得意   anger〔'æŋgə〕 *n.* 忿怒

Questions 43-45 are based on the following introduction.

> Frank. This is Paul Stewart. Paul is the director of studies at the International Business School. He's here to brief us on the new management program, which they have just started at the School. In fact, why don't you come in for the meeting? Frank is one of the people managing the selection program here.

** director〔də'rɛktə〕*n.* 主任　　***director of studies*** 教務主任
brief〔brif〕*v.* 做簡報　　program〔'progræm〕*n.* 課程;方案
selection〔sə'lɛkʃən〕*n.* 選擇　　***selection program*** 選任方案

43. (**D**) Who is Frank?
　　　A. Company president.　　　B. A student.
　　　C. Stewart's friend.　　　D. Program manager.

44. (**A**) Why is Paul visiting?
　　　A. To give a briefing on a new study program.
　　　B. To join a new management program.
　　　C. To select the next batch of trainees.
　　　D. He is looking for work.
　　　* briefing〔'brifɪŋ〕*n.* 簡報　　select〔sə'lɛkt〕*v.* 挑選
　　　　batch〔bætʃ〕*n.* 一組　　trainee〔tren'i〕*n.* 接受訓練的人

45. (**B**) Which one of the following is NOT true?
　　　A. Frank manages the selection program.
　　　B. Paul has been selected for training.
　　　C. Frank and Paul are being introduced.
　　　D. A new program has been introduced.
　　　* introduce〔͵ɪntrə'djus〕*v.* 介紹;採用

High-Intermediate Level
Listening Comprehension Test

This listening comprehension test will test your ability to understand spoken English. In this test, each conversation, short talk and question will be spoken JUST ONE TIME. They will not be written out for you. There are three parts to this test. Special instructions will be given to you at the beginning of each part.

Part A

In part A, you will hear 15 questions. After you hear a question, read the four choices in your test book and decide which one is the best answer to the question you have heard.

Example:

<u>You will hear</u>: Mary, can you tell me what time it is?

<u>You will read</u>: A. About two hours ago.
B. I used to be able to, but not now.
C. Sure, it's half past nine.
D. Today is October 22.

The best answer to the question "Mary, can you tell me what time it is?" is C: "Sure, it's half past nine." Therefore, you should choose answer C.

1. A. For three years now.
   B. Until next April.
   C. I've always been
      very tall.
   D. My position remains
      neutral.

2. A. We have lots of tall
      buildings.
   B. The Radio Tower
      on Main Street.
   C. I do not like those
      tall buildings.
   D. I'm afraid of heights.

3. A. A good accountant
      is hard to find.
   B. There's accounting
      done in this
      department.
   C. It's down the hall, last
      office on the left.
   D. Accounting is the
      biggest department
      in this company.

4. A. It's almost 10:30.
   B. The best is yet to come.
   C. The report is not
      finished yet.
   D. Let me help you and
      we'll be finished in
      no time.

5. A. No, I'm all out of
      quarters.
   B. I used to work there.
   C. No, thanks. I'm not
      hungry right now.
   D. Yes, I've never been
      to LA.

6. A. Yes, it's my first day.
   B. I just bought it.
   C. Yes, here it is.
   D. It's not new anymore.

7. A. They are not giving out any raises now.
   B. You'll need to fill out a salary advance request form.
   C. It's possible for a good worker to advance.
   D. Advancement requires hard work and dedication.

8. A. I'll get it for you.
   B. I'll call them soon.
   C. Here is your menu.
   D. I'll check on the situation.

9. A. She's worked here a long time.
   B. She'll be out all day.
   C. Yes, she will.
   D. It's really beyond expectation.

10. A. I wish the temperatures would fall.
    B. It seems like a bad plan.
    C. They're very hot.
    D. I know. I'll get a new heater.

11. A. No, I don't care what you think.
    B. No, we're fine. Thank you.
    C. No, anything else thanks.
    D. What else would you like?

12. A. He was here a few minutes ago.
    B. It seems he doesn't want to say anything.
    C. It was a very big contract, wasn't it?
    D. He didn't explain how to operate this machine.

13. A. Boxing has always been my favorite sport.
    B. Dogs hear things people can't.
    C. I couldn't help but hear; my office is next to Doug's.
    D. The manager used to be a prizefighter.

14. A. The garage is far away.
    B. Tom's daughter did.
    C. That garage is very good.
    D I always park my car in the garage.

15. A. There are no fleas here.
    B. Yes, but not in the market.
    C. It's about 10 minutes from here.
    D. I don't think they sell fleas at the market.

Part B

In part B, you will hear 15 conversations between a man and a woman. After each conversation, you will hear a question about the conversation. After you hear the question, read the four choices in your test book and choose the best answer to the question you have heard.

Example:

<u>You will hear</u>: (Man)   May I see your driver's license?
(Woman)   Yes, officer. Here it is. Was I speeding?
(Man)   Yes, ma'am. You were doing sixty in a forty-five mile an hour zone.
(Woman)   No way! I don't believe you.
(Man)   Well, it is true and here is your ticket.

Question: Why does the man ask for the woman's driver's license?

<u>You will read</u>: A. She was going too fast.
B. To check its limitations.
C. To check her age.
D. She entered a restricted zone.

The best answer to the question "Why does the man ask for the woman's driver's license?" is A: "She was going too fast." Therefore, you should choose answer A.

16. A. The man wants to file
a suit.
B. The woman is lying.
C. They'd like to avoid a
suit.
D. Tony is handing the case.

17. A. Too many strange
people are coming into
the building.
B. The birds fly into the
office.
C. Security guards are
overpaid.
D. The security guards are
spending too much
time out.

18. A. He went shopping.
B. He stayed at the office.
C. He was watching TV.
D. He had an interview.

19. A. He wants to borrow
money.
B. He wants to open an
account.
C. He's applying for a job.
D. He wants to make friends
with the bank manager.

26. A. He's looking for a
consultant.
B. He came to make an
appointment.
C. He needs some
information from the
company.
D. He's looking for
buyers for his annual
reports.

21. A. Business schools
teach nothing really
important.
B. Tenacity is not a
character thing.
C. Smartness and
tenacity are two
different things.
D. It is important to be
right.

22. A. She asked for Chris.
B. She took something
from Chris' drawer.
C. She left something
in Chris' drawer.
D. She waited for Chris
for something.

23. A. They are going to
       gather evidence.
    B. They are going away
       forever.
    C. They are going to get
       a taxi.
    D. They are going to
       evade taxes.

24. A. The weather may be
       too cold for her.
    B. She has too much to
       carry.
    C. The weather may be
       too hot.
    D. She might miss the
       cold weather.

25. A. The world's auto
       industry is in a crisis.
    B. Environmentalists
       like what's happening
       in Japan.
    C. Japan has no
       environmentalists.
    D. Japanese cars are
       selling very quickly.

20. A. They have to pay more
       taxes.
    B. They will have more
       disposable income.
    C. They will start retailing.
    D. They will move up
       the social ladder.

27. A. He forgot Stella.
    B. He went to the hospital.
    C. He slept too much.
    D. He forgot Stella isn't
       coming.

28. A. He may find himself
       out of work.
    B. The woman may lose
       her job.
    C. He may be transferred
       to sales.
    D. The woman is pretty.

29. A. Costs.
    B. Prices.
    C. Computers.
    D. Offices.

30. A. Never call again.
    B. Call later.
    C. Write a letter.
    D. Drop by.

Part C

In part C, you will hear several short talks. After each talk, you will hear 2 to 3 questions about the talk. After you hear each question, read the four choices in your test book and choose the best answer to the question you have heard.

Example:

<u>You will hear</u>:

Thank you for coming to this, the first in a series of
seminars on the use of computers in the classroom.
As the brochure informed you, there will be a total
of five seminars given in this room every Monday
morning from 6:00 to 7:30. Our goal will be to show
you, the teachers of our school children, how the
changing technology of today can be applied to the
unchanging lessons of yesterday to make your students'
learning experience more interesting and relevant to the
world they live in. By the end of the last seminar, you
will not be computer literate, but you will be able to
make sense of the hundreds of complex words and
technical terms related to the field and be aware of the
programs available for use in the classroom.

Question number 1:   What is the subject of this seminar
series?

You will read: A. Self-improvement.
B. Using computers to teach.
C. Technology.
D. Study habits of today's students.

The best answer to the question "What is the subject of this
seminar series?" is B: "Using computers to teach." Therefore,
you should choose answer B.

Now listen to another question based on the same talk.

You will hear:
Question number 2:   What does the speaker say
participants will be able to do after
attending the seminars?

You will read: A. Understand today's students.
B. Understand computer terminology.
C. Motivate students.
D. Deal more confidently with people.

The best answer to the question "What does the speaker say
participants will be able to do after attending the seminars?" is
B: "Understand computer terminology." Therefore, you should
choose answer B.

31. A. At a 2-stall garage.
    B. At a shopping mall.
    C. At an ATM.
    D. At a convenience store.

32. A. Someone parked illegally.
    B. Someone stole a light truck.
    C. A car was set on fire.
    D. Someone requested information.

33. A. Entered a new business.
    B. Imported baby food.
    C. Relocated to Europe.
    D. Reduced the birth rate.

34. A. Europe is more profitable.
    B. Europe has the largest market.
    C. Birth rates in Europe are falling.
    D. The company wanted more challenge.

35. A. The company has reduced the number of employees.
    B. The company has increased exports to Brazil.
    C. The company did not manufacture baby food before.
    D. The company is going to close its main plant.

36. A. To inform employees of a new policy.
    B. To tell employees to shorten their breaks.
    C. To question the purpose of implementing policies.
    D. To advertise a new café.

37. A. To encourage tardiness.
    B. To discourage punctuality.
    C. To monitor employee attendance.
    D. To allow more coffee breaks.

38. A. The number "1".
    B. The number "2".
    C. The number "3".
    D. The number "4".

39. A. Press "0".
    B. Call another number.
    C. Wait.
    D. Press "4".

40. A. A new TV dinner product.
    B. An ethnic restaurant.
    C. A real estate agency.
    D. A travel agency.

41. A. It serves exotic food.
    B. It is located on a corner.
    C. It is open twenty-four hours a day.
    D. It offers delicious meals.

42. A. The curator of the museum.
    B. An employee of a tour agency.
    C. A housekeeper at the museum.
    D. A tour guide at the museum.

43. A. Their group leader will tell them.
    B. An announcement will be made.
    C. There are signs posted at each entrance.
    D. If there is no rope, it is okay.

44. A. On a Pacific cruise liner.
    B. On a luxury yacht.
    C. On a commercial airplane.
    D. On a roller coaster.

45. A. To relate safety procedures.
    B. To advertise air-safety.
    C. To encourage smoking.
    D. To admonish the passengers against buckling up.

中高級聽力測驗詳解 ⑧

Part A

1. (**A**) How long have you been in this position?
    A. For three years now.
    B. Until next April.
    C. I've always been very tall.
    D. My position remains neutral.

    * position 〔 pə'zɪʃən 〕 *n.* 職位；立場
      neutral 〔'njutrəl 〕 *adj.* 中立的

2. (**B**) Which is the tallest building in your city?
    A. We have lots of tall buildings.
    B. The Radio Tower on Main Street.
    C. I do not like those tall buildings.
    D. I'm afraid of heights.

    * tower 〔'tauɚ 〕 *n.* 高樓；塔   height 〔 haɪt 〕 *n.* 高處

3. (**C**) Could you tell me where the accounting department is?
    A. A good accountant is hard to find.
    B. There's accounting done in this department.
    C. It's down the hall, last office on the left.
    D. Accounting is the biggest department in this company.

    * accounting 〔 ə'kauntɪŋ 〕 *n.* 會計；記帳
      accountant 〔 ə'kauntənt 〕 *n.* 會計師
      hall 〔 hɔl 〕 *n.* 大廳

4. (**D**) How am I ever going to finish this report on time?

    A. It's almost 10:30.

    B. The best is yet to come.

    C. The report is not finished yet.

    D. Let me help you and we'll be finished in no time.

    * yet〔jɛt〕*adv.* 遲早

    The best is yet to come. 最好的情況終將來到。

    in no time 很快

5. (**B**) Have you ever been to the headquarters in Los Angeles?

    A. No, I'm all out of quarters.

    B. I used to work there.

    C. No, thanks. I'm not hungry right now.

    D. Yes, I've never been to LA.

    * ***out of*** 用完

    quarter〔ˈkwɔrtɚ〕*n.* 二十五分硬幣

6. (**A**) You're new here, aren't you?

    A. Yes, it's my first day.

    B. I just bought it.

    C. Yes, here it is.

    D. It's not new anymore.

    * new〔nju〕*adj.* 新來的；陌生的

7. (**B**)　Is it possible to get an advance on my salary?

    A.　They are not giving out any raises now.

    B.　You'll need to fill out a salary advance request form.

    C.　It's possible for a good worker to advance.

    D.　Advancement requires hard work and dedication.

    *　advance〔əd'væns〕*n.* 預付　*v.* 進步

      salary〔'sælərɪ〕*n.* 薪水　　***give out*** 公佈

      raise〔rez〕*n.* 加薪　　***fill out*** 填寫

      request form 申請表

      advancement〔əd'vænsmənt〕*n.* 升遷

      dedication〔,dɛdə'keʃən〕*n.* 投入；奉獻

8. (**A**)　Could you bring me the check, please?

    A.　I'll get it for you.

    B.　I'll call them soon.

    C.　Here is your menu.

    D.　I'll check on the situation.

    *　check〔tʃɛk〕*n.* 支票　　menu〔'mɛnju〕*n.* 菜單

      check on 檢查

9. (**B**)　When do you expect Ms. Greene to be back?

    A.　She's worked here a long time.

    B.　She'll be out all day.

    C.　Yes, she will.

    D.　It's really beyond expectation.

    *　expectation〔,ɛkspɛk'teʃən〕*n.* 期待

      beyond expectation 出乎意料的

10. (**A**) What do you think of this terrible heat wave?

A. I wish the temperatures would fall.

B. It seems like a bad plan.

C. They're very hot.

D. I know. I'll get a new heater.

* ***What do you think of~?*** 你認為～如何？
  heat wave 熱浪　temperature〔'tɛmprətʃə〕n. 氣溫
  fall〔fɔl〕v. 下降　heater〔'hitə〕n. 暖氣機

11. (**B**) Would you care for anything else?

A. No, I don't care what you think.

B. No, we're fine. Thank you.

C. No, anything else thanks.

D. What else would you like?

* ***care for*** 想要　care〔kɛr〕v. 在乎

12. (**B**) Did the manager explain why we are stopping the
project?

A. He was here a few minutes ago.

B. It seems he doesn't want to say anything.

C. It was a very big contract, wasn't it?

D. He didn't explain how to operate this machine.

* explain〔ɪk'splen〕v. 說明
  project〔'prɑdʒɛkt〕n. 計畫
  contract〔'kɑntrækt〕n. 契約
  operate〔'ɑpə,ret〕v. 操作

13. (**C**) Did you hear about the fight between Doug and the manager?

    A. Boxing has always been my favorite sport.

    B. Dogs hear things people can't.

    C. I couldn't help but hear; my office is next to Doug's.

    D. The manager used to be a prizefighter.

    * fight〔faɪt〕 *n.* 爭吵　　boxing〔'bɑksɪŋ〕 *n.* 拳擊
    couldn't help but* + *V. 不得不～
    next to 在～旁邊　　***used to* + *V.*** 以前曾經
    prizefighter〔'praɪz,faɪtɚ〕 *n.* 職業拳擊手

14. (**B**) Who took your car to the garage for you?

    A. The garage is far away.

    B. Tom's daughter did.

    C. That garage is very good.

    D. I always park my car in the garage.

    * garage〔gə'rɑʒ〕 *n.* 車庫；（汽車）修理廠
    park〔pɑrk〕 *v.* 停（車）

15. (**C**) Is there a flea market anywhere near here?

    A. There are no fleas here.

    B. Yes, but not in the market.

    C. It's about 10 minutes from here.

    D. I don't think they sell fleas at the market.

    * flea〔fli〕 *n.* 跳蚤　　***flea market*** 跳蚤市場

Part B

16. (**C**) W：Matt, we just got a complaint from one of our clients. It's quite serious actually. Someone over there just warned me that the manager is seeking litigation.

M：That's ridiculous. They haven't even tried to settle with us. In fact, this is the first time I've heard about the case.

W：I was just checking the files and I found letters from 13 months ago. Tony must have been handling this and after he left no one seems to know what's going on.

M：Now we are in a jam because Tony didn't have anyone take over his mess.

Question：Which one of the following statements is true about the conversation?

A. The man wants to file a suit.

B. The woman is lying.

C. They'd like to avoid a suit.

D. Tony is handling the case.

* complaint〔kəm'plent〕*n.* 抱怨；投訴

client〔'klaɪənt〕*n.* 客戶

seek〔sik〕*v.* 尋求　litigation〔ˌlɪtə'geʃən〕*n.* 訴訟

ridiculous〔rɪ'dɪkjələs〕*adj.* 荒謬的　settle〔'sɛtl̩〕*v.* 和解

case〔kes〕*n.* 案件　handle〔'hændl̩〕*v.* 處理

jam〔dʒæm〕*n.* 困境　***take over*** 接管

mess〔mɛs〕*n.* 混亂的東西

file〔faɪl〕*v.* 提起（訴訟）　suit〔sut〕*n.* 訴訟

17. (**A**) W: How come we have so many hawkers in the building?

M: The security guards let them in.

W: Tell the security guards not to let in any more hawkers. This is an office building, not a market.

M: Okay. I'll get on it.

W: While you're at it, have the security guards tell the hawkers to leave.

M: Yes, ma'am,

Question: What's the woman not happy about?

A. Too many strange people are coming into the building.

B. The birds fly into the office.

C. Security guards are overpaid.

D. The security guards are spending too much time out.

* ***How come~?*** 爲什麼~？　　hawker〔'hɔkə〕*n.* 街上小販
security guard 警衛　　***get on*** 進行
while you're at it 當你在處理的時候
overpay〔'ovə·'pe〕*v.* 薪水過多

18. (**D**) W: By the way, did you watch television last night?

M: No. Why?

W: The CEO had an interview. It was great.

M: Really? Too bad I missed it.

W: I taped it. If you want to watch it later, I'll bring it to you.

M: If you can do that, it'll be great.

Question：What did the CEO do last night?

A. He went shopping.

B. He stayed at the office.

C. He was watching TV.

D. He had an interview.

* **by the way** 順便一提；對了

CEO 總裁 (= *Chief Executive Officer*)

interview〔'ɪntə،vju〕*n.* 訪談　　tape〔tep〕*v.* 錄影

19. (**A**) M：Hello. I want to know something. Is it possible for
a foreign business organization to get a loan from a
local bank?

W：I'll refer you to the bank manager. Please hold on.

M：Sure.

Question：What does the man want?

A. He wants to borrow money.

B. He wants to open an account.

C. He's applying for a job.

D. He wants to make friends with the bank manager.

* organization〔،ɔrgənaɪ'zeʃən〕*n.* 組織

loan〔lon〕*n.* 貸款　　local〔'lokl̩〕*adj.* 本地的

refer〔rɪ'fɝ〕*v.* 叫～求助於 < *to* >

hold on 稍候；不要掛斷電話

account〔ə'kaʊnt〕*n.* 帳戶

apply for 應徵　　**make friends with** 和～交朋友

20. (**C**)　M : I'm from Prime Consulting Incorporated.　I was wondering if it was possible to obtain your annual report.

　　　　　W : Yes, we do give out our annual reports, but you're a little too early.　Can you come back later or leave us your address and…

　　　　　M : Actually our office is just on the next floor.　I can drop by next Monday if that's okay.

　　　　　W : That will be even better.　We'll have it ready for you on Monday.

　　　Question : What does the man want?

　　　A.　He's looking for a consultant.

　　　B.　He came to make an appointment.

　　　C.　He needs some information from the company.

　　　D.　He's looking for buyers for his annual reports.

　　　* consulting〔kən'sʌltɪŋ〕 *adj.* 顧問的
　　　　incorporated〔ɪn'kɔrpəˌretɪd〕 *adj.* 股份有限的 (= *Inc.*)
　　　　obtain〔əb'ten〕 *v.* 獲得　　annual〔'ænjʊəl〕 *adj.* 年度的
　　　　give out 發出　　***drop by*** 順道拜訪
　　　　consultant〔kən'sʌltənt〕 *n.* 顧問
　　　　appointment〔ə'pɔɪntmənt〕 *n.* 約會

21. (**C**)　W : I think this has nothing to do with how smart you are.　You just need tenacity.

　　　　　M : You're right.　And that's not something you get from business school.

　　　　　W : Exactly.　It's a character thing.

Question : What are they saying?

A. Business schools teach nothing really important.

B. Tenacity is not a character thing.

C. Smartness and tenacity are two different things.

D. It is important to be right.

* ***have nothing to do with*** 和～無關

　tenacity〔tɪ'næsətɪ〕 *n.* 固執

　character〔'kærɪktə〕 *n.* 性格

22. (**B**)　W : Chris, Nancy was here.

　　　　　M : Did she want to see me?

　　　　　W : She didn't say a word, but I think she took something from your drawer.

　　　　　M : She did what!? What did she take? Why didn't you stop her?

　　　　　W : Hey. She wasn't exactly the friendliest person in the world. Besides, she said that you have something of hers.

　　　　　Question : What did Nancy do?

A. She asked for Chris.

B. She took something from Chris' drawer.

C. She left something in Chris' drawer.

D. She waited for Chris for something.

* drawer〔drɔr〕 *n.* 抽屜

　friendly〔'frɛndlɪ〕 *adj.* 友善的　　***ask for*** 求見

23. (**A**) W：The first thing you need to do is to go through all the old records.

M：But that's going to take forever.

W：I know, but we have to do that to prove we didn't evade taxes.

M：These IRS audits can really cause havoc on people's otherwise quiet routine.

W：You know what they say — there are only two things for certain in life, death and taxes.

Question：What do the man and woman want to do?

A. They are going to gather evidence.

B. They are going away forever.

C. They are going to get a taxi.

D. They are going to evade taxes.

* ***go through*** 仔細檢查 (= *examine*)
evade〔ɪ'ved〕*v.* 逃避　　tax〔tɛks〕*n.* 稅
IRS 美國國稅局 (= *Internal Revenue Service*)
audit〔'ɔdɪt〕*n.* 查帳　　havoc〔'hævək〕*n.* 大破壞
otherwise〔'ʌðɚˌwaɪz〕*adv.* 在另外情況下
routine〔ru'tin〕*n.* 日常工作；例行公事
for certain 確定地　　gather〔'gæðɚ〕*v.* 收集
evidence〔'ɛvədəns〕*n.* 證據

24. (**A**) W：Should we bring some cold weather clothes?

M：I heard that it's still quite warm this time of the year.

W：I hope you are right. I don't want to freeze.

M：Oh, trust me. It's not going to be cold.

Question：What is the woman worried about?

A. The weather may be too cold for her.

B. She has too much to carry.

C. The weather may be too hot.

D. She might miss the cold weather.

* freeze〔friz〕v. 凍死　　carry〔'kærɪ〕v. 攜帶
miss〔mɪs〕v. 想念

25. (**B**)　M：Did you read the latest about Japan's car industry?

W：Yeah. It's a real crisis and I wonder how that's going to affect the rest of the world economy.

M：It's good news for the environmentalists.

W：I don't think people are going to worry too much about the environment when they realize they can't put food on the table.

M：What's the point in worrying about food on the table when the earth is too polluted for people to live on?

Question：Which one of the following statements is true?

A. The world's auto industry is in a crisis.

B. Environmentalists like what's happening in Japan.

C. Japan has no environmentalists.

D. Japanese cars are selling very quickly.

* **the latest** 最新消息　　industry〔'ɪndəstrɪ〕n. 工業
crisis〔'kraɪsɪs〕n. 危機　　**the rest** 其餘
economy〔ɪ'kɑnəmɪ〕n. 經濟
environmentalist〔ɪn‚vaɪrən'mɛntḷɪst〕n. 環保人士
point〔pɔɪnt〕n. 意義
polluted〔pə'lutɪd〕adj. 受到污染的
live on 靠～生活　　auto〔'ɔto〕n. 汽車 (= automobile)

26. (**B**) M : The tax break for the middle class is good news for retail businesses.

W : Do you think it's going to spur consumer demand?

M : I have no doubts that it will. Many researchers seem to think the same way.

W : They've been saying that for years and business hasn't really picked up.

M : I have a feeling this time will be different.

Question : What changes will occur for the middle income earners?

A. They have to pay more taxes.

B. They will have more disposable income.

C. They will start retailing.

D. They will move up the social ladder.

* ***tax break*** 減稅　　***middle class*** 中產階級

retail (ˋritel) n. v. 零售　　business (ˋbɪznɪs) n. 行業

spur (spɝ) v. 刺激　　demand (dɪˋmænd) n. 需求

doubt (daʊt) n. 懷疑　　researcher (riˋsɝtʃɚ) n. 研究員

pick up 增加

disposable (dɪˋspozəbl̩) adj. 可自由使用的

move up 提升　　***social ladder*** 社會階層

27. (**D**) W : Where's Stella?

M : I think she has a doctor's appointment.

W : Oh, you are right. How could I forget that?

M : You are so absent-minded. She said she wasn't going to be able to come yesterday.

M : You're right. I had completely forgotten about it.

Question：What did the man do?

A. He forgot Stella.

B. He went to the hospital.

C. He slept too much.

D. He forgot Stella isn't coming.

* absent-minded〔'æbsṇt'maɪndɪd〕adj. 心不在焉的
  completely〔kəm'plitlɪ〕adv. 完全地

28. (**A**)　M：I don't think the outlook is going to change.　I feel
　　　　　I should start looking for a job somewhere else.

　　　W：Do you really think we are going to be laid off?

　　　M：I think you're pretty safe, but for those of us in the
　　　　　sales division, things don't look too good.

　　　W：It can't be that bad.　You're just being pessimistic.

　　　M：I may be.　But I still think I should have something
　　　　　else lined up just in case I get the pink slip.

　　　Question：What is the man worried about?

A. He may find himself out of work.

B. The woman may lose her job.

C. He may be transferred to sales.

D. The woman is pretty.

* outlook〔'aʊt,lʊk〕n. 前景　　*lay off* 解雇
  pretty〔'prɪtɪ〕adv. 相當地　adj. 漂亮的
  division〔də'vɪʒən〕n. 部門
  pessimistic〔,pɛsə'mɪstɪk〕adj. 悲觀的
  line up 做適當安排　　*in case* 以免
  pink slip 解雇通知書　　*out of work* 失業的
  transfer〔træns'fɝ〕v. 調任

29. (**A**) M：Do you think we should get some more computers for the office?

W：Do you see it as something that's going to cut costs?

M：I don't know about that, but computers are much cheaper now.

W：We need to focus on cutting costs, not increasing costs.

M：With the new computers, we'll save a lot on maintenance in the long run.

Question：What's the woman concerned about?

A. Costs.　　　　　　B. Prices.
C. Computers.　　　　D. Offices.

* *focus on* 集中；專注於

maintenance〔'mentənəns〕 *n.* 維修

in the long run 最後

30. (**B**) W：Can you ask him to call back later?

M：All right.　Shall I say an hour?

W：Who was he, by the way?

M：I don't know.　He wouldn't tell me.　Are you seeing someone?

W：No!　Besides, nobody knows this number…, except for my brother.

M：Well, he said he'll call back.

Question：What should the caller do?

A. Never call again.　　B. Call later.
C. Write a letter.　　　D. Drop by.

* *by the way* 順便一提；對了　　see〔si〕 *v.* 會見

except for 除了～之外　　*drop by* 順道拜訪

Part C

Questions 31-32 are based on the following message.

> Will the owner of a light brown Chevy Blazer, license plate number 4R3 6H8, please report to the information booth. You are blocking the main entrance. Once again that's a light brown Chevy Blazer, license plate 4R3 6H8. Please report immediately to the information desk. Thank you.

** light〔laɪt〕*adj.* 淡的　　Chevy〔'tʃɛvɪ〕*n.* 雪佛蘭（車廠名）
license plate 車牌　　*report to* 向～報到
information booth 服務台（= *information desk*）
block〔blɑk〕*v.* 堵住　　entrance〔'ɛntrəns〕*n.* 入口

31. (**B**) Where is this announcement most likely being made?
　　　A. At a 2-stall garage.　B. At a shopping mall.
　　　C. At an ATM.　　　　　D. At a convenience store.

　　　* stall〔stɔl〕*n.* 車位　　*shopping mall* 購物中心
　　　ATM 自動櫃員機（= *Automated Teller Machine*）

32. (**A**) What seems to be the problem?
　　　A. Someone parked illegally.
　　　B. Someone stole a light truck.
　　　C. A car was set on fire.
　　　D. Someone requested information.

　　　* illegally〔ɪ'ligḷɪ〕*adv.* 違法地　　*light truck* 小型卡車
　　　set on fire 放火燒　　request〔rɪ'kwɛst〕*v.* 要求

Questions 33-35 are based on the following talk.

> Well, our company has expanded its line of products. Now we are producing baby foods. This is a very challenging area, yet very profitable. We are currently building a plant in Brazil and we are sure to make good profits. We decided that Europe wasn't the place for us since birth rates there are constantly falling.

** expand〔ɪk'spænd〕*v.* 擴大

line of products 生產線

challenging〔'tʃælɪndʒɪŋ〕*adj.* 有挑戰性的

area〔'ɛrɪə〕*n.* 領域

profitable〔'prɑfɪtəbḷ〕*adj.* 賺錢的

currently〔'kɝəntlɪ〕*adv.* 現在

plant〔plænt〕*n.* 工廠　　Brazil〔brə'zɪl〕*n.* 巴西

profit〔'prɑfɪt〕*n.* 利潤

make good profits 獲得很好的利潤

birth rate 出生率　　constantly〔'kɑnstəntlɪ〕*adv.* 持續地

33. (**A**) What has the company done?

    A. Entered a new business.

    B. Imported baby food.

    C. Relocated to Europe.

    D. Reduced the birth rate.

    * relocate〔ri͵loʹket〕*v.* 遷移

      reduce〔rɪʹdjus〕*v.* 降低

34. (**C**) Why has the company decided to relocate?

    A. Europe is more profitable.

    B. Europe has the largest market.

    C. Birth rates in Europe are falling.

    D. The company wanted more challenge.

    * profitable〔ʹprɑfɪtəbḷ〕*adj.* 有利可圖的

      challenge〔ʹtʃælɪndʒ〕*n.* 挑戰

35. (**C**) Which one of the following statements is true?

    A. The company has reduced the number of employees.

    B. The company has increased exports to Brazil.

    C. The company did not manufacture baby food before.

    D. The company is going to close its main plant.

    * manufacture〔͵mænjəʹfæktʃɚ〕*v.* 製造

Questions 36-37 are based on the following notice.

> As of April 1st, the company has implemented a policy regarding tardiness. From now on, all employees are required to punch in and out whenever entering or leaving the office respectively. This includes coffee, lunch, and cigarette breaks.

** ***as of*** 從～開始

    implement〔'ɪmplə,mɛnt〕*v.* 實施

    policy〔'paləsɪ〕*n.* 政策

    regarding〔rɪ'gɑrdɪŋ〕*prep.* 關於 (= *about*)

    tardiness〔'tɑrdɪnɪs〕*n.* 遲到   ***from now on*** 從現在起

    require〔rɪ'kwaɪr〕*v.* 需要   ***punch in*** 打卡上班

    punch out 打卡下班

    respectively〔rɪ'spɛktɪvlɪ〕*adv.* 分別地

    cigarette〔'sɪgə,rɛt〕*n.* 香煙

    break〔brek〕*n.* 休息

36. (**A**)　What is the purpose of this notice?

　　A.　To inform employees of a new policy.

　　B.　To tell employees to shorten their breaks.

　　C.　To question the purpose of implementing policies.

　　D.　To advertise a new café.

　　* notice〔'notɪs〕*n.* 通知；公告

　　　inform〔ɪn'fɔrm〕*v.* 通知 *< of >*

　　　shorten〔'ʃɔrtn̩〕*v.* 縮短

　　　question〔'kwɛstʃən〕*v.* 質疑

　　　advertise〔'ædvɚˌtaɪz〕*v.* 廣告

　　　café〔kæ'fe〕*n.* 咖啡廳

37. (**C**)　Why has the policy been implemented?

　　A.　To encourage tardiness.

　　B.　To discourage punctuality.

　　C.　To monitor employee attendance.

　　D.　To allow more coffee breaks.

　　* encourage〔ɪn'kɝɪdʒ〕*v.* 鼓勵

　　　discourage〔dɪs'kɝɪdʒ〕*v.* 防止

　　　punctuality〔ˌpʌŋktʃʊ'ælətɪ〕*n.* 守時；準時

　　　monitor〔'mɑnətɚ〕*v.* 監控

　　　attendance〔ə'tɛndəns〕*n.* 出席

　　　allow〔ə'laʊ〕*v.* 允許

Questions 38-39 are based on the following message.

> Thank you for calling Norton Electronics. This is a computer-generated voice. To expedite your call, we have installed this automatic switchboard system. To use the system, you must have a touch-tone telephone. If you know the extension of the office or person you want to talk with, dial the extension number now. If you need extension number information, press "1" now. If you want to speak to a customer service representative, press "2" now. If you want product information, press "3". If you are using a rotary phone, or want to speak with an operator, hold on and your call will be answered by the next available operator.

** electronics〔ɪ͵lɛk'trɑnɪks〕*n.* 電器用品店

generate〔'dʒɛnə͵ret〕*v.* 產生　　expedite〔'ɛkspɪ͵daɪt〕*v.* 加快

install〔ɪn'stɔl〕*v.* 安裝

automatic〔͵ɔtə'mætɪk〕*adj.* 自動的

switchboard〔'swɪtʃ͵bord〕*n.* （電話）總機

automatic switchboard system 自動電話轉接系統

touch-tone〔'tʌtʃ͵ton〕*adj.* 按鍵式的

dial〔'daɪəl〕*v.* 撥（號）　　press〔prɛs〕*v.* 壓；按

extension〔ɪk'stɛnʃən〕*n.* （電話）分機

representative〔͵rɛprɪ'zɛntətɪv〕*n.* 代表

customer service representative 客服人員

rotary〔'rotərɪ〕*adj.* 旋轉的　　***rotary phone*** 轉盤式電話

operator〔'ɑpə͵retɚ〕*n.* 總機人員　　***hold on*** （電話）不要掛斷

38. (**C**) What number should you dial if you want product information?
  A. The number "1".
  B. The number "2".
  C. The number "3".
  D. The number "4".

39. (**C**) If you want to speak with an operator, what does the message say you should do?
  A. Press "0".
  B. Call another number.
  C. Wait.
  D. Press "4".

Questions 40-41 are based on the following advertisement.

> Tired of the same thing for dinner, night-in and night-out? Why not try something exotic and fresh tonight at Papa Spiro's Greek House. Try our mouth-watering shish kebabs. Our gyros will be sure to please, and our salads are a must for any gourmet. Papa Spiro's is located on the corner of First and Main and is open from 9 to 2 a.m., seven days a week.

** **_night-in and night-out_** 每晚;日復一日

exotic〔ɪgˈzɑtɪk〕*adj.* 有異國風味的

fresh〔frɛʃ〕*adj.* 新鮮的　　Greek〔grik〕*adj.* 希臘的

mouth-watering〔ˈmauθˈwɔtəˌɪŋ〕*adj.* 令人垂涎三尺的;美味的

shish kebab〔ˈʃɪʃkəˌbab〕*n.* (蕃茄、洋蔥串在一起的)烤肉

gyro〔ˈgaɪro〕*n.* 希臘烤肉三明治

please〔pliz〕*v.* 使滿意　　**_sure to please_** 保證滿意

must〔mʌst〕*n.* 不可少的東西

gourmet〔ˈgurme〕*n.* 美食家

be located~ 位於

40. (**B**) What is being advertised?

A. A new TV dinner product.

B. An ethnic restaurant.

C. A real estate agency.

D. A travel agency.

* advertise〔'ædvə͵taɪz〕 v. 廣告

ethnic〔'ɛθnɪk〕 adj. 民族的；異族的

real estate〔'rilə'stet〕 n. 不動產

agency〔'edʒənsɪ〕 n. 公司　　***travel agency*** 旅行社

41. (**C**) What information is untrue about Papa Spiro's Greek House?

A. It serves exotic food.

B. It is located on a corner.

C. It is open twenty-four hours a day.

D. It offers delicious meals.

* serve〔sɝv〕 v. 供應（食物）　　meal〔mil〕 n. 一餐

Questions 42-43 are based on the following announcement.

> Good morning. I'm Bob Landers and I'll be your guide this morning as you tour the Bastonia Museum. The Bastonia has eighty-four rooms. We'll be touring thirty of them. But first, some rules of the house: Photos are not allowed in certain rooms. Every room has a sign at the entrance telling you whether or not it is okay to take pictures. Please obey these signs. Also, we ask that everybody stay with the tour group. Please do not wander off. We don't want anybody to get lost. Finally, some exhibits are roped off. Please stay behind the ropes. Okay then, shall we start?

** guide〔gaɪd〕*n.* 導遊　　tour〔tʊr〕*v.* 在～參觀
certain〔ˈsɝtn̩〕*adj.* 某些的　　sign〔saɪn〕*n.* 告示牌
entrance〔ˈɛntrəns〕*n.* 入口
whether or not 是否　　obey〔oˈbe〕*v.* 遵守
wander off 與同伴走散；迷路
exhibit〔ɪgˈzɪbɪt〕*n.* 展示品
rope off 用繩子隔開　　rope〔rop〕*n.* 繩子

42. (**D**) Who is Bob Landers?

    A. The curator of the museum.

    B. An employee of a tour agency.

    C. A housekeeper at the museum.

    D. A tour guide at the museum.

    * curator〔kjuˈretɚ〕*n.* 館長

      tour agency 旅行社

      housekeeper〔ˈhaʊsˌkipɚ〕*n.*（博物館、醫院之）清潔人員

43. (**C**) How can visitors determine whether photography is allowed?

    A. Their group leader will tell them.

    B. An announcement will be made.

    C. There are signs posted at each entrance.

    D. If there is no rope, it is okay.

    * determine〔dɪˈtɝmɪn〕*v.* 判定

      photography〔fəˈtɑɡrəfɪ〕*n.* 照相

      group leader 領隊

      announcement〔əˈnaʊnsmənt〕*n.* 宣佈

      post〔post〕*v.* 張貼

Questions 44-45 are based on the following announcement.

> Passengers are reminded to keep their seats in an upright position and to keep their seat belts on for the duration of the landing. We would also ask that you remain seated until the plane comes to a complete stop. At this moment we would like to thank you all for flying Pacific Heights, where the sky is the limit where hospitality and quality service are concerned.

** remind〔rɪ'maɪnd〕v. 使想起;提醒

upright〔'ʌp'raɪt〕adj. 直立的

position〔pə'zɪʃən〕n. 位置

duration〔djʊ'reʃən〕n. 期間

landing〔'lændɪŋ〕n. 登陸;降落

remain〔rɪ'men〕v. 保持 **remain seated** 留在座位上

come to a complete stop 完全停妥

at this moment 現在 pacific〔pə'sɪfɪk〕n. 太平洋

height〔haɪt〕n. 高(此指「航空公司」)

limit〔'lɪmɪt〕n. 範圍

hospitality〔,hɑspɪ'tælətɪ〕n. 殷勤招待

quality〔'kwɑlətɪ〕adj. 高級的

concern〔kən'sɝn〕v. 關心

44. (**C**) Where is this announcement most likely being made?

    A. On a Pacific cruise liner.

    B. On a luxury yacht.

    C. On a commercial airplane.

    D. On a roller coaster.

    * cruise〔kruz〕*n.* 航遊

      liner〔'laɪnə〕*n.* 定期輪船

      cruise liner 遊輪   luxury〔'lʌkʃərɪ〕*adj.* 豪華的

      yacht〔jɑt〕*n.* 遊艇

      commercial〔kə'mɝʃəl〕*adj.* 商用的

      roller coaster〔'rolə'kostə〕*n.* 雲霄飛車

45. (**A**) What is the main point of the announcement?

    A. To relate safety procedures.

    B. To advertise air-safety.

    C. To encourage smoking.

    D. To admonish the passengers against buckling up.

    * relate〔rɪ'let〕*v.* 敘述

      procedure〔prə'sidʒə〕*n.* 步驟；措施

      advertise〔'ædvə‚taɪz〕*v.* 宣傳

      air-safety 飛航安全   encourage〔ɪn'kɝɪdʒ〕*v.* 鼓勵

      admonish〔əd'mɑnɪʃ〕*v.* 告誡

      admonish sb. against ~ 告誡某人不要 ~

      buckle up 繫安全帶

劉毅英文「中高級英檢保證班」

高中同學通過「中級檢定」已經沒什麼用了，因為這個證書本來就應該得到。你應該參加「中高級英檢」認證考試，有了這張證書，對你甄試申請入學，有很大的幫助。愈早考完，就顯示你愈優秀。

I. 上課時間： 台北本部： A班：每週二晚上19：00～21：00
B班：每週日下午2：00～4：00

台中總部： 每週日上午9：30～11：30

II. 上課方式： 初試課程→完全比照財團法人語言訓練中心「中高級英檢初試」的題型命題。一回試題包括45題聽力測驗，50題閱讀能力測驗，我們將新編的試題，印成一整本，讓同學閱讀複習方便。老師視情況上課，讓同學做聽力測驗或閱讀測驗，同學不需要交卷，老師立刻講解閱讀能力測驗部份，聽力部份則發放詳解，讓同學回家加強演練，全面提升答題技巧。

複試課程→完全比照全真「中高級複試」命題標準命題，我們將新編的試題，印成一整本，以便複習，老師分析試題，一次一次地訓練，讓同學輕鬆取得認證。

III. 保證辦法： 同學只要報一次名，就可以終生上課，考上為止，但必須每年至少考一次「中高級英檢」，憑成績單才可以繼續上課，否則就必須重新報名，才能再上課。報名參加「中高級英檢測驗」，但缺考，則視同沒有報名。

IV. 報名贈書： 1.中高級英檢1000字
2.中高級英語克漏字測驗
3.中高級英語閱讀測驗
4.中高級英文法480題
5.中高級英語聽力檢定
（書＋CD一套）

V. 上課教材：

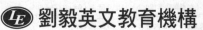 劉毅英文教育機構

台中總部：台中市三民路三段125號7F（李卓澔數學樓上）　　TEL：（04）2221-8861
台北本部①：台北市重慶南路一段10號7F（火車站前・台企大樓）　TEL：（02）2361-6101
台北本部②：台北市許昌街17號6F（火車站前・壽德大樓）　　　　TEL：（02）2389-5212
新竹群益補習班：新竹市東大路一段95號（蘇永年數學）　　　　　TEL：（03）522-8351

劉毅 TOEIC 700 分保證班

✓ 一次繳費，終生上課
✓ 學費全國最低
✓ 獨家研發教材 (非賣品)
✓ 一次繳費，所有多益班皆可上課

1. **問：什麼是「TOEIC 700 分保證」？**

   答：凡是報名保證班的同學，我們保證你考取 700 分。如果未達到 700 分，就可以免費一直上課，考上 700 分為止，不再另外收費，但是你必須每年至少考一次 TOEIC 測驗，考不到 700 分，可憑成績單，繼續上課，考上 700 分為止。

2. **問：你們用什麼教材？**

   答：我們請資深美籍老師，根據 TOEIC 最新出題來源改編，全新試題，市面上沒有，但是考試必有雷同出現。

3. **問：「TOEIC 700 分保證班」如何收費？**

   答：「TOEIC 700 分保證班」終生無限上課，僅收 19,800 元。一次繳費，所有多益班皆可上課。

4. **問：你們有什麼贈書？**

   答：報名後贈送「TOEIC Model Test ①～④」及聽力原文、「TOEIC Writing Test ①～⑧」、「TOEIC Speaking Test ①～⑧」、「TOEIC 口說測驗」、「TOEIC 必考字彙」、「TOEIC 文法 700 題」、「TOEIC 字彙 500 題」、「TOEIC 聽力測驗 ①」。我們全力協助同學應試，只要有關「多益」的書籍，通通贈送給你。

5. **上課時間：**

班級		上課時間
台北	TOEIC 台北 A 班	每週一晚上 7:00～9:00
	TOEIC 台北 B 班	每週日晚上 7:00～9:00
	TOEIC 台北寫作班	每週三晚上 7:00～9:00 外師免費不限次數批改
	TOEIC 台北口說班	每週二晚上 7:00～9:00
台中	TOEIC 台中 A 班	每週六下午 2:00～5:00
	TOEIC 台中 B 班	每週四晚上 7:00～9:00
	TOEIC 台中口說班	不限次數約定上課

※ 以上課表會依實際上課情形調整。

劉毅英文教育機構

台中總部：台中市三民路三段125號7F（李卓澔數學樓上）　　TEL：（04）2221-8861
台北本部③：台北市重慶南路一段10號7F（火車站前・台企大樓）　TEL：（02）2361-6101
台北本部②：台北市許昌街17號6F（火車站前・壽德大樓）　　TEL：（02）2389-5212
新竹群益補習班：新竹市東大路一段95號（蘇永年數學）　　TEL：（03）522-8351

TOEFL-iBT 100分保證班

「劉毅英文」自從開「TOEIC 700分保證班」以來，同學反應奇佳，我們以最短的時間，教最多東西，學起來很輕鬆，但卻很扎實。應同學的要求，我們花費鉅資，請外籍專家按照「托福」出題來源，編寫上課教材，設計「TOEFL-iBT 100分保證班」。

1. **問**：什麼是「TOEFL-iBT 100分保證班」？
   答：新制TOEFL-iBT滿分是120分，我們讓同學考到100分以上為止，如果沒達到100分，就可以免費上課，不再另外收費，但是每年必須拿出成績單，證明你去考過。

2. **問**：什麼是「TOEFL-iBT」？
   答：凡是申請美加地區大學或研究所的學生，都必須參加網路化測驗（Internet-Based Testing, iBT），透過網際網路，隨時連線至ETS（Educational Testing Service）。

3. **問**：是不是採取嚴格的模考方式？
   答：不，由於成年人在社會上已有地位，考低分不好意思，所以我們將新編的試題印成一整本，讓同學閱讀複習方便。老師視上課情況讓同學做聽力測驗或閱讀測驗，但同學不需要交卷。

4. **問**：TOEFL-iBT難不難？
   答：比TOEIC難一點，但是只要練習，熟悉題型，認真上課，就可以得高分。

5. **問**：「口說測驗」怎麼教？
   答：我們以「一口氣英語」方式，三句為一組，九句為一段的方式讓同學背。練習多了，自然會。

6. **問**：TOEFL-iBT考些什麼？
   答：

閱讀	1.題數：36~70題 2.內容：3~5篇學術性文章 　新增2個特殊功能： 　①Glossary—簡單的單字解說 　②Review—快速地檢視已填寫的答案 3.測驗時間：60-100分鐘 4.題型：選擇題（包含完成表格、將句子插入文章中適當的位置、同義字、代名詞、看圖選項…等的單選題或複選題）	口說	1.題數：6大題 2.內容：看完或聽完題目後，有一段準備時間，然後再回答問題。準備時間與作答時間皆有限制。 3.測驗時間：20分鐘 4.題型：2種題型—①聽一段對話或演說後作答。 　　②先看一篇文章再聽一段說明或對話後，再作答。
聽力	1.題數：34-51題 2.內容：2~3段對話，包含兩個或兩個以上的對話者 　4~6篇演說，學術性演講或學生在課堂中討論的對話 3.測驗時間：60-90分鐘 4.題型：選擇題（含單選及複選題）	寫作	1.題數：2題 2.測驗時間：50分鐘 3.內容：應試者根據電腦所指定的題目，於電腦上打字作答。 4.題型：2種題型— 　①看一篇文章，再聽一段說明或對話後，寫一篇相關的文章，測驗時間20分鐘。 　②就一個題目寫一篇文章，測驗時間30分鐘。

- **上課時間**：　台北本部：每週四晚上7：00～9：00
  　　　　　　　　台中本部：每週五晚上7：00～9：00

- **報名贈送**：1. TOEFL-iBT Model Test　　2. TOEFL-iBT 聽力測驗原文
  　　　　　　　3. TOEFL-iBT 托福口說原文　4. 一口氣托福口試①
  　　　　　　　5. 托福字彙進階

中高級英語聽力檢定②

主　　　編 / 劉　毅

發　行　所 / 學習出版有限公司　　　☎ (02) 2704-5525

郵 撥 帳 號 / 0512727-2 學習出版社帳戶

登　記　證 / 局版台業 *2179* 號

印　刷　所 / 裕強彩色印刷有限公司

台 北 門 市 / 台北市許昌街 10 號 2 F　　☎ (02) 2331-4060・2331-9209

台灣總經銷 / 紅螞蟻圖書有限公司　　　☎ (02) 2795-3656

美國總經銷 / Evergreen Book Store　　☎ (818) 2813622

本公司網址　www.learnbook.com.tw

電 子 郵 件　learnbook@learnbook.com.tw

書 + MP3 一片售價：新台幣二百八十元正

2009 年 1 月 1 日二版一刷

ISBN 978-986-231-013-7